# HOW TO MURDER A MILLIONAIRE

## MOVIE CLUB MYSTERIES, BOOK 3

### ZARA KEANE

BEAVERSTONE PRESS LLC

## HOW TO MURDER A MILLIONAIRE
### (Movie Club Mysteries, Book 3)

### *Murder. Millionaires. Mankinis.*

Armed with her newly issued private investigator's license, Maggie Doyle is on the case…of a sheep that went missing twenty-two years ago. When she trips over a dead body on the first day of the investigation, Maggie realizes there's more to this cold case than a fight over lamb chops.

An invitation to spend the weekend with her grandmother's oldest friend and her family, the super wealthy Huffingtons, gives Maggie the perfect excuse to sniff out the killer. After the family patriarch is electrocuted in the swimming pool, Maggie finds herself embroiled in yet another murder inquiry. With the body count rising, can Maggie catch the killer before they strike again?

**Join my mailing list and get news, giveaways, and an exclusive FREE Movie Club Mystery serial!**

**http://zarakeane.com/newsletter2**

## A NOTE ON GAELIC TERMS

Certain Gaelic terms appear in this book. I have tried to use them sparingly and in contexts that should make their meaning clear to international readers. However, a couple of words require clarification.

The official name for the Irish police force is *An Garda Síochána* ("the Guardian of the Peace"). Police are *Gardaí* (plural) and *Garda* (singular). Irish police are commonly referred to as "the guards".

The official rank of a police officer such as Sergeant O'Shea is Garda Sergeant O'Shea. As the Irish frequently shorten this to Sergeant, I've chosen to use this version for all but the initial introduction to the character.

The official name for the Whisper Island police station would be Whisper Island Garda Station, but Maggie, being American, rarely thinks of it as such.

The Irish police do not, as a rule, carry firearms. Permission to carry a gun is reserved to detectives and specialist units, such as the Emergency Response Unit. The police on Whisper Island would not have been issued with firearms.

Although this book follows American spelling conventions, I've chosen to use the common Irish spelling for proper names such as Carraig Harbour and the Whisper Island Medical Centre. An exception is the Movie Theater Café, which was named by Maggie's American mother.

# 1

## *Whisper Island, Ireland*

WHEN I ROLLED out of bed at the butt crack of dawn, I had no idea my day would start with a missing sheep and end with a dead dude in a crotchless mankini.

Averting my gaze from the dead guy's man junk, I kneeled beside the body and felt for a pulse. As I'd expected, there was none. The man's skin was cold to the touch, indicating he'd been dead a while. I stood and scanned the barn for clues, but the cause of death was obvious: the rake sticking out of his chest was hard to miss.

I swore under my breath. How the heck could this be happening to me again? In the five months since I'd swapped my cheating ex and crumbling career in the San Francisco PD for life on a remote Irish island,

I'd stumbled into two murder investigations. Becoming involved in a third was *not* on my to-do list.

Swallowing a sigh, I reached for my phone and hit speed dial.

My neighbor, and not-so-secret crush, answered on the second ring. "Sergeant Reynolds, Whisper Island Garda Station."

His deep rumble and Irish accent affected me like a comforting blanket. "Liam, it's me. You're not going to believe what I've just found."

"Maggie?" He groaned. "Aw, no. Why didn't I check caller ID?"

"That's a lovely way to greet the woman who cooked you dinner last Saturday," I said indignantly. "You could muster up a little enthusiasm."

"When said woman only contacts me at my work number to report finding dead bodies, I have good reason to be wary."

"Well, actually…" I let the words hang in the air a moment.

"No way." There was the sound of a chair scraping the floor on the other end of the line. "Don't tell me you've found another one."

"It's not like I *plan* to find dead people. It just sort of…happens." I didn't add that this particular corpse *happened* to be wearing a lime green mankini that hadn't been designed with swimming in mind. I'd let Reynolds enjoy that sight when he got here.

He muttered something in Gaelic that I was pretty sure I didn't want translated. "Tell me who's dead and where you are, and I'll get over there right away."

"Jimmy Wright is our vic." I rattled off the address of the Wright farm. "It's a thirty-minute drive from the station, give or take."

"I know the place. That's where I had to arrest an animal activist a few months ago. You sure Jimmy's dead?"

I regarded the rake sticking out of the farmer's chest and the pool of blood staining the straw beneath his body. I tasted bile, and my grip on the phone tightened. "No doubt about it. All he's good for now is fertilizer."

"Once a cop, always a cop, right down to the black humor," he said in a bone-dry tone. "I'll be there in forty. If no ambulance is required urgently, I'll swing by the Whisper Island Medical Centre on my way to the Wright farm and get Dr. Reilly to join me."

"You do that. And bring a forensics kit," I added as an afterthought. "It looks like murder."

"Why am I not surprised? You have a magnetic attraction to people who die unnatural deaths."

I tried to muster some righteous indignation, but failed. He had a point. I did have an uncanny nose for murder. "I'll see you soon."

"Wait a sec, Maggie." Reynolds's voice deepened a notch. "Promise me you won't touch anything. Your P.I.'s license doesn't give you permission to trample all over crime scenes."

Trample all over the place? What did he take me for, an amateur? "Sure thing, Sarge," I drawled. "I'll stay out of the barn."

I disconnected before Reynolds's sharp mind guessed my intentions and ordered me off Wright's property.

Shoving my phone into my purse, I exited the barn and jogged across the farm courtyard. Although it was gone eight-thirty in the evening, the sun still shone brightly and would do so until around ten o'clock. Just as I'd had to get used to the longer hours of darkness during an Irish winter, I had to adjust to the longer hours of sunlight now that it was June.

When I reached my new car, I pulled my keys from my pocket. I say "new," but the vehicle was my cousin's cast-off. Julie had sold it to me for a steal when she'd upgraded to an SUV last month. I opened the passenger door of the MINI, trying to ignore the wobbly door handle. There was a reason the car had been cheap, but I'd spent the last of the money from my successful investigation into the Whisper Island Hotel hauntings on rent, equipment for my new profession, and my day-old private investigator's license. Besides, the MINI was an improvement over the last rust bucket I'd driven.

I reached under the passenger seat and grabbed my mini detective kit. In the glove compartment, I located a pair of disposable rubber gloves, plastic overshoes, a cover for my hair, and a can of pepper spray. The latter was probably overkill—experience told me Jimmy'd been dead a while. I didn't think his killer was lurking on the farm, but I wasn't taking any risks.

I glanced at my watch. I had around thirty-five minutes before Reynolds arrived. I could spend it sweating in the barn with Jimmy Wright's earthly remains, or I could sneak into his house and start the investigation I'd been sent here to conduct. As long as I didn't have to pick the lock, I was golden.

I hurried toward the farmhouse and slipped on my protective gear. On instinct, I tried the back door first. *Bingo.* No breaking and entering required. I pushed open the unlocked door and stepped inside.

A small mudroom separated the back door from the kitchen. I surveyed the scene. Wright was a tidy man. Each shoe, boot, and coat was arranged on its respective shelf or hanger. When I ventured into the kitchen, it was a similar story. The dishwasher gurgled gently as it cleaned its load. A bushy tortoiseshell cat meowed at me from her vantage point in front of the dishwasher.

"Hey, there." When I bent down to pet her, she purred and nuzzled my arm. As a newly minted cat owner, I checked to make sure she had food and water in her bowls before I searched the premises.

The kitchen revealed nothing of interest. I moved from room to room, rooting through drawers, shelves, and closets. When I reached the reluctant conclusion that the first floor held no clues, I headed up the creaky staircase. My feline friend followed, meowing a message I couldn't decipher.

"If you saw Jimmy's murderer, you can't tell me." *Pity.* I'd have paid good money to see Reynolds's face when I presented him with the cat as a potential witness.

On the landing, the cat made straight for a bedroom. A quick glance around the neat room told me it was Jimmy's. My preliminary research indicated that he was divorced and lived alone. He ran the farm with the aid of two employees, neither of whom had been in evidence since my arrival.

A couple of photographs adorned the nightstand. They were the first photos I'd seen in the house, so I checked them out. The first depicted a young Jimmy on his wedding day, beaming with pride at his new bride. The second photo was of a kid on a trike. I examined the clothes. Mid-Eighties was my guess. I replaced the frame on the nightstand and turned my attention to the drawer underneath.

I was leafing through papers when my phone buzzed with an incoming call. I glanced at the display and groaned. With a good fifteen minutes before Reynolds was due to arrive, I had time to take the call, even if I didn't want to. After a moment's hesitation, I hit speakerphone. "Hey, Paddy. What's up?"

"Have you found her?" my client demanded. "Have you found my Nancy?"

I rolled my eyes. Why had I let my aunt talk me into accepting Paddy Driscoll as my first client? I'd known it was a bad idea the moment he'd marched into my newly furnished office in his Sunday best— semi-clean gumboots, and a stained checked shirt. I'd had the feeling that the assignment wouldn't be one I'd want to take, and my instinct had been correct.

"Nancy's been missing for more than twenty-two years," I said, moving to Wright's bedroom closet, "and I've been on the case for less than twenty-two hours. You can hardly expect me to find her that fast."

"You don't seem to care, Maggie. Your aunt assured me you'd give my case the same consideration you'd give any other."

*Gee, thanks, Noreen.* "Listen, I'm doing my best, but you've got to admit that finding a missing sheep after two decades is a long shot."

Paddy grunted. "I don't expect her to be alive. I'm not a fool. I just want to know what happened to her. I've always suspected foul play was involved."

And, according to what Paddy had told me in my office this morning, he'd always suspected Jimmy Wright was the culprit. I paused in my perusal of Wright's clothes, and the unpleasant suspicion that Paddy had killed Wright in a fit of anger flashed across my mind. But if Paddy had murdered Jimmy, why would he draw suspicion upon himself by sending me over to the Wright farm? The guy had a temper, but he wasn't stupid.

I closed the closet and moved to the next room, Jimmy's cat at my heels. "I told you I'd try to find out what happened to Nancy, and I meant it. But you're going to have to be patient."

"Patient?" the man roared. "I've waited twenty-two years for answers. Neither Sergeant O'Shea nor the fool who had the post before him took me seriously. And now this young fella—what's his name again?"

"Sergeant Reynolds," I supplied.

"When I asked Reynolds to reopen the case, he looked at me like I'd sprouted horns. I came to you because I was desperate."

Not exactly a ringing endorsement of my detective skills, but I took no offense. Paddy was grumpy at the best of times, and today was definitely not his day. His lousy mood would nosedive when he found out Jimmy was a dead end—literally.

The next room I entered was a home office. I paused in the doorway, and Paddy's litany of complaints faded from my consciousness. In stark contrast to the rest of the house, Jimmy's office was a hot mess. Papers lay strewn across the floor, and drawers had been emptied of their contents. Someone had been in here—maybe the killer—but had they found whatever they'd been looking for? For the first time since I'd entered the house, a shiver of unease snaked down my spine.

On the phone, Paddy droned on about the failure of the Whisper Island authorities to take him seriously, and my shortcomings as a P.I. I held the phone in place with my neck while I rifled through the mess of papers. "You can't expect me to solve the mystery in a day."

"Have you at least spoken to Jimmy Wright?"

A vision of Wright's body loomed before me, and a giggle surged up my throat at the reminder of the lime green mankini. And then I thought of the rake and the blood... "Not exactly."

"What do you mean, 'not exactly'?" Paddy snapped. "Either you have, or you haven't."

"Questioning Jimmy is proving to be difficult," I hedged. Reynolds would not be pleased if I blabbed about Wright's murder before he'd had a chance to examine the body.

"Wright knows something," he muttered. "I'm sure of it."

Whatever Jimmy Wright had known was unlikely to come to light now, but I refrained from sharing this observation. "I'll call you tomorrow evening with an update. How does that sound?"

"It sounds like you're fobbing me off," Paddy retorted with his customary tact. "If you want me to pay your ridiculous fee, you'd better work for it."

The charge I'd quoted him was a one-time first-client deal and well below my usual fee, but I had neither the time nor the desire to argue with the man. "As I said, I'll call you tomorrow. Bye, Paddy."

I slipped my phone back into my bag and made a last-ditch effort to rifle through Jimmy Wright's papers. A glance at my watch told me to give it up as a lost cause. The clock was ticking. If anything relevant to the murder was in this room, the intruder had probably found it, and I highly doubted Jimmy had kept info relating to Paddy's missing sheep, assuming he'd had anything to do with her disappearance.

The cat and I left the office and walked down the upstairs hallway. Under my feet, an uneven floorboard creaked. I stopped in my tracks. *Could it be...?* I tested it again, shifting my weight back and forth. My heart rate kicked up a notch. I stepped off the board and rolled back the strategically placed rug.

Sure enough, one of the wooden floorboards underneath was slightly out of alignment with the others. I took my flashlight out of my detective kit and shone it along the edges of the rogue floorboard. I slid a ruler into the gap and eased up the board. I shone my light inside the exposed space underneath. The space was larger than I'd anticipated. I lay on my stomach and peered inside. My stomach performed a dance worthy of an acrobat. Wedged in the space, I spied some papers and a laptop. In the distance, I heard Reynolds's siren.

I whipped out the laptop and flipped it open. My heart sank at the sight of the demand for a password, but it was hardly surprising. If Jimmy Wright had gone to the trouble of hiding his laptop, he'd password protect it. My mind whirred. What could Wright have used as a password? A super-complex one like Lenny insisted I used? Or something simpler and easy to guess? The cat rubbed against my leg and jogged a memory.

I reached for the red collar around her neck. Engraved on the metal tag was the name, Mavis. "Perfect."

My fingers flew over the keyboard. On my third attempt, I struck gold with Mavis2014. Heart pounding, I pulled the external hard drive from my backpack and contemplated my options. Cloning a murder victim's laptop was a major no-no, but then, searching his house before the police arrived wasn't exactly within the parameters of the law.

I stared at the external hard drive with longing. I'd been dying to try it out ever since Lenny had talked me through the steps of computer cloning, but common sense prevailed. With a sigh, I shoved it back into my bag. My first day as a private investigator was a little soon to get stripped of my license.

Instead of trying out my new tech skills, I performed a cursory check of Jimmy Wright's files. I didn't know what I was expecting to find relating to a sheep that had disappeared so long ago. Probably nothing, but I just might turn up something that related to his murder. I'd been the one to find his body, after all. It was only natural for me to take an interest in the case.

The sound of the approaching police car grew louder. I had to act fast. I fingered the bag containing the external hard drive and itched to take it out. Man, it was hard to do the right thing sometimes, especially seeing as my being in Wright's house was far from correct procedure. I'd have to 'fess up to

Reynolds, but I'd cross that wobbly bridge when I had to.

I clicked and scrolled my way through Jimmy's Documents folder. At first glance, there was nothing nefarious among them. Perhaps I'd have better luck with his internet searches. When I pulled up his recent history, two site names leaped out at me. So Jimmy Wright had used online dating portals? I made a mental note of the URLs before closing the laptop and returning it to the space under the floor.

The siren rose to a crescendo. Adrenaline shot through my body. With a pounding heart, I flipped through the papers I'd found with the laptop. I snapped a photo of the top two with my phone, barely registering their contents. Inside my rubber gloves, my palms were damp with sweat. I returned the papers to the hiding place under the floor, and replaced the floorboard and rug. Then I jumped to my feet and ran.

## 2

————

I'D BARELY MANAGED to close the back door behind me and stuff my protective gear into my bag when the squad car pulled into the yard. I forced air into my lungs and schooled my features into a calm expression. Beside me, Mavis perched on the top step, regal as a queen. She'd darted out of the house an instant before the door had slammed behind us, leaving me with no time to coax her back inside.

Sergeant Liam Reynolds leaped out of the driver's side and sprinted toward us. For a moment, my anxiety at being caught searching Wright's house evaporated. During the five months I'd lived on Whisper Island, my relationship with the police officer had evolved from vaguely flirtatious to on-the-verge-of-dating—if, that was, we ever managed to go on a date without being interrupted by an emergency.

When his gaze met mine, Reynolds's frown relaxed. The by-now familiar spark of awareness crackled through my veins and reignited the jumble of emotions I felt every time I was in his company.

"Maggie." His dark blue eyes never left my face. "How are you?"

"I'm okay. Doing better than Jimmy Wright." I nodded toward the barn. "Want to go take a look?"

"Yeah. We'd better get it over with." He gestured for me to follow him, and Mavis interpreted the invitation as extending to her. Reynolds regarded the cat with amusement. "I see you've found a friend."

"I think she sees me as a source of food and cuddles. Smart cat. With Jimmy gone, I don't know who'll look after her."

"I don't suppose Noreen wants to add to her cat collection?" he asked with a grin.

My aunt had eight cats, not counting the kittens who'd been born a few months ago. "I don't know. I can ask her." My steps slowed as we neared the barn. "It's not a pretty sight in there."

This was an understatement. Despite the seriousness of the situation, I swallowed a laugh. Reynolds would bust a gut when he saw Jimmy's fashion statement.

The arrival of Dr. Reilly spared us the sight of the corpse for a few extra seconds. The owner of the Whisper Island Medical Centre parked his red Jaguar behind the police car and hurried to catch up with us. He cast an impatient glance at his watch as he speed-walked the short distance to the barn. Reilly was an okay guy, but I'd never warmed to him. He was too puffed up in his self-consequence for my taste. Still, he was the only doctor available. Given the cause of death, I was confident that Wright's body would be sent to the mainland for an autopsy by a pathologist.

Judging by Dr. Reilly's dour expression when he recognized me at the barn door, my dislike of him was reciprocated. "Good evening, Ms. Doyle."

"Let's get these on before we go inside." Reynolds removed packages of rubber gloves and disposable overshoes from his backpack and handed them to us. The three of us dutifully kitted up before we trooped into the barn. Mavis scooted in behind us and yowled in protest when Reynolds scooped her up and put her on the wrong side of the barn door. "Sorry, sweetheart. Can't have you in here contaminating the corpse." The cat summarily disposed of, he turned his attention to the crime scene. Reynolds reeled back at the sight of Jimmy's body. "Whoa. What is he wearing?"

"I believe it's called a mankini," I supplied, my tone deadpan, "but I suspect that particular model is only found at sex shops."

Reynolds shook himself and blinked several times. "Whatever that is, it's not a good look."

"Nope," I agreed. "It gives the phrase 'I wouldn't be seen dead in that' a whole new meaning."

Dr. Reilly took a cautious step toward the body and examined the rake. "The cause of death seems clear."

*Talk about stating the obvious.*

Even though I'd seen it already, the pool of blood under Jimmy's body turned my stomach. The muggy June weather had attracted flies, and they swarmed around the corpse with glee. I concentrated on the strap of Jimmy's lime-green mankini. Throwing up wasn't an option.

Reynolds pulled out a camera from his bag. "I'll take a few photos before you examine him, Tom."

The doctor and I gave Reynolds space while he took shots of the body from every angle. When he was satisfied with the results, he nodded to the doctor. "Your turn."

Dr. Reilly kneeled before the corpse and began his examination, careful to avoid disturbing the rake.

Letting the doctor do his thing, I followed Reynolds around the barn while he took more photos. "Only one entrance," I observed, "and no security cameras that I can see. There don't appear to be any around the yard, either."

"Why are you here, Maggie?" His frown slid back into place. "Is it something to do with your work? Do you know anyone with a grudge against Wright?"

It was on the tip of my tongue to prevaricate and deny any knowledge of Jimmy Wright's potential enemies, but Reynolds and I had danced that jig on a previous case, and it hadn't ended well for me. After a moment's hesitation, I said, "Paddy Driscoll hired me to look into a matter of a missing sheep. Paddy thinks Jimmy Wright had something to do with her disappearance."

"Ah, no. Not this crazy cold-case sheep business again."

My lips twitched. "Paddy said he'd mentioned it to you, and that you didn't treat the matter with the seriousness he felt it deserved."

"The sheep's been missing for twenty-something years," he said in exasperation. "How does he expect me to find her? Assuming the sheep didn't just fall off a cliff, anyone involved in her disappearance has probably left the island by now."

He had a point. Whisper Island's population had dwindled since my father's generation had come of age. It had always been a place that was ripe for emigration: few jobs beyond family farms, and a brain drain of young people who left for higher education on the mainland and rarely returned.

"Paddy seems genuinely distressed. He says he's asked every Whisper Island police chief to look into the case since it happened, and none of you have."

Reynolds's eyes creased in amusement. "So he decided to hire you."

"Bingo."

He grinned. "A cold case involving a missing sheep is a great first job for your private investigation business."

"Laugh away. I've had my private investigator's license for a day, and I already have a paying client." Okay, a job involving a missing farm animal hadn't been what I'd been expecting, but my business had to start somewhere, right?

His amusement evaporated when he snapped a few extra shots of the barn. "On a more serious note, do you think Paddy hated Jimmy enough to kill him?"

"I've thought about that, but the pieces don't fit. Why would Paddy hire me the day before he intended to kill Jimmy? Why would he send me to the farm to question Jimmy if he knew I'd find the man dead? It doesn't make sense."

"I agree, but I'll need to talk to Paddy." He nodded in the direction of the doctor. "Looks like Tom's finished his examination. Want to hear what he has to say?"

"Sure." I'd expected him to kick me out of the barn before the doc voiced his conclusions, and I was grateful he was letting me stay. Being honest about Paddy had been the right move. As long as Reynolds didn't find out I'd searched the house before I was ready to reveal this information, I was good to go.

Dr. Reilly lumbered to his feet, puffing a bit from the effort. The doctor wasn't fat, but he had the pudgy appearance of a man who didn't always practice what he preached regarding healthy eating and exercise.

Reynolds propelled me toward the body. "What's the verdict?"

The doctor brushed straw off the blazer of his suit before he answered. "Wright's been dead at least four hours. Probably closer to five."

"That puts the time of death between four and

five o'clock." Reynolds turned to me. "What time did you get here, Maggie?"

"Around eight-fifteen. When Jimmy didn't answer the house door, I figured I'd find him somewhere around the farm." I cast an involuntary glance at the body and swallowed hard. Now was not the moment to focus on the mankini. "I didn't expect to find him like…this."

Reynolds moved to the other side of the body and examined the position of the rake. "What else can you tell us, Tom?"

"On cursory inspection, the cause of death is exactly what it appears to be—multiple stab wounds from the prongs of this rake, two of which more than likely perforated the heart. He also has a gash on the back of the head, but I can't examine that too closely without disturbing the rake."

"The head wound was probably caused by the fall," Reynolds mused. "We'll know more when the forensics team gets here and we can move the body. Was there any sign of defensive wounds?"

"None that I can see," Dr. Reilly replied. "Wright's nails are clean. Whatever he was doing in the barn didn't involve getting his hands dirty."

We all regarded the remains of Jimmy Wright and the outfit he probably hadn't planned to die in.

"Jimmy must have been meeting someone," I said. "Unless he usually strolled around his farm wearing lime-green strings of Lycra."

An expression of repulsion flickered over Dr. Reilly's face, but Reynolds grinned. "Not as far as I know," the policeman said, "and I doubt Jimmy was heading to the pub in that outfit. A romantic rendezvous is my guess."

On Reynolds's initiative, we turned away from the corpse and strolled out of the barn. Mavis was waiting for us on the other side of the door, with her ears pricked up in anticipation. Of what, I wasn't sure, but Mavis didn't strike me as the kind of cat who liked to be kept away from the action. A gal after my own heart.

"Maybe Jimmy got his kicks out of wearing weird outfits for booty calls," I said while we walked back across the yard. "That theory implies he was expecting a visitor."

"A visitor who could be our perp. Did you see anyone near the property when you arrived, Maggie?" Reynolds asked. "Or any sign that someone other than Wright had been here recently?"

I shook my head. "I looked, but I saw no one. There are tire tracks all over the yard, but that's hardly surprising. Wright was a farmer. He drove trucks and farm vehicles through here all the time."

Reynolds looked up at the cloudy sky. "I'll need to photograph all the tracks before the rain comes. We're due for a downpour overnight."

The doctor looked at his watch again, and his body vibrated with impatience. "Do you need me for anything else, Liam? If not, I'll be off. It's Maria's birthday, and we have reservations at the hotel restaurant."

"Go on," Reynolds said. "I can handle it from here. There's not a lot I can do until the forensics team arrives, and that won't be for a couple of hours."

"See you tomorrow, Liam. Goodbye, Ms. Doyle." Dr. Reilly nodded brusquely at me and walked back in the direction of his car.

After he'd left, I turned to Reynolds. "Do you need me to stay? I could help you sift through the evidence."

An amused twinkle sparkled in his eyes. "Nice try, Maggie. I'll need to take your statement, but that can wait until tomorrow. Can you call by the station in the morning?"

"Sure. I need to open the café for Noreen anyway. How does ten-thirty sound? My aunt will be in by then."

"Sounds perfect. Will you ask your aunt about the cat?"

I laughed. "In other words, will I take her with me and save you one hassle for this evening?"

"Pretty much." Reynolds's slow-burn smile turned my knees to jelly.

I picked up Mavis and started to walk to my car.

"Maggie?"

I turned back, knowing what he was going to say before he'd had a chance to utter a word. "Yes?"

"Leave this case to me. No interfering. Is that understood?"

"Of course," I said, my tone sweet. "However, I'll need to continue my investigation into what happened to Paddy Driscoll's sheep. If I come across any information pertaining to your murder inquiry, would you like me to share it?"

A muscle in his jaw flexed. "Forget the sheep. Concentrate on finding stray cats or cheating spouses. That's the sort of work a P.I. on a small island should expect to get."

"Stray cat, stray sheep." I shrugged. "What's the difference? Tell you what, Sarge. You concentrate on the dead guy in a sex suit, and I'll concentrate on my case. Deal?"

"Maggie, I—"

I opened the door of my car and slid behind the wheel, depositing Mavis on the back seat before I put on my belt. I gunned the engine and rolled down my window as I drove past him. "By the way, you'll find Wright's laptop and some papers under a floorboard upstairs. If you discover any mention of Paddy Driscoll and his sheep, do let me know. Have a great evening."

I gave the slack-jawed Reynolds a cheery wave and left him in the dust.

## 3

WORD TRAVELED FAST on Whisper Island. The news of my discovery of Jimmy Wright's body was no exception. When I pulled up in front of my aunt's café at seven o'clock the next morning, Lenny was waiting for me at the entrance. My friend's lanky frame quivered with excitement, and he danced from foot to foot like a toddler who needed to pee. *Aw, man.* The last thing I wanted to deal with this morning was a barrage of questions.

Sure enough, Lenny accosted me the instant I stepped out of the car. "The sarge says you found another corpse."

So much for living down my reputation as a dead-body magnet. "There's no need for you to look so cheerful about it." I slipped the key into the lock and let us into the café, bowing to the inevitable. "Want a coffee before I set up for opening?"

"Sure. I'll help you get ready when we're done."

I laughed. "In return for me telling all?"

A wide grin spread over my friend's bony face. "Of course."

"All right. We have a deal. But you'll need to keep what I tell you to yourself. I haven't even made a formal statement to the police yet."

After I'd put my purse and jacket under the counter, I fixed him a frothy cappuccino with the Movie Theater Café's huge Italian-made machine. I made a less flashy double espresso for me and brought our coffees over to the Doris Day table. Each table was named after an old movie star and had their black-and-white photo, plus movie paraphernalia, inlaid under the glass surface. My aunt had purchased Smuggler's Cove's abandoned movie theater a couple of years back, and she'd turned it into a café. Every month, the Movie Club she'd founded met to watch a classic movie in the old theater. Lenny and I were among the club's most enthusiastic members.

My friend wiped milk froth off his scraggly goatee. "I want all the deets. How'd Jimmy Wright wind up dead?"

"A rake through the chest," I said without preamble.

Lenny leaned forward. "Accidental?"

"I doubt it. If he'd tripped and fallen onto the rake, he should have been lying face down. Reynolds is treating the death as suspicious."

"Awesome." My friend beamed like a kid who'd

been promised a trip to a theme park. "Is a forensics team coming to the island?"

"Yeah. They came last night." I took a sip from my espresso cup. "What do you know about Jimmy Wright? Did he have any enemies?"

"Nah. Jimmy was a boring old git. I can't imagine anyone wanting to kill him. His murder is the most exciting thing about the guy."

A vision of the mankini sprang to mind. *Not quite a boring old git.*

"Apart from one of his bulls being shot a few months ago when an animal activist trespassed on his property, I don't know much about Jimmy Wright." I toyed with the rim of my cup. "Except that Paddy Driscoll wasn't his greatest fan."

"Paddy Driscoll…" Lenny drew his brows together. "I heard something about that, but wasn't their quarrel old news?"

"Paddy hired me yesterday to look into the disappearance of one of his sheep—" I paused for dramatic effect, "—twenty-two years ago."

Lenny snorted milk foam. "Don't tell me Paddy's still looking for Nancy," he spluttered, coughing and laughing simultaneously. "Wow. Does he think Jimmy had something to do with it?"

"Yeah, but he can't prove it." I sighed into my espresso. "It doesn't make sense. Why would Jimmy take Paddy's sheep? I thought Jimmy concentrated on dairy farming with a side business in breeding bulls."

"He does. Did," Lenny corrected himself. "I can

ask my parents what they know. I was a little kid at the time. I only have vague memories of a sheep going missing. I don't think people took Paddy seriously. Sheep go missing all the time on the island. They wander off, fall into bogs, or tumble off cliffs." He shrugged. "That's life."

"Listen, would you be willing to do some work for me? I need your internet search expertise."

My friend perked up. "Sure. Hey, if you're looking for an assistant, I'm your man."

My stomach clenched. It was an idea I'd toyed with before but rejected. "I'd love to hire you, but I can't afford to take on an assistant before I have a few paying clients. I was talking about a one-off job."

Lenny's cheerful mood deflated, and I felt bad for letting him down. "I just thought you could do with a tech guy on your team," he said, "especially as you ask me to help you anyway."

This was true. I'd insisted on paying Lenny for helping me get set up with computer equipment for my P.I. business, but I was pretty sure he'd under-charged me for his services.

"I don't have a team yet. As soon as I'm in a posi-tion to hire help, you'll be the first person I call."

He looked at me hopefully. "I'll work for free until you get more work. You can pay me back when you have the money."

The pleading look in my friend's eyes was hard to resist. "That's very kind of you, but I can't ask you to do that. It wouldn't be fair."

"You're not asking. I'm offering." Lenny's expression grew grave. "Maggie, I'm going crazy at my parents' shop. They don't let me have any say in the products we sell. The computer repair business keeps me sane, but there's not enough work on the island to make it a full-time gig."

I'd never considered how he felt about working for his parents. Despite his easygoing persona, he was a smart guy. I could imagine that being a store assistant wasn't exactly his dream job, even if it was at a place that sold electronic goods.

"You can't quit your job on the basis of what work I might have in the future. Why don't we compromise? You can help me for a few hours a week, and we'll see how it goes. Even I can manage to pay you for three to five hours of work a week." Barely, but I'd figure it out somehow.

Relief flooded over my friend's face. "Thanks, Maggie. You won't regret this."

I knew I wouldn't. One day, Lenny would make a fantastic full-time assistant—if I could ever afford to pay him a salary and fund his P.I. training. "As your first official job for Movie Reel Investigations, I'd like you to take a look at Jimmy Wright's internet history." I gave him the *Reader's Digest* condensed version of my search of Jimmy's house and outlined the sites I'd memorized from his laptop's search history. "Is there any way for you to hack into the computer without the police finding out?"

"Yeah, but there's a reason you hesitated before

cloning Wright's laptop. I hate to say it, but we've got to play fair with Sergeant Reynolds, especially while the ink is barely dry on your P.I. license."

"I know. It's just frustrating to know he has the laptop and we can't look at it." I checked my watch. "The forensics team is probably still on the island, but they'll take the laptop with them when they leave."

Lenny grinned. "Then you'll just have to charm Reynolds into letting you take a look at the laptop before it heads to the mainland. Better still, persuade him to give you permission to copy its contents."

"He'll never agree to that. But…he might be persuaded to let *you* take a peek before the forensics team takes it away. Let's face it—if there was someone on the force on the island who had the technical know-how to do a forensic search, Reynolds wouldn't need to send it to the mainland."

"You mentioned you'd snapped a few photos of the papers Jimmy kept under the floor with the laptop. Anything interesting?"

I shook my head. "I don't know. They were bank statements regarding the transfer of money to an American bank account, but it didn't name the recipient. I'll need to take another look at them."

"So what's the plan?" Lenny asked, glancing at his watch. "I need to get to my parents' shop to open up, and I said I'd help you set up here."

"Never mind about helping me. Noreen will arrive in a sec. It won't take three of us. Could you get away from the shop at around ten-thirty and join me at the station? I'm due to give my formal statement. We could tackle Reynolds together and see if he'll let us take a look at Wright's computer."

"If I can square it with Mum, I'll be there."

Lenny drained his coffee cup and was about to stand up when Noreen burst into the café. My aunt was pleasantly plump with huge green eyes and jet-black curls. She possessed an energy and zest for life that belied her fifty-six years. This morning, she was bouncing from foot to foot in the way she always did when she had news.

"I guess you heard about Wright," I said dryly, wondering how many times I'd be expected to tell that story this morning.

"What? Oh, you mean about you falling over Jimmy Wright's body?" My aunt waved a hand in a dismissive gesture. "Sure, you're always finding corpses, love. That's yesterday's news."

I exchanged a look with Lenny. He shrugged and made a "beats me" expression. I turned back to my aunt. "Come on, Noreen. Spill. You know you want to."

Noreen plunked herself onto a chair at our table and dropped her voice to a stage whisper. "Do you remember that mysterious silent investor in the Whisper Island Hotel?"

"The one Paul and Melanie are terrified to upset? Yeah. What about him?"

"His entourage arrived on Whisper Island on the first ferry. And you'll never guess who he is."

"Nope, but I'm sure you'll tell us."

She beamed as though she were the bearer of fantastic tidings. "Huff Huffington."

"Huff Huffington?" I screwed up my forehead. "Not the *Huff's Puffs* guy?"

My aunt nodded excitedly. "That's the one. He's your grandmother's best friend's son. Remember the school friend who exchanged movie magazines with Mammy? Helen is his mother."

"Wait...*Helen Huffington* is from Whisper Island?" I didn't pay much attention to the Forbes 500 list, but even I'd heard of Helen Huffington and Huffington Enterprises.

Lenny wore a baffled expression. "Who's Helen Huffington? And what are *Huff's Puffs*?"

"Helen Huffington is one of the wealthiest women in America," I explained. "Her late husband founded a fast food chain, and it became a colossal success. Think gross fried balls of chicken. This was in the fifties, so her husband was the public face of the business, but it was an open secret that Helen Huffington was the brain behind their success. I had no idea she was Irish."

"That's right," Noreen continued. "Now Helen's son runs the company, and it seems he invested in the Whisper Island Hotel."

I whistled. "No wonder Paul and Melanie are scared. Huff Huffington has a reputation for being a tyrant. Apparently, he was short-listed to host the

reality show *Future Tycoons*, but he behaved so outra-
geously on a test episode that they couldn't air it
on TV."

"I remember now." Lenny straightened in his seat,
and his expression grew animated. "Snippets ended
up on YouTube, complete with all the bleeped-out
swearing. The guy was totally out of control."

"I'm rather hoping he's *in* control this evening,"
Noreen said. "Maggie and I have been invited to join
his family for dinner at the hotel restaurant."

I blinked. "We have? But I'm supposed to cater to
the Detectorists Club meeting tonight."

"I know, but I called Kelly and asked if she'd be
willing to take your shift."

"In other words, you're strong-arming me into
attending this dinner," I said wryly. "Let me guess—
Huff Huffington has a single son."

Noreen's grin was sly. "He does. And he's a handsome lad from what I could see through my
binoculars."

"Binoculars? You spied on them?" I laughed.
"Why am I even asking? Of course you did."

"Well, just for a minute," Noreen replied, not in
the least abashed. "I saw the ferry arriving at Carraig
Harbour on my way to the café, and I knew the Huffingtons would be on it. Helen phoned me last night to
arrange the dinner, and she mentioned when they'd
be arriving."

I could picture the scene perfectly. My aunt

leaning over the cliff at a perilous angle, just to get a look at a potential husband for me or my cousin Julie.

"You'll come, won't you?" She smiled at me as though my answer were a foregone conclusion. "It'll be worth your while."

Dinner sounded good, just not in the company of a bunch of strangers, one of whom had the reputation for shouting at people. "I'm sorry, but I need to work on Paddy's case and give him an update."

"Ah, but by attending the dinner, you will be working on the case."

I frowned. "How?"

"Now surely Lenny remembers why?" Noreen turned to my friend, who exchanged a perplexed look with me. "Don't you remember Helen Huffington's history?"

"I'm afraid not, Noreen. I'm not much interested in the island's old fogies. Besides, Helen must have left long before I was born."

She clucked her tongue in disapproval. "Honestly, the youth of today has no respect for our island's history. Helen Huffington was Helen Wright before she married."

A light bulb of comprehension flashed in my mind. "She was related to Jimmy. How?"

"His aunt." Her mouth stretched into a triumphant smile. "I told you you'd want to go to that dinner."

## 4

———

AT TEN-THIRTY ON THE DOT, I strode into Whisper Island Garda Station and gave Sergeant Reynolds my formal statement in the station's one and only interrogation room. After we'd crossed I's and dotted T's, I tackled him about the laptop.

"Could I have a quick look at Jimmy Wright's laptop? Or would you let Lenny take a peek?" I treated him to my most charming smile. "I helped you find it, after all."

He slid me a half amused, half exasperated side-eye. "You shouldn't have broken into the house, Maggie. I could write you up for that."

I adopted an expression of supreme innocence. "I didn't break in. The door was open."

"As in, wide open with a 'Welcome Maggie' sign dangling over it?"

"Well, not exactly," I conceded. "More like unlocked."

Reynolds chuckled, and his deep, rumbly laugh warmed me from the inside out. "What am I going to do with you, Ms. Doyle? You were a menace before you got your private investigator's license, and now…" He let the unspoken words hang in the air between us.

"You agreed to write me a letter of recommendation when I applied for the license."

"A moment of madness." His teasing grin took the sting out of his words. "Seriously, you know I wish you well in your new business, but I can't let you break the law."

"You told me not to trample all over the crime scene. I promised to leave the barn alone, and I fulfilled that promise. Besides, I gave you a heads-up about the loose floorboard," I said sweetly. "That saved you time."

"Yeah, and thanks, but you shouldn't have been fiddling with it in the first place."

"But I did fiddle with it, and I saw the laptop and papers hidden underneath. Would you please let Lenny take a look at Wright's internet searches and files? He's a whiz at all things computer-related."

Reynolds spread his palms wide. "No can do. You should know better than to ask."

"Come on. You owe me a favor."

His mouth stretched into the slow-burn smile that never failed to make me weak at the knees. "If I owe you anything, I've repaid it by not charging you with ransacking Jimmy Wright's house after you'd found him dead."

I gave him the evil eye. "If you're referring to Wright's home office looking like it had been attacked by a frenzied orangutan, that wasn't me."

"No?" He crossed his arms over his broad chest and grinned at me. "As far as I'm aware, you were the only person in Jimmy Wright's house after his death. Please tell me you had the sense to wear gloves."

My smile was smug. "Please. I went the whole hog. I even sprang for a hair cover."

Reynolds shook his head. "Some would say that was indicative of you wanting to cover your tracks from the police."

"And yet I informed you about my search, and I did you a favor by dealing with the cat." I needed to steer the conversation away from my impromptu house search and back to the laptop, and I figured the hairball dominatrix would do the trick.

"How's Mavis?" Reynolds asked, taking the bait.

"A terror. She marched into my house, took one look at Bran and the kittens, and proceeded to mark her territory by peeing all over the house."

The policeman winced. "Does this mean Mavis's stay with you will be of short duration?"

"I hope so. It's not fair on Bran and the kittens for Mavis to muscle them out of their home." I grimaced. "Unfortunately, I made the mistake of telling Noreen about Mavis's outrageous behavior before I asked her if she wanted the cat."

Reynolds laughed. "Mavis might calm down once she settles in."

"She's probably missing Jimmy." I treated him to my most sultry smile. "I'm assuming you've looked through his computer files."

"You have a lovely smile, Maggie, but I'm still not giving you any info."

"Could you at least provide Lenny a list of the sites Wright looked up? I only had a chance to memorize a few."

"Even if the contents of Wright's laptop weren't connected to a murder investigation, I couldn't let you or Lenny look at my official notes."

"Lenny's waiting outside." I gave him my most appealing wide-eyed look. "Why don't you let him have a quick look?"

His shoulders heaved with laughter. "You're incorrigible. You never give up, do you?"

"Nope." I crossed my arms over my chest and stared him down. My efforts had little effect.

Laughing, Reynolds stood and held the door of the interrogation room open for me. "You're out of luck, Maggie. The laptop left for the mainland half an hour ago."

I put my hands on my hips and gawked at him. "No fair. You've been stringing me along all this time."

"Yeah." He grinned down at me, reminding me just how tall he was. "It was fun."

"Meanie. The laptop was my only potential way of discovering a connection between Jimmy Wright and Paddy Driscoll's sheep."

"What a load of nonsense. Even if Jimmy took Paddy's sheep twenty-two years ago, why would any mention of the event be on his three-year-old laptop? You just want in on the murder investigation."

"Of course I do." I pressed my lips into a prim line. "I found Jimmy's body, after all."

"I'll keep you informed—up to a point."

His dazzling smile failed to appease me, sexy though it was. I didn't miss the paperwork and politics of being a cop, but, man, I itched to get my teeth into an interesting investigation.

I turned the situation over in my mind while Reynolds led me down the hall and into the waiting room. "I hope the tech crowd can turn up some clues. If Jimmy was kinky, I bet he met his partners online. I doubt there are many people on Whisper Island with a penchant for wearing lime-green sex suits."

Lenny, sleepy-eyed and slumped over a computer magazine, underwent a visible one-eighty. "Did you mention a lime-green sex suit? Like with weird straps that don't cover much?"

Reynolds and I looked at each other, and then back at my friend. "Did you see Jimmy Wright yesterday?" Reynolds demanded. "If so, when?"

"Huh? I didn't see Jimmy." The implication dawned on Lenny, and his thin face grew animated.

"Wait…Wright was murdered while wearing one? Dude, that's awesome."

"Not exactly awesome for Mr. Wright," Reynolds said dryly. "Am I to understand that you saw *someone else* wearing an outfit like Jimmy's?"

"Yeah," Lenny said. "When I was driving over to visit Granddad yesterday, I saw a person running alongside the wall wearing a weird outfit. Sort of a crotchless leotard."

I shuddered. "Please don't tell me fluorescent crotchless outfits are becoming a trend on Whisper Island. If so, I might need to rethink my decision to move here permanently."

Lenny grinned. "No chance. Folks around here are more into wellies and tweed caps. I'd never seen one of those outfits before yesterday, and I consider myself a connoisseur of online porn."

I raised my eyebrows. "I did *not* need to know that."

Reynolds cleared his throat. "Let's focus on the person you saw, Lenny. Are you sure it wasn't Jimmy?"

"Unless he developed boobs before he died, nope."

"Hang on a sec." Liam leaned in. "You saw a woman?"

"Yeah. She was creeping along behind the wall, kind of furtive, but the seat in my van is pretty high. I could see all of her. In every sense of the word."

"You didn't think to tell me this earlier?" I asked,

outraged by my friend's failure to share a scintillating piece of island gossip with me.

Lenny shrugged. "I don't care what other people do for kicks, as long as they're not hurting anyone. I was more interested in hearing about Jimmy's murder."

"Where, exactly, is the field where you saw this woman?" Reynolds pointed to the map of Whisper Island that decorated the wall behind the station's reception desk.

Lenny stepped forward and examined the map. After a moment, he indicated an area that wasn't far from Jimmy's farm. "Must have been around here. It was just before I passed the old windmill."

"What time did you see her?" Reynolds whipped out his notebook and pen.

Lenny considered the question for a moment. "I guess it must have been around four-thirty. Definitely before five."

Reynolds looked at me. "That ties in with Dr. Reilly's estimation of the time of death."

"Whoever the woman was, she must have been meeting Jimmy," I said. "There has to be a connection. I can't imagine many people on the island run around wearing those outfits."

Reynolds's mouth quivered. "You'd be surprised. But yeah. It's unlikely that she wasn't connected to Jimmy. The pertinent question is whether or not she had anything to do with his death."

"Or saw something that could point to the killer," I added. "You say she was running, Lenny?"

"Yeah." He scrunched up his forehead. "Acting furtive for sure. I put it down to the outfit. I figured she'd been sleeping with someone she shouldn't and had to make a run for it when his wife came home."

"Or she'd just witnessed a murder," I suggested, "and was fleeing in terror."

"Or she'd just *committed* a murder," Reynolds countered, "and was making her getaway."

"Surely a woman who'd just killed a man wouldn't make a getaway half naked," I said. "Wouldn't she have gotten dressed first?"

"Did you see any discarded women's clothing in the house or barn?" Reynolds asked.

I shook my head. "You?"

"No." He sighed. "I don't like this. We have to find that woman. Can you give us an exact description, Lenny? Age? Build? Height?"

"Hard to tell height with her crouched so low. As for age…" Lenny considered the point. "I dunno. Forties? Older than us at any rate. Her hair was the sort of blond that reminds me of my sister's dolls. It was…bouffant? I dunno how to describe it. I'm not an expert on hairstyles."

I flipped through my mental photo book of hairstyles. "Big? Do you mean like a beehive? Or an Eighties backcombed look?"

"I'm not sure. It looked kind of weird, but then the outfit wasn't exactly what I usually see people wearing on Whisper Island, so I just put it down to her being eccentric."

Reynolds rubbed the back of his neck. "Okay. I'll need you to give me a formal statement, Lenny. Maggie, thanks for your time."

"You can't just dismiss me like that," I said in tones of outrage. "Not when things are getting interesting. If I hadn't asked Lenny to meet me at the station, you'd never have heard about this half-naked woman running around the fields."

One corner of his mouth curved. "Maybe, maybe not. Either way, I'm in charge of investigating crimes on Whisper Island."

I began to protest, but he cut me off.

"Go back to the café, Maggie. Maybe your P.I. business will turn up an interesting case for you to work on."

I glared at him, but I knew when I was beaten. "Okay. Please let me know if you discover anything relevant to Paddy Driscoll's missing sheep."

Reynolds's expression darkened. "After I take Lenny's statement, I intend to pay Paddy a visit."

Poor old Paddy. Even though I was irritated by the man's impatience for progress on an impossible case, I didn't envy him that interview with Sergeant Reynolds. "Be nice. I don't think he had anything to do with the murder."

"Thank you for sharing your opinion with me. Now go and let me do my job."

I turned on my heel and stomped out of the

police station. I walked back to the café in a state of
frustrated preoccupation, weaving through the crowds
of people. This time of year, Smuggler's Cove was
alive with tourists. They poured out of every store,
café, and business, including my bank.

I bit back a sigh. Jimmy's murder was a million
times more interesting than Paddy's missing sheep,
but however much I wanted to be involved in the
murder inquiry, my bank balance demanded that I
concentrated on paying cases. All the same, I'd use
tonight's dinner to pump the Huffingtons for info on
Jimmy. Outside the café, I flexed my shoulders. Time
to serve scones and field questions about my latest
dead body.

DESPITE MY BEST INTENTIONS, I barely made it to the
Whisper Island Hotel on time that evening. My shift
at the café had been busy, leaving me with no spare
moments to devote to the Case of the Missing Sheep,
and the few tidbits I'd gleaned from customers at the
café weren't sufficient to justify my expenses. Juggling
shifts at the café and a new case was no easy feat, but
I wasn't in a financial position to scale back on the
work for my aunt.

When I pulled into the Whisper Island Hotel's
parking lot, I snagged the last available spot. I
rummaged through my purse and found my phone.
I'd told Paddy I'd call him with an update, and I'd

follow through, even though I had nothing of substance to report.

"Hey," I said when he answered. "I'm calling to check in with you as promised. I'm going to need a few more days before I can type up my initial report."

Total baloney. At this rate, my report would consist of one sentence.

"I'll pay your fee until the end of next week," Paddy muttered. "If you've made no progress by then, we'll call it quits."

"That sounds like a plan." And way more reasonable than I'd expected him to be after last night's rant.

"I might have overreacted last night," Paddy said, unconsciously echoing my thoughts. "Sorry about that. I get emotional when it comes to Nancy."

This was an understatement, but I let it slide. "Don't worry about it. I get that it's a difficult topic for you."

His only response was a grunt. "I heard you found Jimmy Wright's body."

"Yes." I paused for a beat, and my naturally suspicious nature kicked in. "I'd just found him when you called."

"I guess we might never know the truth now."

Paddy's tone was morose and defeatist and hammered home to me how much discovering the sheep's fate meant to him. However absurd I found his obsession, I had to respect his dedication to finding out the truth. However, I couldn't help wondering how much Paddy knew about Jimmy's death. Was the timing of his call yesterday a coincidence? He was aware I intended to talk to Jimmy, and he could have guessed I'd do it when my shift at the café ended.

I glanced at the clock on my dashboard. Time to wrap this up. "Let's wait and see what I uncover over the next few days. The right question could jog someone's memory."

"Okay," Paddy said. "I'll let you get going to that fancy dinner of yours."

"How did you—?" The pieces clicked into place. "Noreen mentioned it to you."

"She did. I never had time for Jimmy Wright, but I'd like to get a look at his rich aunt." He chuckled. "Helen went to school with my father. He said she was quite a looker."

"You might be in luck. If I know Noreen, she'll do her best to persuade the Huffingtons to come to tomorrow night's Movie Club meeting."

"Yeah. She probably will. I'll see you then."

"Bye, Paddy."

I slipped my phone back into my purse. After a quick makeup check in the rear view mirror, I got out of the car and smoothed the bodice of my royal blue strapless midi dress. I'd paired the dress with nude strappy sandals, and kept my jewelry to the silver loops my mother had given me for Christmas, and a simple Irish triskelion pendant that I'd won at a pub quiz a few weeks ago. No doubt I'd pale in comparison to the Huffington family's finery, but I wouldn't disgrace my grandmother's memory in front of her oldest friend.

I took a deep breath and squared my shoulders. Somehow, I'd steer the conversation toward Jimmy Wright's murder. An elderly aunt wasn't likely to know much about how her nephew met a sticky end, but it was worth a shot.

## 5

IN STARK CONTRAST to earlier in the year, business at the Whisper Island Hotel was booming. The tourist season was in full swing, and the lobby teemed with guests. I cut a path across the slick marble floor and almost crashed into Melanie Greer, de facto hotel manager, and my teenage nemesis.

Her eyes widened when she saw me. "Maggie? What are *you* doing here?"

"That's a lovely way to greet a restaurant guest," I said smoothly. "I have a dinner date with your mysterious silent partner."

At the mention of Huff Huffington, Melanie's tanned face paled. "You know Huff?"

"Not yet. His mother was my grandmother's best friend. They've invited my family and me to join them for dinner."

"So that's why I saw Julie and Philomena going

into the restaurant," she mused. "I thought it was out of their price range."

"Tactful as ever," I said dryly. "Now if you'd let me past…"

She placed a tentative hand on my arm, halting my progress. "If you could put in a good word for Paul and me, we'd be very grateful. As you know, things have been…difficult…over the last year."

"If the topic comes up, which I doubt, I'll put in a good word for *you*," I said pointedly. While I didn't intend to blab about Paul's embezzlement now that he'd reimbursed the hotel for the money he'd stolen, I wasn't prepared to lie about his stellar management skills.

Melanie bit her lip and inclined her neck in acknowledgment. "Thanks. I appreciate it."

Leaving her with a worried expression on her expertly made-up face, I hurried into the restaurant.

A waiter hailed me the instant I walked into the room. He looked me up and down and gave a low whistle. "Hello, Maggie. Long time, no see. You look good out of your maid's uniform."

"No one looks good in that uniform. How are you doing, Piotr?" I smiled warmly at the tall Polish waiter with the basketball player's build. I didn't know him well, but we'd crossed paths during my undercover investigation at the hotel earlier this year.

"I'm pretty good, thanks." He grinned. "It's not so quiet as when you worked here."

"I can see that." Like the lobby, the restaurant was packed.

Piotr glanced at the computerized register. "You're here to join the Huffington party with your aunts and cousin?"

"That's correct."

He motioned for me to follow him. "Come on. I'll show you to the table."

On our way through the packed restaurant, I spotted Noreen, sitting at a table near a window and waving madly at me. Philomena and Julie sat beside her, both in more formal attire than I was used to seeing them in beyond our Movie Club nights. As I'd suspected, all of our finery paled in comparison to the designer dresses worn by the other women at the table. My gaze swept over our hosts, taking in an elderly woman who must be Helen Huffington, two younger women, two men in their thirties, and a large man at the head of the table who had to be the infamous Huff Huffington.

Noreen stood and hauled me to the only free seat at the table, beside a handsome young man of around thirty. "Everyone, this is my other niece, Margaret."

*Margaret?* No one had ever called me that, not even my mother. I sat down and exchanged a quizzical look with Julie, who shot me a commiserating expression from the other side of the table.

Helen Huffington was a tiny, bird-like woman in her eighties. She smiled warmly at me from her end of the table. "It's lovely to meet you. You're the spitting image of May." At my blank expression, she laughed. "That's what I used to call your grandmother when we were in school. She hated the name, Peggy."

"It's lovely to meet you, too, Mrs. Huffington. I enjoy reading the old movie magazines you sent my grandmother. My aunts kept her collection."

Helen clapped her hands together as though I'd just completed a performance she'd found pleasing. "How delightful. I like knowing those magazines are being enjoyed by a new generation. Living so far apart, and with little time to write long letters, exchanging magazines was our way of keeping in touch over the years. And please, call me Helen, dear. Mrs. Huffington sounds stuffy."

"Helen, then." The name felt strange on my tongue. With her carefully styled snowy-white hair and expensive but tasteful jewelry, Helen looked as regal as the Dowager Countess in *Downton Abbey*.

"Let me introduce you to the rest of my family." Helen turned to the man seated to her left. "This is my grandson, Rosie, and his wife, Candace."

Rosie, presumably Ambrose J. Huffington IV, winced, and his scowl didn't enhance his homely looks. "Amb, Grandmother. I prefer to go by Amb."

A guffaw of laughter drew my attention to the head of the table. I needed no introduction to know who this was. Ambrose J. "Huff" Huffington III was a large man in every sense of the word. He wasn't fat, but he was well padded, and he had the look of a college athlete gone to seed. Huff had a magnetic presence that, while not charming, made him the central focus of the table, even while his mother had taken the reins on the introductions. I took an instant dislike to the guy.

"Amb?" he sneered. "What sort of a name is that? I've called you Rosie since you were in diapers, and Rosie you'll stay."

A flush crept over his son's face, right up to his receding hairline. Amb opened his mouth as if to speak, but his wife laid a hand on his arm.

"I believe Margaret is our new neighbor, honey. She's one of the permanent residents at the complex." Candace gave me a brittle smile that wasn't reflected in her iron-gray eyes. "Such quaint little houses. Where do you put all your stuff?"

"Oh, you know. Shoeboxes under my bed," I said breezily, ignoring my aunt's warning look. "So you're the family who's rented the other houses at Shamrock Cottages until the end of the month?"

"That's right. Candy and Rosie are in Number One, and I'm staying in Number Two." The guy beside me smiled, displaying even, pearly white teeth. "I'm Doug, the black sheep of the family."

His laugh implied that he was anything but. Doug was good-looking in a clean-cut frat boy kind of way with a wide jaw, high cheekbones, and hazel eyes. His confident appraisal of me sent a warning prickle down my spine. I couldn't put my finger on why—

maybe it was the frat boy look—but Doug Huffington reminded me of my ex.

I snuck a glance across the table. My cousin bit her lip but failed to control her heaving shoulders. Her mother, Philomena, gave me a grin and a conspiratorial wink. I bit back a groan. My aunts would never stop trying to matchmake me with every single man who crossed our paths.

"And last but not least," Helen said, "my son, Huff, and his wife, Brandi."

"That's Brandi with an 'i'," Doug whispered, leaning closer to me than I cared for. "The 'i' is very important."

I focused on Doug's father. Huff Huffington gave me a cursory once-over and scowled as though I hadn't passed muster. His wife barely glanced my way and didn't deign to acknowledge me. She couldn't have been older than her mid-twenties. Younger than Julie and me at any rate. Her blond hair had been teased into a style that would have made Dolly Parton proud, and her enormous breasts didn't fit her petite frame. Still, there was no denying the expensive cut of her dress, and I'd bet the diamonds on the elaborate choker around her neck were the real deal.

Once the introductions were over, I waited for the menus to appear, but none did. In response to my raised eyebrow, my cousin whispered, "Huff's already ordered."

I blinked. Hey, I wasn't *that* late. "But I haven't had a chance to look at a menu."

"Dad likes to order for everyone," Doug explained in a breezy voice, once again leaning into my space in a presumptuous fashion. "If we don't want to eat what Huff likes, tough luck."

*Wow.* Even my former mother-in-law hadn't been that domineering.

By the time the first course arrived, I deeply regretted giving in to my aunt's pressure to attend this dinner. The food was good, even if Huff's menu choices were on the conservative side, but it irked me that he dominated the conversation. On the couple of occasions that Noreen attempted to get a word in edgewise, the man talked over her. We were treated to a list of all his family members' failings, complaints about the service at the hotel, and a list of reasons why the Irish were backward and lazy.

The only person who appeared to have any influence over Huff was his mother, but Helen seemed content to play with her food and listen to her son drone on about people we didn't know and insult each of his relatives in turn.

I swallowed a bite of my steak and pounced on the next conversational lull before Huff could start again. "I found a dead body yesterday."

All eyes at the table were drawn to me, some curious, and others aghast. I took a sip of my wine and weighed my next words with care. I had no idea how well Helen had known her nephew. She didn't give the impression of a woman in mourning, but I didn't want to be insensitive. "I understand you knew the deceased."

Helen coughed into her napkin. Huff turned puce. An ominous silence fell over the table.

"Maggie says he was murdered," Julie piped up. "She's always finding dead bodies."

"Not always," I amended, "but I have found the occasional corpse during my time on Whisper Island."

"That sounds fascinating," Helen said, recovering her composure. "Noreen tells me you're a private investigator."

"That's correct, although my job had little to do with me finding Jimmy Wright's body."

Noreen gave me a swift kick under the table. I ignored her and kept my attention on Helen. Her face remained a perfect blank. "Tell me about this missing sheep, dear. Your aunt mentioned the case. A farmer looking for a sheep after twenty years sounds just like the Whisper Island I remember."

I swallowed a sigh but obliged her with a brief overview of the case. As soon as I got to the part about going to Jimmy's farm to question him, Huff's booming voice drowned me out.

"I don't know why you're complaining about that cottage. The listing said it sleeps up to four people. That's plenty big for you, Candace, and the kid. Aren't they plenty big, Maggie? You live in one, don't you?"

It was the first time this evening that Huff had

engaged me in conversation. I doubted the timing was a coincidence. "They're fine for one or two people. More would be a squash, but they're designed for holidaymakers, not permanent residents. My neighbor and I are the exceptions."

"I don't see why Hailey couldn't join us for dinner tonight," Amb muttered. "She likes steak."

"Once she's out of diapers, she's welcome to join us," Huff said. "Until then, she stays with a sitter."

Candace reared up in indignation. "Hailey is almost six years old. She's been potty trained for years."

"Then why did she pee her pants the last time she visited me?" Hailey's less-than-adoring grandfather demanded. "All I did was ask her to clear her playthings off the lawn."

*Whoa.* The sip of wine in my mouth turned to vinegar. What a total boor.

"You intimidate her." Candace's tone was flinty. "She was too scared to say she needed to use the restroom."

Huff's nostrils flared. "If I scare her, it's only because you've raised a wimp. I'm her grandfather. Why should she be scared of me?"

If Amb held the stem of his wine glass any tighter, it would snap. "She doesn't like it when you shout."

His father's sneer made me want to slap the man. "The child needs to toughen up. If you and Candace would hurry up and give her a brother, the kid would soon learn to stand up for herself."

Amb's face turned chalky white. Beside him, Candace's ramrod-straight posture faltered, and her heavily Botoxed forehead threatened to display emotion. It didn't take a degree in psychology to see that Huff's remark had hit them like a bucket of acid.

"Has Hailey had a chance to try out the playground or the games room at Shamrock Cottages?" I directed the question at Candace, who looked as though she was about to burst into tears, and her husband flashed me a grateful look.

The woman swallowed, and a hint of a smile broke through her stiff expression. "I believe that was her plan for this evening. Martha—my sister-in-law—stayed behind to look after her."

"It'll be nice to see the family facilities get some use. For the last few months, the only residents have been me and my neighbor, and neither of us has kids living with us."

"The 'family facilities,' as you call them, would get more use if my children were more inclined to reproduce." Huff drained his wine glass in one go and slammed it on the table. "Doug here is divorced with no children, and Rosie and Candy only have one kid. I'd hoped for more grandchildren by now."

"Well, don't waste your time waiting for Martha to get married, honey," Brandi said, a catlike smile on her lips. "At least she makes a good babysitter."

I experienced a pang of sympathy for the absent Martha. It couldn't be easy living with a domineering father and a stepmother who was younger than her.

Huff puffed out his chest and patted his wife's hand. "Maybe you can take her shopping, honey. Give her a few tips. Lord knows she needs 'em."

I was on the verge of putting my size eights into my mouth and calling Huff several uncomplimentary monikers when Helen intervened. "Now, Huff, dear," she said in her soft, lilting voice that had never quite erased the Irish tones of her childhood. "This is a friendly family gathering with my oldest friend's daughters and granddaughters. Save the family squabbles for an appropriate time." She turned to me and gave me a beatific smile. "Before you arrived, Noreen had just invited me to attend your Movie Club meeting tomorrow night. It sounds fun."

I swallowed my unspoken diatribe against her son and focused on the elderly lady. "We'd love to have you. We dress up, drink cocktails, and watch classic movies. Tomorrow night's movie is *How to Marry a Millionaire*."

"Wonderful." Her eyes grew misty. "May would have loved that club. I have very few regrets about the decisions I made during my life, but not returning to Ireland while she was still alive is one of them."

"Mammy adored the old movie theater in Smuggler's Cove," Noreen said. "I inherited my interest in old films from her. Renovating it into the Movie Theater Café was a dream come true."

"Well, I'm looking forward to seeing it. Maybe I can persuade Candace and Martha to join me." She glanced at her oldest grandson. "You don't mind looking after Hailey tomorrow evening?"

For the first time that evening, Amb's face lit up. "Sure I'll stay with her. We can check out the games room at Shamrock Cottages." He turned to me. "Is the games room worth investigating?"

"Definitely. I'd have loved it as a kid. There's table tennis, foosball, snooker, and a stack of board games."

At his end of the table, Huff cleared his throat in an exaggerated manner and began a loud and interminable story about some guy he'd beaten at golf earlier that day. Amb's relaxed expression vanished, and the rest of the meal dragged on. I tried to engage Helen in conversation a couple of times, but either she didn't hear me, or she was deliberately avoiding any discussion about her nephew's untimely demise.

After a dessert that I barely tasted, we were finally set free by Huff's announcement that he was hitting the bar. His goodbyes to us were cursory at best, and I didn't care for the steely glint in his eyes when he shook my hand. "Good luck with your new business venture, Maggie."

He pronounced the words "business" and "venture" like they were poison. No, his interruption earlier had been no accident. But why? Was he protecting his mother from my curiosity because she was grieving and putting on a brave face for her dinner guests? Or did Huff know something about Jimmy's death? I dismissed this last observation. The

Huffingtons hadn't arrived on Whisper Island until this morning, hours after Jimmy was murdered.

Huff moved on to Noreen, and I shook hands with Amb, Candace, and Doug in turn. The latter held my hand longer than I liked.

"I hope to see you again soon, Maggie," Doug whispered into my ear, his finger caressing my palm. "I've only been on the island for a few hours, and I'd love to get a tour of the hot spots from one of the residents. Maybe we can go out for a drink while I'm on Whisper Island."

Or maybe *not*.

With a tight smile, I extricated my hand from his grasp and resisted the urge to wipe it clean. I didn't peg Doug as a predator, but his cocky self-assurance and presumption that I'd fall at his feet reminded me of Joe, my soon-to-be ex-husband. Joe had the same easy charm and seemingly off-the-cuff compliments that I'd since discovered were well-rehearsed lines.

Amb helped Helen to her feet while Candace supplied the older woman with her cane.

"Thank you so much for coming. It's lovely to see May's family." Helen turned to me. "Did anyone mention the weekend trip to you, Margaret? We might have discussed it before you arrived."

Weekend trip? I suppressed a shudder. Any trip involving Huff Huffington wasn't one I intended to join. "No, but I have plans this weekend."

"If you mean your shifts at the café, I've already sorted that out." Noreen beamed at me. "Kelly and one of her friends have agreed to cover for both of us."

"We're throwing a party on Gull Island on Saturday evening," Helen interjected before I could respond to my aunt. "Just a small gathering. I hope you'll come along."

"Of course she——" Noreen began, but I cut her off. She'd twisted my arm to come to tonight's dinner, and I hadn't even had the opportunity to talk to Helen about Jimmy Wright. No way was I spending a weekend trapped on Gull Island with Huff.

"I have a case to investigate, but thank you for the invitation."

Helen patted my arm. "If you change your mind, the invitation still stands. The family is going over early on Saturday morning, and I've arranged for a boat to take your aunts and cousin over in the afternoon."

"I hope you all have a great time," I said diplomatically. "See you tomorrow at the Movie Club."

As we exited the restaurant, I turned the evening's events over in my mind. Huff had acted shifty, and Helen was hiding something. I had no idea if their behavior was connected to Jimmy Wright's murder, but I intended to get answers.

## 6

THE MORNING after my dinner with the Huffingtons, I got up early to get in a run before work. I left Mavis snoozing at the foot of my bed. She'd decided that my bedroom was hers but thankfully refrained from peeing all over it to make her point.

By the time I'd pulled on my running gear, Bran, the Border collie-Labrador mix I'd inherited from Noreen, was prancing in front of the cottage door, eager to get moving. I scratched his head. "You're so impatient. You know I need to feed the kittens first."

At the mere sound of me opening a can of cat food, Sukey and Felix appeared at my side, meowing and rubbing against my legs. I bent down and stroked their soft fur. I'd been reluctant to take on pets when I hadn't been sure how long I'd stay on Whisper Island, but now that the move looked to be permanent, I'd warmed to the idea of having company in the cottage. The kittens were the progeny of Noreen's cats, Roly and Poly, and had just turned five months old.

From his position in front of the door, Bran whined with impatience. I ignored him and filled the kittens' bowls with fresh water and cat food. I added bowls for Mavis for when she deigned to wake up. Once Sukey and Felix were busy with their breakfast, I laced up my running shoes and took Bran outside.

The sun was just beginning to rise. A gorgeous orange glow lit up the semicircle of houses that formed the Shamrock Cottages complex. Outside the cottages occupied by the younger members of the Huffington clan, Candace and a short woman I didn't recognize were setting tables for breakfast. Torn between impatience to start my run and curiosity to meet Huff's only daughter, I tugged on Bran's leash to rein him in. The decision was made for me when Candace spotted me and waved.

I jogged over to join them, Bran pulling me forward at a rapid pace. "Morning."

Candace wore a light linen summer dress and strappy sandals. Even at five-thirty in the morning, her makeup was perfect. "Hello, Margaret. I hope you slept well."

"Yes, thanks. And I prefer Maggie."

"Ah." A thin smile appeared on her lips. "I wondered."

She made it sound like an insult, but I let it pass. I focused on the woman beside her. In spite of Martha's shapeless beige dress and a face free from makeup, I judged her to be no older than her early thirties. I stretched out a hand. "I'm Maggie Doyle. I live at Number Eight."

The woman darted a glance at Candace before shoving a strand of mousey hair behind one ear. "Martha Huffington."

"I was sorry to miss you last night," I said in a warmer tone than I'd used with her sister-in-law. "I hope you can make the Movie Club meeting tonight."

"Well, I—" Martha looked flustered, and her pale hand fluttered to the string of pearls around her neck. What was it about dedicated spinsters and strands of pearls?

"Of course she'll be there." Candace squeezed her sister-in-law's shoulder. "You enjoy old movies, don't you, Martha?"

The woman inclined her neck a fraction. "I guess so."

"Then that's settled." Candace turned to me. "What time do we need to be there?"

"Eight o'clock would be good," I replied. "We drink cocktails before the movie begins."

"That sounds lovely." This time Candace's smile was reflected in her eyes. "We'll see you then."

AFTER MY RUN, I showered, dressed, and drove the thirty-minute distance from Shamrock Cottages to the Movie Theater Café. I didn't bother with breakfast—

I'd grab a scone at the café and wash it down with some of Noreen's excellent coffee.

My day passed in a blur of waiting tables, baking scones, and snatching spare moments to hunt down the missing sheep. By the time the café closed that evening, I had to conclude that my investigation was not progressing well. The few people who remembered the sheep incident were of the opinion that Nancy had wandered off and fallen off the cliff.

"Paddy's rift with Jimmy Wright was well known," Noreen said while we were setting up the café for the Movie Club meeting. "No one took it seriously. Sure, we all know Paddy has a temper, but he's all bark and no bite."

I glanced up from the James Cagney table, where I was going over the accounts with Julie. "What triggered the feud? The missing sheep, or something before that?"

"Oh, that's been going on for years. Jimmy and Paddy used to be best friends…until Jimmy married Paddy's ex-girlfriend."

I recalled the wedding photo I'd seen in Jimmy's bedroom. "I heard they got divorced."

"Poor old Jimmy," Julie said. "Mum said Sally had departed for the mainland before the ink was dry on the marriage certificate."

With, presumably, the kid I'd seen in the photograph beside Jimmy's bed. "Did Paddy have contact with his son?"

An expression of surprise flooded my aunt's face, and Julie looked equally perplexed.

"Son?" Noreen shook her head. "Ah, no. Jimmy was quiet about his private life, but he'd have said if Sally had been pregnant."

"He had a photo of a little boy on his nightstand, taken in the Eighties."

"Really?" Noreen considered this for a moment. "Are you sure it wasn't one of the Huffington boys?"

"I guess it could be."

"They'd be about the right age," Julie said. "Only why would Jimmy have a photo of just one of them and not the other?"

"Exactly," I added. "And what about Martha?"

Noreen frowned. "I don't know. Perhaps Jimmy was godfather to one of the boys."

"That's a possibility." If Jimmy was close enough to the Huffingtons to be a godfather to one of Huff's boys, why had they acted so cagey yesterday when I'd mentioned the murder? A thought struck me. "Who's Jimmy's next of kin?"

"Helen Huffington, I suppose," Noreen said. "Jimmy's only brother died a few years back, and there's no one else. Why don't you want to go to Gull Island, Maggie? The Huffingtons have rented Marley House for the occasion. It's bound to be a lovely weekend."

I arched one eyebrow. "Don't you mean *Margaret*?"

Julie giggled.

Noreen had the good grace to blush. "I'm sorry. I

don't know what came over me last night. Those people were so…formal. And Huff…well, you saw what he's like. I got nervous."

"Huff's an uncouth boor," I said with feeling. "There's no need to make my name posh for him."

"The man is a pig," Julie added. "You missed him insulting his wife, Maggie. He flat-out told her she was stupid."

"She doesn't strike me as book smart," I said, "but she's got a certain cunning. She's smart enough to dress in a way she knows will please Huff."

"Won't you reconsider the weekend trip, Maggie?" Noreen's eyes were pleading. "You haven't been out to Gull Island since you moved to Whisper Island. We took you a couple of times when you visited as a child."

"I remember. We visited Dolphin Island, too. I have fond memories of both, but I don't want to spend the weekend with Huff just to see Gull Island again."

"You don't have to hang out with Huff," Noreen argued. "He's made it perfectly clear he's not interested in us. But Doug seems to like you."

I rolled my eyes. "I get the impression that Doug likes every female from puberty to menopause."

"He is on the slimy side," Julie agreed, pushing a stray auburn curl behind her ear.

"See?" I said to Noreen. "Even Julie agrees, and she's got arguably worse taste in men than I do."

"A low blow," my cousin said dryly. "I figure we're about even in the bad taste stakes."

A vision of Sergeant Liam Reynolds flashed through my mind, and the butterflies in my stomach took flight. "We can make a conscious decision to change. We don't have to settle for bad guys."

"Never settle for bad coffee, bad men, and bad books," Philomena said, staggering through the café door laden with a stack of movie magazines. "If Maggie doesn't want to go to Gull Island, leave her alone."

I raised an eyebrow. Philomena was usually just as much a matchmaker as her sister. "Why does your support worry me?"

Philomena dumped the magazines on a table with a complacent smile. "Money is all very well and good, but I'd like you and Julie to settle down with men likely to stay on the island."

"Of course you would." I exchanged an amused glance with my cousin. If it were left up to my aunts, Julie and I would be dragged down the aisle with the nearest farmers.

While Julie and I finished the accounts, I considered the information about Jimmy Wright. The farm and its surrounding land must be worth a chunk of change, but the Huffingtons were multi-millionaires. Jimmy's farm would have little impact on their financial situation. Besides, the Huffingtons hadn't arrived on Whisper Island until after Jimmy's murder.

I was still mulling over the strange circumstances

of Jimmy's murder when Lenny arrived. He always volunteered to help us set up for the Movie Club meetings, and he was responsible for the tech side of screening the movies.

"Hey, ladies." Lenny grinned at me. "Still chasing sheep, Maggie?"

I groaned. "That case is a disaster. I don't think I can justify charging Paddy. I haven't been able to discover anything half the island doesn't know."

My friend slapped me on the back. "I have faith in you. Something'll turn up."

I glanced at my watch. "You'd better get up to the projection room."

"Ahem," he said, grinning. "Don't you mean your office?"

I pulled a face. "An office I haven't had a chance to use."

"I've put the word out that you're in business," Noreen said, bustling into the café with a tray loaded with clean cocktail glasses. "You'll soon have more clients."

I exchanged an amused look with Lenny. I just hoped that future clients wouldn't want me to look for long-dead sheep.

Lenny departed to make sure everything was in working order for the screening later, and I helped Julie and my aunts get snacks ready for the meeting. When I had a quiet moment between cleaning tables and polishing cocktail glasses, I slipped upstairs to join him in the projection room that doubled as my office for Movie Reel Investigations.

I ran my finger over the shiny new sign on the door and felt a wistful pang in my stomach. Setting up as a private investigator was a risk. If the business failed, I had no reason to stay on Whisper Island. Over the last few months, it had become abundantly clear to me that this wasn't a vacation or a temporary stay. I'd never felt as at home as I did on the island, and I was determined to make a life here.

I knocked lightly on the door and went in. Lenny was fiddling with cables. "Sorry I didn't call you yesterday, Maggie. We had a computer emergency at the shop, and I had to stay late to fix it."

"No problem. I haven't exactly made great progress with the sheep case." I perched on the side of my desk. "Did you have any success with those websites I mentioned?"

"Jimmy Wright was into online dating, but we'd guessed that already." Lenny winked at me. "Admit your interest in Jimmy's love life has nothing to do with Paddy's sheep."

"I found his body. Of course I'm interested in the murder investigation. There's also the odd coincidence that Paddy hired me the day before Jimmy died, and specifically suggested I talk to the man."

"I still can't see Paddy sticking a rake in Jimmy over a sheep that went missing more than twenty years ago," Lenny said. "It's probably just a coincidence."

"I agree, but I'm a former cop. Cops don't like coincidences, and neither do private eyes." I shifted my weight to my other leg. "Tell me more about Jimmy's dating sites."

"They catered to people with unusual tastes."

"Hence the mankini."

"Exactly." Lenny's grin widened. "I managed to hack into his online profiles and read his messages."

My ears pricked up. "Seriously? That's awesome. Did they reveal anything about who he was seeing?"

"Sort of. He had regular hookups with two women from what I could tell, but I suspect not all of their communication was through the website."

"And we don't have access to his phone," I added.

"Right. But I can tell you that one of the women lived in Galway and went by the online moniker of Nene68. The other woman called herself Sally. She made a reference to meeting Jimmy on the island last month, so she might be the person I saw."

"Did you check out their profile pictures?"

"Of course. And that's where it gets complicated. In their photos, both women are heavily made up and wearing costumes. That was Jimmy's kink. It's hard to tell what they'd look like without the wigs."

"Wigs?" My brain whirred. "You said the woman in the field had weird hair."

Lenny nodded. "Yeah. It could have been a wig that had gone askew while she was running."

"In other words, we can't rely on her being a blonde," I mused. "Pity."

"Sorry the search wasn't more helpful." Lenny wrinkled his brow. "I still don't see how Jimmy's sex life can have any connection to Paddy's missing sheep."

"Neither do I, but seeing that I found his body, I have a vested interest in Jimmy Wright's murder."

My friend laughed. "I'd say Sergeant Reynolds is thrilled about that."

"Not remotely. He warned me not to dig for info."

"Which you promptly ignored by asking me to use my Google-fu skills."

I grinned. "Guilty as charged."

Julie burst into the room, out of breath. "The Huffingtons have arrived. Noreen's all aflutter and wants you downstairs."

"I gotta get a look at the YouTube star," Lenny exclaimed, leaping to his feet. "He was unbelievably obnoxious in the clips I saw."

"He's just as bad in real life," I said with a sigh. "Why's Noreen freaking out? The Huffingtons aren't visiting royalty."

"They've got money and an eligible bachelor. That qualifies them as royalty in Noreen's book." Julie's eyes twinkled. "She and Mum want you to entertain Doug."

"Doug's here?" I groaned and followed her out of my office and down the stairs that led to the café. "Why aren't they throwing *you* at him?"

"Because Mum has set her heart on me getting

together with Günter," Julie said over her shoulder. "Like that will ever happen."

"The lady doth protest too much, methinks," Lenny whispered behind me, making me giggle.

I had my suspicions about my cousin's true feelings about Günter, but tonight wasn't the moment to dwell on Julie's love life. I had a wily old lady to interrogate.

## 7

TO MY SURPRISE, the entire Huffington clan, minus Amb and Hailey, were gathered by the bar. Huff and Doug had gone all out and wore tuxedoes. Helen and Candace had opted for elegant evening gowns, while Brandi wore a low-cut dress so short that it barely covered her shapely behind. In contrast to her relatives, Martha was dressed in a drab pantsuit of an indeterminate color that was somewhere between beige and vomit.

"Oh, my," Julie murmured under her breath. "That girl needs a fashion intervention."

"From what I could ascertain from our admittedly brief encounter this morning, Martha Huffington's lack of fashion sense is the least of her problems."

Julie dragged me forward, and I greeted Helen warmly, introducing Lenny as an old friend.

"I remember your grandfather well," Helen said to him. "Is Gerry still with us?"

"He's alive and kicking," Lenny said. "He might stop by tonight if he can tear himself away from his latest brew of poteen."

I left Helen reminiscing about the island's old fogies and welcomed the rest of her family to the Movie Theater Café. Once again, Doug took the opportunity to hold my hand for longer than was socially acceptable. When he leaned down to whisper in my ear, his breath smelled of whiskey. "Want to skip out on the movie and go somewhere nicer?" His slurred speech indicated that he was well on the way to getting drunk.

I yanked back my hand and glared at him. "If you'd rather go elsewhere, the door's to your left." I plastered on a smile and moved on to Candace. I kept up the smile for almost all of them, but my reception of Huff was mutually cool. "I wouldn't have thought you'd be interested in old movies," I said sweetly. "Given the comments you made last night about the Irish being obsessed with history and living in the past."

Noreen shot me a warning look, but I ignored her.

Huff eyed me properly for the first time that evening. "I don't much care for old movies, but Mother likes them. It was important to her that I come."

*Interesting.* So Helen exerted more influence over her son than I'd thought. Pity she didn't persuade him to stop belittling his family.

Lenny left to mix cocktails, and Helen drifted over

to my side. "I'm looking forward to the film. *How to Marry a Millionaire* was one of the first films I saw after I moved to America."

"And then Grandmother went and did just that." Doug flashed his white teeth at us.

"So I did, young man," Helen said tartly. "And if I hadn't, your grandfather would never have made a success of Huffington Enterprises."

Doug snorted. "Pity Brandi is unlikely to work the same magic on the company."

Candace cleared her throat. "Martha and I were just saying how charming your aunt's café is, Maggie. It's not the usual sort of place we frequent, of course."

*Of course.* I took a step closer to Helen and deftly maneuvered her out of earshot of the others. "May I ask you a question?"

"Sure, dear. Is it about your grandmother?" A hint of her perfume tickled my nose. It reminded me of the scent my former mother-in-law had favored.

"No, it's not about Granny." I hesitated for a moment. "Actually, it's about your nephew. I think I put my foot in it last night. I'm sorry if I upset you."

An emotion passed over Helen's face so quickly that I might have missed it had I not been paying attention. I'd been a cop too long not to recognize fear when I saw it. When she spoke, Helen was in full control of her feelings. "It's a terrible tragedy. I believe you found his body?"

"Yes." I paused for a moment, allowing her composure to settle. "Were you and Jimmy close?"

Her glance darted to the left before focusing on me. "No, I'm afraid we weren't. I left Whisper Island several years before he was born."

"What a shame he died the day before you came back."

She looked at me sharply and didn't respond for a long moment. "According to the newspapers, Jimmy was killed on Wednesday. Huff, Brandi, and I got here on Monday."

Now it was my turn to be surprised. "I thought you arrived on the ferry yesterday morning."

"Oh, the others did." Helen's smile didn't quite meet her eyes, but I gave her credit for her acting skills. "Huff had business to attend to at the hotel. He, Brandi, and I have rooms at the hotel, and the others are staying at those cottages where you live."

So Huff and Helen had been on the island for two whole days before Jimmy Wright had died? I filed this information away for future reference. If Helen had barely known her nephew, I couldn't think of a reason why she or her son would be involved in Jimmy's murder, but they were relatives, and the connection was worth checking out.

Philomena appeared with a tray of cocktails, and Helen's shoulders visibly relaxed. "Here's a martini for you, Helen. I made one for you, too, Maggie." My aunt handed around cocktails to the group. "Here you go, Huff. A Maple Old Fashioned, just like you asked for. I followed Maggie's recipe."

Huff took a sip, not bothering to wait until we'd said *sláinte*. "Not bad," he said grudgingly to me. "Where'd you learn to make cocktails? I suppose you waited bars. You're the type."

"If you mean I'm the type to pay my way through school, then yes. College degrees don't come cheap, even at state schools. But then, you wouldn't know about that, would you?"

Huff laughed. "You've got balls, lady. I wish you'd give them to my son."

"I assume you're not referring to me, Dad." Doug sidled over to us and gave me a practiced smile. "I've got plenty."

"Do you work at Huffington Enterprises, too?" I asked, my curiosity getting the better of me.

Doug laughed. "No way. I don't want to play second fiddle to my brother. Besides, I'm not a board-room kind of guy."

"You're a fool, but at least you have a sense of adventure." Huff's lip curled. "It makes me sick to think of the family business passing to someone without my abilities."

"Amb is perfectly capable of running Huffington Enterprises," Candace said, bristling with hauteur.

"Yeah." Huff sneered. "Right into the ground. The boy's too much of a wimp to crush his opponents. That's what you gotta do in business."

A muscle flexed in Candace's jaw. She looked like

she wanted to say more, but pressed her plump lips together in a visible effort not to antagonize her father-in-law further.

I, however, had no such reservations. "I guess Amb isn't destined to become a YouTube sensation," I said over the rim of my martini glass. "I saw the clip of you hurling your scotch glass at a guy's head. Is that an example of you crushing your opponents?"

Huff's face turned a deep purple.

Noreen moved speedily, grabbed my arm, and hauled me off. "I need Maggie to serve the club members. Back in a sec." When we were out of earshot, she demanded, "What are you doing, Maggie? Huff can be brash, but please try to be polite to him."

"Sure. As long as he's polite to everyone else."

"We both know that's not going to happen." My aunt's shoulders tensed. "He's a difficult man, but Helen was Mammy's oldest friend. I want their visit to Whisper Island to go well, for Mammy's sake."

I exhaled a sigh. "Fine. I can do polite. Just keep me away from Huff. And Doug, too. The man's a pest."

"I was disappointed when you didn't want to join us on Gull Island, but now I'm relieved. I don't want tension this weekend." Noreen shot a glance in the Huffingtons' direction. "And I think I made a mistake trying to bring you and Doug together. He's so drunk he can barely stand straight."

"Are you sure you don't want to cancel the trip?

You could come over to my place. I'm planning to spend my weekend looking for Paddy's sheep and watching Bette Davis movies."

"Part of me wants to, but I'd like a chance to get to know Helen better." My aunt glanced at her watch. "Speaking of movies, we'd better get everyone into the theater."

I laughed. "I thought you wanted me to serve drinks."

"I only said that to get you away from Huff. Philomena and Lenny have the drinks under control."

Fifteen minutes later, I'd helped my aunts to get everyone into the movie theater, and Lenny had started the movie for us. I sat next to Lenny. Julie, to her annoyance, ended up beside Günter, our friend from the Unplugged Gamers club and the guy Philomena was determined to make her son-in-law, and that Julie—for reasons I had yet to discover—was equally determined to avoid. I slid a look at Günter, who was his usual clean but disheveled self, complete with his battered German Army jacket, thick beard, and wild blond hair. Günter was the only member of the Movie Club who didn't dress up for our meetings, mainly because he didn't own a suit.

The movie proved to be as entertaining as I remembered. Judging by the applause at the end, it was one of our better recent choices. We all filed out of the movie theater, and the club members began to collect their coats and head home.

Just as the Huffingtons were about to leave, the bell above the café door jangled, and Sergeant Liam Reynolds strode in. My stomach leaped in that way it always did when I saw him, even if our paths had crossed several times that day.

Reynolds sought me out and made a beeline in my direction. When he stopped in front of me, his crinkly smile made his blue eyes twinkle. "Maggie, love. I thought I'd missed you."

And to my utter astonishment, he kissed me right on the lips.

I inhaled sharply, but Reynolds's mouth silenced my gasp. His lips were warm, soft, and tender—everything I'd imagined when I allowed myself to contemplate what it would be like to kiss him. I'd hardly had time to register what was happening when he broke the kiss and stepped back, leaving me red-faced and breathless. I stared up at him in stunned silence.

"Is this your young man, Maggie?" Helen's curious voice cut through the haze of my thoughts.

I dragged my gaze away from Liam. Behind the Huffingtons, Lenny, Julie, and my aunts formed a tableau of slack-jawed incredulity. In contrast, Günter seemed utterly unfazed by the course of events.

"N—" I began, but Liam beat me too it.

"Yes." He stepped forward and took Helen's hand. "I'm Liam Reynolds, Maggie's boyfriend."

I slow-blinked. What was he up to? Icy humiliation washed over me, stinging my skin from head to toe. Had he kissed me to get an in with the Huffing-tons? If so, why?

"Nice to meet you, Liam," Helen said. "I'm Helen Huffington."

"It's a pleasure to meet you, Mrs. Huffington. Are you enjoying your time on Whisper Island?"

She beamed. "Oh, yes. A lot has changed on the island, but so much is just as I remember from my girlhood."

"Are you doing much traveling while you're in Ireland?" he asked.

Helen laughed the sexy tinkling laugh that must have won over Ambrose J. Huffington II all those years ago. "Not I. The long flight tired me out. But we're planning to spend the weekend on Gull Island, and I'm very much looking forward to that." She gave me a sly glance. "It's a pity Maggie can't join us. She could have brought you along as her date."

"Oh, didn't she tell you?" Reynolds put his arm around my shoulders and squeezed me tight. "She rearranged her schedule so she can go."

I breathed in sharply, and his grip around me tightened in warning.

"How wonderful." Helen appeared to be genuinely pleased. "Will you join us, Mr. Reynolds?"

"The name's Liam. And I'd love to." He turned to me, and I read the message in his eyes as clearly as if he'd written it with neon ink. "If that's okay by you, Maggie?"

No, it was not okay. That rat had used me to

further his investigation. Had the kiss meant nothing to him? Despite my anger and confusion, my rational side replayed the last few minutes on fast forward. He'd introduced himself as Liam Reynolds, conveniently forgetting to add the "Sergeant" part, and he'd made no reference to living in the same complex as the younger Huffingtons. Whatever was going on, he needed my assistance in getting onto Gull Island and crashing their party. Which meant he had a lead on the Wright murder case, and that lead had to concern Helen or Huff. No way was I passing up an opportunity to glean insider info on Jimmy Wright's murder.

I looked up at Reynolds's handsome face, smiling benignly down at me, and resisted the urge to kick him in the gonads. "Of course, Liam. We'll have a blast."

"Excellent. I'm glad that's settled." Helen turned her attention to my cousin, who was helping Günter load a tray with dirty cocktail glasses. "Is this young man your boyfriend? Would he like to join us?"

Julie's eyes widened, but before she could respond, her mother and Noreen said "yes" in hearty unison.

"Günter, *dear*," my cousin said in a voice laced with sarcasm, "you said you had plans this weekend."

"Nothing I can't change, *mein Schatz*," Günter said, not missing a beat. "I haven't been over to Gull Island since last summer. I'd love to join you if I may."

"Splendid." Helen beamed at us. "I just know we'll all have a wonderful time."

I snuck a glance at my "date" for the next two

days and flashed him a wicked grin. The trepidation I read in his eyes pleased me. If Sergeant Reynolds wanted to use me to help his investigation, I'd milk the situation to my advantage. I raised my glass to him. "*Sláinte*. Here's to a wonderful weekend."

## 8

THE BOAT the Huffingtons had hired to take us to Gull Island was the polar opposite of the Whisper Island ferry. A uniformed porter helped Günter and Reynolds haul Noreen's and Julie's numerous cases up the wooden ramp and onto the vessel. I'd packed the bare essentials, and Reynolds was similarly light on baggage. Günter didn't appear to have brought more than a small backpack and his usual calm demeanor.

Julie's phone rang the instant she climbed on board. When she looked at the display, she groaned. "Please don't let this be another substitute teacher mess-up."

When my cousin moved to the other side of the boat to take her call, I regarded the pile of suitcases at Noreen's side and chuckled. "We're there for less than forty-eight hours. You guys have brought enough stuff for a month's vacation."

"We need options, especially now that you and

Julie have brought companions along. You need to dress the part." Noreen lowered her voice. "I do hope Günter makes an effort with his appearance. I had a word with him last night. This is his chance to impress Julie and turn a fake date into the real deal."

I glanced over at Günter, who was leaning against the rail and laughing at something Reynolds had said. The German was a good-looking guy, even with his wild hair and beard. "Günter's fine as he is. Don't try to change him. And please stop with the matchmaking. You'll make Julie run."

"I'll try to keep it under control, but I promised Philomena I'd do my best. She'd love to see Julie settled."

"Speaking of Philomena, where is she?" I scanned the pier, but there was no sign of my aunt or uncle. "It's not like her to be late."

"Oh, she's not coming. She and John have a sixtieth birthday party to attend."

I laughed. "Did Huff scare her off?"

"My sister's made of tougher stuff than that buffoon," Noreen said with feeling. "No, the party plans were already made, and Philomena didn't want to back out."

"If you don't like Huff, why were you so insistent that we go to this party?"

"For Helen's sake. Her son can go and jump in the ocean and swim back to America for all I care." Noreen's hard expression softened. "Like I said last night, Mammy would have wanted us to make Helen welcome, and that's what I'll do."

Julie marched over to us, red-faced and still clutching her phone. "Honestly. My boss *knew* I was away this weekend."

I cocked an eyebrow. "Problem at work?"

"Cormac forgot to arrange a substitute for this morning's Beginner Irish class. Somehow he thinks it's my fault." My cousin blew out her cheeks. "I asked for this weekend off well before the Huffingtons made their plans."

"How are the Saturday morning classes going?"

Julie rolled her eyes. "A disaster. The classes were Cormac's brainchild. He thought it was a great way to earn extra money for the school during the tourist season. Unfortunately, we have a small staff, and few of us are keen on giving up part of our weekends. Officially, the Beginner Irish class is taught by Oisin and me. We're each supposed to work every other Saturday. In reality, I'm landed with three or four Saturdays a month because Oisin always has sporting events. It's not fair."

"And because Oisin is his son, the school principal takes his side," I finished.

"Exactly." Julie shoved a stray auburn curl behind her ear. "Anyway, let's forget about it. I want to enjoy the weekend and not dwell on work. Besides——" she flashed me a wicked grin, "——you need to tell us when you and Reynolds became an item."

I opened my mouth to tell her that Reynolds and

I weren't an item—at least, not yet—but I held my tongue. While we hadn't had an opportunity to discuss the situation, I knew he needed me to stay silent about the true state of our relationship. As for Julie, she was giving Günter a pointed cold shoulder, but he appeared to be indifferent to her icy treatment.

The boat's horn saved me from answering Julie's question. A moment later, we were off and powering out to sea in the direction of Gull Island. Reynolds sidled over to us and deftly maneuvered me away from the others. We strolled down the deck at a casual pace—or as casual as one could be when a strong Atlantic wind hit the deck.

When we were out of earshot, Reynolds's grip around my waist relaxed. "Thanks for playing along last night. I'm sorry I haven't had a chance to talk to you alone since then."

The memory of his kiss made my heart beat a little faster. I took a deep breath of salty sea air and aimed for cool, calm, and semi-collected. "Don't worry about it. I guessed it was about Jimmy Wright's murder, and my hunch was cemented when you didn't return to the cottages last night."

*Oh, ouch.* Had I just admitted I'd waited up for him? When he hadn't returned by two o'clock in the morning, I'd given up and gone to bed.

"I stayed over at Günter's new place." Reynolds rubbed his freshly shaven jaw, drawing my attention to his strong hands. "I was pretty sure none of the Huffingtons had seen me yet, and I wanted to use that to my advantage."

"Who's looking after your cat?"

Reynolds's expression lit up at the mention of the kitten he'd rescued last winter. She was part of the same litter as Sukey and Felix. "I heard on the Whisper Island rumor mill that Miss Flynn and Miss Murphy were looking after Bran and your cats for the weekend. I asked if they'd be willing to take mine as well."

"What have you discovered?" I asked, curious to know why Reynolds was desperate to spend the weekend with the Huffingtons. "Did Helen visit her nephew before he died? Or did Huff?"

"They say not. Sergeant O'Shea questioned Helen and Huff on Thursday, but new information has come to light since then. I decided to trade on our acquaintance in the hope of snagging an invitation to this weekend's shindig on Gull Island. I apologize for ambushing you like that." A slow smile spread across his face, revealing his barely there dimples. "Can't say I didn't enjoy our first kiss, even if I'd have chosen for it to happen under other circumstances."

My cheeks burned, and I cursed myself for blushing like a teenager. "I didn't expect it to happen in front of half of Whisper Island."

"Neither did I." His grin widened. "But I liked it."

So had I. Far more than was good for me. I cleared my throat. Time to focus on a topic that didn't involve getting hot and bothered by the sergeant.

"Does the new info you've discovered implicate Helen or Huff? When I spoke to Helen about Jimmy, she swore she barely knew him."

Reynolds snorted. "Define 'barely.' Jimmy worked for her company for five years during the Eighties. I don't know how much contact they've had since he moved back to Ireland, but they definitely knew each other then."

I digested this information. "Why did Helen try to give me the impression they didn't? She didn't outright deny knowing her nephew, but she made it sound like they'd never met because she hadn't been back to Whisper Island since she emigrated."

"That's not true." His mouth twisted into a frown. "Well, maybe the part about Helen not returning to Ireland before this summer. However, Jimmy spent several summers with the Huffingtons when he was a kid, and Helen paid for him to go to college in the U.S. After he graduated, she hired him to work for her company."

"Wow. That's a lot more than a bare acquaintance." I recalled the flash of fear I'd picked up during my conversation with Helen last night. It had been gone so fast that I could have imagined it, but I didn't think so. "Why would she downplay her connection to Jimmy?"

"That's one of the many questions I'd like to pose to her and her son." Reynolds's jaw tightened. "The district supervisor warned me to tread carefully with such influential suspects." His voice dripped with sarcasm.

I felt his pain. I'd been there, more than once, during my time on the force back in San Francisco. "Same old story everywhere. Money doesn't talk, it roars."

"Pretty much." He stretched his neck from side to side and leaned against the railing. "Not that the friendly warning will stop me from doing my duty."

"I didn't think it would. That's why you're a good cop." My gaze drifted over the sea, and I sifted through the new information Reynolds had shared with me. "Did the Huffingtons deny knowing Jimmy when Sergeant O'Shea questioned them? It seems foolish if they did. They have to know that sort of info can easily be checked."

"They didn't deny that Jimmy had worked for them, but they didn't volunteer the information, either. O'Shea had to confront them with it, and then they were vague about the details. He had the feeling they were holding something back."

The unspoken implication hung in the air—if even the incompetent Sergeant O'Shea thought the Huffingtons were prevaricating, the situation stank.

"Helen and Huff knew Jimmy, but that doesn't necessarily mean they're connected to his murder. Have you found a concrete link?"

"Nothing definite, but I'm working on it. Whatever about Helen, Huff had motive and opportunity." Reynolds leaned closer, and his warm breath tickled my ear. "Last year, he and Jimmy fell out over money. Apparently, Huff persuaded Jimmy to invest in the Whisper Island Hotel."

I raised an eyebrow. "Seriously? I understood the only owners of the hotel were Paul Greer's parents and their infamous silent investor, whom we now know is Huff Huffington."

"Exactly. Huff told Jimmy that he'd be the investor on paper due to his reputation as a businessman, but he'd pay Jimmy his fair share of the profits."

"So that's what the bank statements under the floor boards were about." I screwed up my nose. "The whole idea reeks. Why did Jimmy go along with the plan?"

"He trusted his cousin, I guess." Reynolds shrugged. "Maybe they were close as kids."

I thought of the photo on Jimmy's nightstand. Close enough for Huff to ask Jimmy to be a godfather to one of his kids? "How much money did Jimmy give Huff?"

"Two hundred thousand euros," Reynolds replied. "A drop in the ocean in comparison to what Huff paid the Greers, but the money represented Jimmy's life savings."

"Wow. What went wrong? Did Huff rip off Jimmy?"

"That's what Jimmy felt." A line appeared between Reynolds's brows. "According to his email records, the man claimed that the payouts he received last year were much lower than they should have been. Huff brushed him off with excuses, but a cursory glance at the paper trail indicates Jimmy was right to feel resentful."

"Do you have evidence that they met in the time between Huff arriving on Whisper Island and Jimmy's murder?"

"I'm waiting for forensics to get back to me on that." His frown lines deepened. "I'm not hopeful that a man as clever as Huff Huffington will have left fingerprints or his DNA all over a crime scene for us to find."

"Unless he killed Jimmy in a fit of temper," I mused. "Huff's a bully."

"Yes, but he's a bully who has the smarts to clean up after himself."

"That's true," I conceded with a sigh. "What are you hoping to discover this weekend?"

"I'm not expecting him to confess to murder, but I'm hoping that he, or one of the others, will let something relevant slip. And if my source on the mainland comes through with the goods—" his expression turned serious, "—then I'll call for backup and make an arrest."

"What's your gut telling you?" I asked. "Do you think Huff did it?"

Reynolds nodded. "My gut says yes, but I have no proof, just a feeling, and a feeling's not going to stand up in court."

I turned my back on the sea and stretched my arms along the railings. "Let's turn this around for a sec. If Huff ripped off Jimmy, wouldn't Jimmy be the one with a grudge strong enough to kill Huff and not the other way around?"

"I've thought about that. I've also considered the possibility that Jimmy attacked Huff, and Huff killed Jimmy in self-defense."

"Huff's a lot bigger than Jimmy," I said. "It wouldn't have been a fair fight."

"There's also Dr. Reilly's opinion, backed up by the pathologist, that Jimmy hadn't been in a physical fight before he died. He showed no signs of having punched someone or defending himself against an attack. Whoever killed Jimmy took him by surprise."

"What about the gash on his head? Could that have been inflicted before he fell?"

"The pathologist doesn't think so. He said the wound was consistent with Jimmy striking his head against the ground when he fell. The straw in that part of the barn was sparse, and not sufficient to cushion a blow."

I stretched my neck back, and the wind whipped my ponytail into my mouth.

Laughing, Reynolds helped me to disentangle myself from my hair. "Your hair's getting long."

"I know. I need a cut, but I've been too busy to find a stylist."

"I like it." Reynolds moved close enough for me to smell his subtle aftershave. "The longer look suits you."

My heart slammed against my ribs. "We're

supposed to be a *pretend* couple, remember?" Even if a huge part of me wanted us to be the genuine article…

Reynolds tugged on a strand of my curly red hair and extended it to its full length before letting it spring back. "Pity. When did you say your divorce from G.I. Joe will be official?"

I burst into laughter. "G.I. Joe? Seriously, if you met him, you'd never call him that. Think designer suit and handmade Italian loafers, not military gear."

Reynolds's eyebrow shot up. "Kind of like Doug Huffington?"

"Same slick lines, but physically more like Doug's older brother, Amb. Doug's got more muscle than Joe."

"Does he indeed?" Reynolds teased. "Have you been checking him out?"

"I had to sit next to him at dinner on Thursday. His muscles were kind of hard to miss." I scrunched up my nose. "So was his massive ego and inability to take no for an answer."

Reynolds's eyebrows shot up. "Has he been hassling you?"

"Nothing I can't handle. He's just full of himself and thinks all women will fall at his feet. And with his family's money, I'd guess most do."

"If you're sure. Any problems with him this weekend, you let me know."

I gave him a mock salute. "Yes, sir."

"Tell me about the rest of the Huffington clan," Reynolds prompted. "Just your observations."

I thought for a moment. "I like Helen, but I don't trust her."

"She certainly did her best to mislead you." He chuckled. "O'Shea dismissed her as a harmless old lady."

"She's a harmless old lady with claws. She didn't turn her late husband's business into the success story it became without possessing a ruthless streak. Of all the family, she's the only one who has any influence over Huff."

"Yeah. I hear he's a difficult character."

"That's putting it mildly. Excluding Helen, he delights in controlling his family and belittling them. Doug and Brandi get off reasonably lightly, but the others come in for a regular battering."

"What's the older son like?" he asked. "He wasn't at the café last night, so all I've got to go on is info I gleaned from the internet."

"I get the impression that he's ruled by his wife, and they're both ruled by his father. He's a weak-willed sort of guy. Not as good-looking as his father and brother, and he lacks the shark instinct needed in high-stakes business. However, I'm willing to bet he has more brains than his father gives him credit for."

"What makes you say that?"

"Just a hunch. I haven't spoken to him at length, or away from his father, but I can rectify that this weekend."

"What about his wife?" Reynolds asked.

"Candace? She can be friendly when she finds a common enemy with you and forgets to be a snob."

He grinned. "You don't like her."

"No, but I like her better than Huff's wife, Brandi."

"The one who looks like a younger version of Dolly Parton?"

"Dolly's got more class," I said. "Brandi is a trophy wife, and she dresses in the fashions men found sexy back in the Eighties. I doubt that's an accident."

Reynolds took out his phone and opened his notes app. "What about Martha? No one seems to know anything about her, except that she's over thirty and unmarried, which is apparently worth mentioning."

I rolled my eyes. "Martha Huffington dresses like a spinster out of a Fifties novel. She's the victim of a lifetime of her father's misogynistic remarks and putdowns. If she has a personality, she's learned to hide it well."

His brow creased. "This whole business is a mess. I'm annoyed at my superintendent warning me to treat the Huffingtons with kid gloves, but I understand he's feeling the heat from above. The higher-ups don't want a wealthy investor implicated in a murder."

"That's total garbage."

"Of course it is." Reynolds grimaced. "I had to pull strings and trade favors to get a look at Huff's financial records."

"Given the sums involved, I can't imagine Jimmy

Wright's two hundred grand made much difference to Huff."

"No, but if the two had a falling out, there might be more to it than just money."

"That's true, but what?"

"That's what I hope to find out between now and Sunday." Reynolds shifted his weight and straightened. "We're almost at Gull Island. We'd better join the others."

## 9

GULL ISLAND WAS EVEN MORE BREATHTAKINGLY beautiful than I remembered. It had the same steep, jagged cliffs as Whisper Island, but that was where the similarities ended. I leaned over the railing to get a better look. "It truly is gorgeous. I'd forgotten about the purple-gray rocks and the old ruins at the center."

My cousin stood beside me at the railing. "Most of the island is covered in a rock surface not unlike that of the Burren in County Clare. I take my school kids out here every year to go for a hike up to the ruins of the medieval monastery. It's exercise and a history lesson rolled into one."

"Smart." I strained my neck back to take another peek at the top of the cliffs, but we were too close to the rocks for me to get a good look.

Reynolds moved to my free side and placed his hand on the small of my back. Despite the T-shirt separating his palm from my skin, an involuntary tingle ran through my body. For a moment, I forgot to breathe.

Reynolds's deep voice jolted me back to reality. "I visited the monastery when I came out here in January. It was so windy and cold that I considered taking refuge in the round tower."

"I hope we get a chance to visit it while we're here." I turned to Noreen. "Do you have any idea what the Huffingtons have planned for the weekend?"

"No, but I'm pretty sure I sold Huff on a trip to the monastery. I gave him an embellished version of the Viking raids during the Middle Ages. He liked the idea of the island being attacked numerous times but never surrendering."

"Historians would disagree," Julie said dryly, "but it is one of the best preserved early medieval monastic settlements in Europe."

The boat bypassed the public harbor and sailed on for another ten minutes to a tiny blink-and-you-miss-it cove on the other side of the island.

"The Huffingtons have rented Marley House for the weekend," Noreen explained. "We'll dock at the property's pier."

"Didn't we visit Marley House when I was a kid?" I asked. "I remember lovely gardens and an ugly house."

"We toured the gardens, yes. The house was only recently renovated and opened to the public. It's available to rent for short periods of time, complete with sole access to the swimming pool and gardens."

"Is the property privately owned?"

Julie shook her head. "Not these days. It used to be the private residence of the local English landowner. When he and his family left during the first part of the twentieth century, the house was abandoned for many years until the state bought it and opened the gardens as a tourist attraction. The house was renovated and reopened a couple of years ago."

"Interesting. I remember a little Japanese-style garden with a bridge."

"That's still there. We can take a look later." Reynolds smiled down at me, banishing all thoughts of my impending divorce and lousy taste in men from my mind. "I want to check out places I can take Hannah when she visits me next month."

"You must be looking forward to showing her around Whisper Island."

Reynolds's face softened as it did every time his daughter came up in conversation. "I'll have her for three whole weeks. That'll be the longest stretch since the divorce."

I squeezed his hand. "I'm looking forward to meeting her."

Our boat docked in a small cove at the bottom of a steep cliff, and we filed down the narrow gangplank onto the pier. Like Whisper Island, the only way up was by means of a rickety metal staircase, or an elevator that had been built into the side of the cliff.

I handed Noreen my bag. "I'll see you at the top."

Julie looked aghast. "Surely you're not planning to walk?"

"Yeah. I'm not fond of enclosed spaces."

Reynolds moved to my side. "I'll join you."

I eyed him skeptically. "Are you sure? You don't have to."

"I know, but I want to." He stretched his neck from side to side. "Besides, I could do with the exercise."

"Okay, but don't look to me for help if you get a fit of vertigo. I'm only slightly more okay with heights than I am with enclosed spaces."

"I'll be fine." He gestured to the first step. "Ladies first."

The climb to the top took us close to twenty minutes. Despite the ominous wobble of the steps beneath my feet, the view on the way up was spectacular. When we reached the top, I was gratified to find that I wasn't out of breath. All those morning runs had been doing me good, even if they hadn't yet helped me shift the last of the stubborn pounds I'd piled on during my post-split food binge and the month I'd spent living with Noreen, Queen of Twenty-Three Helpings.

Reynolds scanned the rocky landscape. "It's beautiful up here. I don't get out here enough."

"Does Gull Island fall under your jurisdiction?" The thought had never occurred to me before, but it would make sense.

"Yeah. Whisper Island Garda Station is responsible for maintaining law and order on Gull Island and Dolphin Island. Beyond my trip out here as a tourist before I started working on Whisper Island, I haven't had a reason to come out here." He grinned at me. "All the dead bodies you keep turning up have kept me busy."

I groaned. "I'm never going to live down my rep as a dead-body magnet."

"At this rate, no." He chuckled and propelled me along the rocky path that led to Marley House. "Promise me we'll have a corpse-free weekend."

"I can't make a promise like that, but I'm certainly not planning on finding any more. Jeez, I didn't plan to find the first few."

The rocky terrain came to an abrupt end a few yards from the wall that surrounded Marley House. A pebbled path cut through lush green grass and led us to a door-sized wrought iron gate that appeared to be the side entrance to Marley House's gardens.

Reynolds tried the handle, and the gate swung open.

"Stellar security system," I said when we stepped through to the garden on the other side. "I guess burglars don't often venture out to Gull Island."

"I'm more concerned with potential murderers than burglars at the moment, but I'll have a word with the council when I get back. Gates shouldn't be left unlocked when the house is rented."

I followed him down a meandering path that led from the gate to the main house. It took us through

Marley House's ornamental gardens. Each area had a theme, including the charming Japanese-style garden I remembered from my long-ago visit. A narrow stream ran through the garden, dividing a Japanese pagoda on one side from stepping stones flanked by a variety of plants and flowers on the other.

"I'd love to explore," Reynolds said, "but I guess we'd better get moving and meet our hosts."

At that moment, my stomach rumbled loudly, making us both laugh. "I hope the Huffingtons have a good cook."

He chuckled. "They do. They've hired Carl Logan from the hotel. He and a few waitstaff will be working here until Sunday evening."

"You're full of gossip."

"Blame the Spinsters. They told me when I dropped off the cat."

The last section of the garden took us past a maze before the front entrance of the house came into view. We passed two gardeners, busy trimming hedges with power tools. "This garden must be a full-time job."

Reynolds shielded his eyes from the sun. "The house, too. It's huge."

Marley House loomed before us. It was a large edifice that had been constructed from the solid, gray-purple stones that covered most of the island. It bore the hallmarks of a residence that had been added to over the generations, and it was difficult to guess its original shape.

"It's impressive in its ugliness," I said to Reynolds, "but the gardens are beautiful."

He looked at me, and his soft smile made my stomach flip. "Ready?"

I knew what he was asking. Was I ready to pretend to be his girlfriend for an entire weekend? Could I fake an intimacy we didn't yet have? Judging by the butterflies in my stomach, I could. "I'm ready."

"Excellent. And Maggie?"

"Is this the part where you warn me to stay out of your investigation?"

"Yes." He grinned. "Will it work?"

"Heck, no. You used me to wrangle an invite. The least you can do is let me in on the action."

"I'm rather hoping there won't be any action," he said dryly, propelling me up the steps to the front door. "At least not any involving you."

"Spoilsport." I pressed the bell, and the loud clang resounded through the house.

A moment later, Candace Huffington opened the door and ushered us inside a large stone hallway flanked by suits of armor on one side, and an array of ugly oil paintings on the other.

Her greeting was stiff but not unfriendly, and Reynolds was treated to the ghost of a smile. "Welcome to Marley House. I'm afraid I can't show you to your rooms just yet." Candace's nose—or what was left of it after multiple surgeries—quivered. "Apparently, there was a mix-up with our arrival time. The cleaners are still working upstairs. Huff is livid. He seems to think I'm to blame somehow." She delivered the last sentence in a staccato burst before collecting herself, a faint flush appearing on her cheeks. "I'm sorry."

While it was obvious that her apology referred to her outburst about her father-in-law, I threw her a lifeline. "Don't worry about it. We don't need bedrooms before tonight."

Candace squared her shoulders and regained some of her composure. "True, but Huff wants us to go on a hike around the island after lunch. You'll need to change for that."

"We can do that in a bathroom," I said. "It's all good."

She treated me to a brittle smile that didn't reach her eyes. "I suppose you're more used to dressing in confined spaces than I am."

That was what I got for making an effort. The woman just couldn't help herself. My smile stiffened. "As you say, I'm more used to slumming it than you are."

Reynolds cleared his throat. "Do you want us to get ready for the hike now?"

"Oh, no. We'll have lunch first." Candace's eyelids fluttered. "Follow me, and I'll take you to the dining room. My father-in-law has some business calls to make, so he won't be joining us."

I snuck a glance at Reynolds. From her tone, it was screamingly obvious that Huff's absence from the lunch table came as a relief to her. Frankly, a meal without Huff would be good for my digestion.

As we trailed after Candace toward the dining room, I deliberately slowed my pace. "Here goes," I whispered to Reynolds. "We have to convince Helen we're in love or she'll grow suspicious."

"I have faith in our acting skills." He slipped his arm around my waist, and his warm breath tickled my skin. "Break a leg, sweetheart."

## 10

Courtesy of Huff's absence, lunch was relaxed and the food superb. Martha had taken Hailey, Amb and Candace's daughter, to visit Dolphin Island for the day. They weren't due back before the evening. Without the family patriarch's snide remarks, the adults blossomed, but their good humor vanished the instant Huff's valet informed them that their father wanted to leave on the hike in ten minutes. Candace, who'd barely touched her food, showed Julie and me to a downstairs bathroom where we could change into our outdoor gear.

"Huff's a dose of misery," Julie whispered when we were alone. "Amb and Candace would be semi-okay if it weren't for his father's constant putdowns."

"I doubt Martha took Hailey on a day trip just to spend time with her niece." I pulled on a pair of gray hiking shorts. "Huff seems to reserve his most cutting remarks for her and Amb."

"Yeah. I won't lie—part of me would love to have the Huffingtons' money. The idea of not having to worry about paying the bills, owning a mortgage-free home, and being able to afford fancy holidays…" She buttoned her blouse and pulled a face at her reflection in the bathroom mirror. "Meanwhile, I have a pile of unopened bills on my kitchen counter that I'll need to tackle when we get back tomorrow evening."

I dragged a brush through my wild curls and redid my ponytail. "Not needing to worry about money sounds awesome, but watching Huff in action is a stark reminder that no amount of money is worth being controlled by a tyrant."

"Exactly. I grumble about Mum interfering with my love life, but she's a dear, really."

"My relationship with my parents can be politely described as strained, yet they'd never make remarks designed to hurt me. If Mom insults me at times, she doesn't mean to." I pulled my hair into a messy bun and applied sun cream. "This is as good as I'll get."

"We're freckle twins," Julie said with a laugh. "Mine always come out this time of year."

In spite of my best efforts to avoid them, the warm June weather had brought out my freckles. I clicked the cap on the bottle shut and slipped it into my backpack. "Ready to face our fate?"

Julie made a mewling sound. "No, but I promised Mum I'd be sociable. I wish I could cry off with a headache like Brandi."

I laughed. "Or claim old age, like Helen. If you

feel like avoiding the Huffingtons, hang back with me. I want you to fess up and tell me exactly why you object to Günter."

My cousin's lightly tanned cheeks flushed a becoming pink. "You don't give up, do you?"

"Nope." I slung my bag over my back and grinned at her. "I'll get it out of you eventually, so you might as well give in and tell me all."

Out in the courtyard, Reynolds and Günter lounged by the fountain in well-worn shirts, shorts, and boots. Amb and Candace looked incongruous in expensive hiking gear that I'd bet had never been worn before. Doug looked more at home in his designer outfit, but Huff had unwisely squeezed himself into clothes a size too small for him.

"Felicity," he roared. "Where are my binoculars?"

A wisp of a woman in a black pantsuit raced out of the house, nearly colliding with Julie and me at the bottom of the steps. "Here you are."

Huff's already red face turned an unhealthy shade of purple. "These are the wrong ones. I wanted the Zeiss binoculars."

"Oh, I'm sorry." The poor woman quivered with tension. "You'd left the Bushnell ones on your bed, and I assumed—"

"I don't pay you to assume," Huff yelled. "I pay you to obey my orders."

"I'm sorry, sir. I'll go back for them now." Felicity raced back up the steps into the house to collect Huff's preferred binoculars.

"Stupid woman," he growled, still holding the offending binoculars. "Too dumb to take these back with her. I'd fire her if I could find a replacement quickly. Guess I'll have to wait until I get home."

"It's not her fault if you forgot to specify which brand you wanted," I said in an acid tone. "How many personal assistants do you go through in a year?"

Huff rounded on me, his eyes bulging.

Before he could roar at me, Candace squeaked, "Maybe we should rethink the hike. Why don't we play a game of tennis? Do you play, Julie?" Not for the first time, her preference for my cousin over me was blatant. No skin off my nose.

Julie, bless her, leaped on the opportunity to distract Huff from bellowing me out. "I know how to play, but I'm out of practice."

"How about a game of mixed doubles?" A note of hysteria heightened Candace's voice. "Amb and me against you and Günter."

"Sounds good to me." Günter cast an amused glance in Julie's direction. "What do you say, *Liebling*?"

"If you call me that one more time, I'll aim a tennis ball at your head," my cousin muttered. "Cut it out."

"But why?" Günter grinned. "It annoys you so much."

"I said we'd go for a hike this afternoon, and we will *all* go for a hike." Huff's voice shook with barely controlled rage.

The unfortunate Felicity reappeared at that moment, holding another pair of binoculars. Huff grabbed them from her and shoved the offending pair into her trembling hands. Thus supplied with his preferred binoculars, Huff stomped off in the direction of the main gate. The rest of us trooped behind.

Reynolds fell into step with me. "That man has serious anger management issues. If I had to investigate *his* murder, I'd have trouble finding people close to him who *didn't* have a motive."

"Tell me about it. The man is vile." I sucked air through my teeth. "I know you need to be here as my date this weekend, but I'm close to packing my bag and catching the next ferry back to Whisper Island."

"Please don't do that." Reynolds put his arm around my shoulders and bent down as though to whisper sweet nothings in my ear. "Slow down so we'll hang behind a little." His lazy smile and razor-sharp eyes told me all I needed to know.

"Sure." We walked slowly until we were behind enough from the others not to be overheard. "Well?" I demanded. "Do you have new info?"

"Nothing concrete about the Wright murder." He scrunched up his face. "Huff's slipperier than an eel. I'm certain he visited Jimmy Wright on the day Wright died. Whether or not he killed the man, I can't say yet."

"Even if Huff did visit Jimmy, he wasn't the only visitor that day. Judging by his preference in online smut, Jimmy didn't dress up in that ridiculous outfit for Huff's sake. He was expecting a female visitor."

"We're still working that angle. No luck in tracking down his dates yet, but we'll get there." His expression turned grim. "I got an email from a friend in the FBI. Apparently, Huff was a suspect in a business rival's murder, but they could never pin it on him."

My investigative instincts kicked in. "Premeditated, or spur-of-the-moment?"

"The victim was whacked over the head with a ceramic chicken."

I stifled a laugh. "So it was a spur of the moment killing. That fits my reading of Huff's personality."

"Mine, too."

A memory stirred. "Was this Ronnie King, the chicken wings guy?"

"That's right." Reynolds raised an eyebrow. "Have you heard of him?"

"He owns—owned—King's Wings," I said. "In addition to selling gross fried chicken balls in supermarkets, the Huff's Puffs brand includes a chain of fast-food restaurants, and King's Wings was their main rival. If I recall correctly, Huff wanted to buy King out, but King refused."

"Exactly, and here's where it gets interesting. After King's death, Huffington Enterprises acquired King's Wings via tactics akin to a hostile takeover. They kept the deal quiet and have continued to run King's Wings under its original name."

"So Huff got his way." I shook my head. "Why doesn't that surprise me?"

"King's murder remains unsolved, although the investigating officer is convinced Huff did it." Reynolds's jaw hardened. "If he killed Jimmy Wright, I'll make sure justice is served."

I slipped my hand into his. "Come on, fake boyfriend. Let's try to enjoy the walk, despite our less-than-genial host. I'm looking forward to checking out the medieval monastery."

We increased our pace and soon caught up with the others. The general mood was subdued. There was an unspoken agreement among us not to antago-nize Huff and trigger another temper tantrum. I wasn't in the mood to bait him. I didn't find bullies amusing, even to goad into losing their cool.

We retraced the path Reynolds and I had taken when we'd gotten off the ferry. As we walked across the rocky landscape, the fresh air and gentle breeze made the unpleasantness of earlier recede. After a thirty-minute trek up a steep slope, we reached the monastery.

I stopped to catch my breath and take in the view. To my left, Dolphin Island looked to be a short swim away, although I knew it was a thirty-minute boat trip. "It's stunning up here."

"Yeah," Reynolds said. "We're a lot higher up than anywhere on Whisper Island."

"The original monastery was built around 600 AD," Candace intoned, reading aloud from her guidebook. "Can you imagine, Amb? Those monks were entirely self-sufficient on a rock in the middle of the Atlantic."

"You can see some of their craftsmanship at the museum on Whisper Island," Julie said. "Archaeologists found a trunk full of old manuscripts."

This information enchanted Candace. "How fascinating. We'll have to take a look next week. Won't we, Amb?"

"Hmm?" His expression was distracted. "What did you say, honey?"

"Have you been listening to a word I've said?" Candace asked but with no rancor in her voice. "Honestly, Julie. He goes off in his own world sometimes, and getting through to him is impossible."

"My mother says exactly the same thing about my father," my cousin said. "Men, eh?"

"Whatever's bugging Amb, I don't think it's normal guy stuff," I whispered to Reynolds. "He's been on edge since we arrived. He barely touched his lunch."

Reynolds slipped an arm around my shoulders, and I stifled a gasp at the ripple of awareness that slid down my spine. "Candace didn't eat much, either."

"True," I said, "but I doubt she ever allows more than the bare minimum of food to pass her lips."

Huff stomped around the ruins of the monastery. "I thought there'd be more to this place," he grumbled. "Candace said it was the main tourist attraction on the island. Some attraction. It's a pile of old rocks.

They ought to raze it to the ground and build something useful."

Candace's face crumpled. "These remains are part of the island's history."

"If they're clinging to a few bits of old rock, no wonder the island's broke." Huff looked at his watch. "Let's head back to the house. It's nearly time for cocktails."

"But Dad, we just got here," Amb ventured, his Adam's apple working overtime. "Candace was looking forward to exploring the monastery."

"No reason why she can't," I cut in. "Come on, Candace. I'll go around with you, and you can show me what's what. I didn't think to bring a guidebook."

Before Huff could object, I'd looped arms with Candace and dragged her into the monastery.

When we reached the remains of an altar, she turned to me. "That wasn't a good idea, Maggie. Huff doesn't like to be thwarted."

"Huff can take a flying leap off a cliff for all I care. I know he's loaded, but why do you allow him to humiliate you?"

A muscle in Candace's cheek twitched. "Amb feels it's his duty to obey his father."

"Why does his duty apply to you?" I demanded. "Why should you put up with Huff's insults?"

"Everything we have—Amb's income, our house, our lifestyle—is dependent on Huff." She interlaced her fingers and began to pace back and forth in a jerky manner that was the polar opposite of her elegant stride. "If it weren't for Amb, I'd leave. I've been out of the workforce for a few years, but I'd find something."

"What's Amb's objection? He can't enjoy the way his father treats him."

"Of course not, but he won't give up his dream of making his father proud." Her smile was wry. "I know. It'll never happen, but he clings to the hope."

"How long are you planning to stick around waiting for Amb to get a reality check?"

She exhaled a sigh. "A year. Maybe less. I can put up with Huff insulting me, but I won't tolerate him being mean to my daughter."

"In your position, I'd have walked long ago."

Candace gave me a sad smile. "You'd never be in my position, Maggie. Money doesn't hold sway over you like it does me. I like being rich. I like designer clothes. I don't want to have to scrimp and save and wonder how to make the next mortgage payment."

I thought of Joe and our fabulous Pacific Heights home and the closet full of designer clothes that I'd only worn to please my husband and his mother. Had the money kept me in the marriage longer than I should have stayed? Probably. And if I'd had a kid to consider, as Candace did, I might have stayed even longer. "If you love Amb, and the issue is Huff, do what you can to persuade him to walk away."

"Believe me, I've tried." Candace blinked back tears, and her rigid posture returned. "I don't know why I'm telling you all this."

"Because I'm easy to talk to, and I'll give it to you straight."

A genuine laugh escaped Candace's lips. "That's true. You certainly stood up to Huff."

"I don't like bullies." I glanced through a gap in the stone wall and spotted Reynolds. He indicated that he was going to walk back with the others. I gave him a thumbs up. He needed to corner Huff alone, and it'd be easier to do it when he wasn't expected to hang with me.

Candace dried her eyes with a lace handkerchief and cleared her throat. "Were you serious about wanting to look around the monastery, or did you say that to separate me from Huff?"

"Both." I gave her a reassuring smile. "I'd far rather look around the monastery without your father-in-law's running commentary driving me into a fury. We have time before dinner, and you might not get another chance to come up here before you leave. Let's make the best of it."

## 11

When Candace and I returned from the monastery, a flustered-looking Martha met us in the entrance hall. Her jittery pace faltered when she saw us, and for a moment, it was as though she didn't recognize us.

"Hey, Martha," I said. "Is everything okay?"

The woman's plump fingers tugged at her rings. "Yes, thanks. There's just a lot to do today, and Hailey and I just got back. Dad's not happy with the dinner menu, and, well, you know how he gets." Her voice was breathier than usual, and wisps of hair had escaped her tight bun.

"Oh, I know very well how Huff gets." A hint of acid touched Candace's voice. "Is Hailey in her room?

"Yes. She's playing with her dolls before dinner."

"I'll go up and spend some time with her before dinner." Candace patted my arm. "Thanks for staying with me, Maggie."

"No problem. I enjoyed the opportunity to explore the monastery."

"So did I. I'll see you later." A rare look of contentment settled over Candace's features. "I'm sure Hailey will want to regale me with stories about her adventures on Dolphin Island."

After her sister-in-law had gone upstairs, I turned to Martha. "Are you acting as hostess for the weekend?"

A wry smile broke through Martha's flustered countenance. "I guess I am."

"Can't Brandi help?"

"She says her headache is too bad for her to come downstairs. That leaves me to deal with the kitchen staff and oversee everything else."

"If there's anything I can do, let me know."

"Thanks, but I'll manage." She smoothed her palms down the front of her linen pants and collected herself. "Your rooms are finally ready, by the way. I've put you upstairs in the blue room. I hope that's okay."

"I'm sure it'll be fine."

"I just showed your boyfriend up, so if you can come with me?"

I opened my mouth to say Reynolds wasn't my boyfriend but clamped it shut. After all, he and I had talked about going out on a proper date, and we'd eaten dinner at each other's houses a couple of times. We both knew we were hovering on the precipice of a real relationship. My only reservation about transforming our fake relationship into the genuine article was an ingrained fear of getting hurt. I'd made lousy choices in the past. Although Reynolds was nothing like my ex, I didn't trust my judgment when it came to men.

Martha led me up a stone staircase before swinging left on the landing. I followed her down a dark corridor until she stopped in front of a door and knocked. A sleepy-eyed Reynolds opened the door, revealing a spacious room with little natural light. A lumpy-looking bed formed the room's centerpiece.

"Sorry, Liam. Did I wake you?"

He stifled a yawn. "No worries. I wanted to hit the shower before dinner."

"Speaking of showers, you're sharing an adjoining bathroom with your cousin and her boyfriend." Martha gestured to a door to my right. "I hope you don't mind."

"Not at all." I bit down a giggle. I had a feeling that Günter and Reynolds would be sharing that lumpy bed tonight. I could only hope that Julie and I had scored the better mattress.

"In that case, I'll leave you to unpack."

Martha retreated, leaving me with a poker-faced Reynolds. "Which side of the bed do you prefer, darling?"

I snorted with laughter and banged on the door of the adjoining bathroom. "Julie? Günter?"

A moment later, the door opened, and my cousin burst into the room, red-faced and vaguely disheveled. *Very suspicious.* I exchanged a glance with

Reynolds. Günter trooped in after her, wearing his usual nonchalant expression. Given Julie's deer-caught-in-the-headlights vibe, I chose to address him.

"I thought—we thought—that Julie and I could share her room, and you and Liam could have this one."

Günter nodded. "Fine by me. Julie snores."

My cousin squawked in outrage. "I most certainly do not. And how would you know whether or not I snore?"

"That time you stayed with your parents when you had the flu?" He gave her a saccharine-sweet smile. "You snored."

Julie put her hands on her hips and glared at him. "I was sick. My nose was blocked."

"All I'm saying is what I heard." Günter slung his bag on the bed. "Now, unless you want to see me naked, you'd better get out of here. I have to dress for dinner."

Julie's eyes stood out on stalks, and her cheeks turned pink. She darted into the shared bathroom and through to what was destined to be our bedroom.

"Play nicely, Günter," I said before I followed her. "Or are you planning to tease her into submission?"

"Not at all. I know she doesn't like me. She's already told me she doesn't go for men with beards."

I eyed him with suspicion. Was it my imagination, or were his shoulders shaking? I looked at Reynolds, but he appeared to be just as baffled as I was.

"Behave yourselves, boys," I said. "We'll see you downstairs for dinner."

After we'd unpacked, Julie and I changed into our evening finery. I'd brought one of the two evening dresses I'd salvaged from my pre-separation closet—a strapless black number with a slit up one side. I no longer had the expensive jewelry to add the final touches to my outfit, but I didn't care. A careful application of makeup, a little magic with the curling iron, and I was ready to go.

Julie added a final application of lipstick and stood back to examine her reflection in the full-length mirror. "Do I pass muster? Don't feel the need to flatter me."

"No flattery is required. You're gorgeous and you know it."

My cousin wore an off-the-shoulder champagne-colored dress that showed off the smattering of freckles on her lightly tanned shoulders and accentuated her shapely figure. She slipped my arm through hers. "Thanks, Maggie. Ready to face Huff?"

I shuddered. "Gosh, no. His performance this afternoon was epic."

"I hear you. I felt so bad for his assistant."

"If she has sense, she'll look for another job the moment she lands stateside."

"I hope dinner is served with lots of alcohol," Julie whispered. "I don't know how else I'll get through an evening of Noreen trying to shove Günter and me together at every opportunity."

"Like Lenny said, you protest way too much. I think you have a secret crush on him."

Julie blushed. "Don't be silly. Maybe I made an effort tonight for Doug."

"Nice try, but I was watching you at the Movie Club. Your eyes strayed in the direction of a guy more than once, and it wasn't Doug Huffington. Are you ever going to tell me why you object to him?"

Julie sighed. "Okay, but you've got to swear you'll keep it to yourself."

"Unless the info's relevant for a murder investigation, I won't blab."

This cracked my cousin up. "I highly doubt it. A couple of weeks before you arrived on Whisper Island, Günter and I kissed at Lenny's New Year's Eve party."

My ears pricked up. "Sooo…did he suck as a kisser?"

"Quite the opposite." Her expression grew dreamy. "It was wonderful."

"Then why didn't you want to follow up on that kiss?"

She looked at me sharply. "Who says I didn't want to? *He* wasn't interested in *me*."

This info surprised me. "Are you sure? Günter's very solicitous toward you."

"Oh, I'm sure. We arranged to go out to dinner on the second of January. About an hour before we were due to meet, I got a text message from him saying he was on a plane to Germany and had to cancel. He gave no explanation, and he didn't contact me when he got back to Whisper Island. The next time I saw him was at the Movie Club meeting when Sandra Walker died. Does that sound like a man keen to go on a date with me?"

"I don't know what to make of his behavior," I mused. "Something must have happened to cause his last-minute trip to Germany, but I doubt it had anything to do with you."

"Then why didn't he call me when he got back?"

"I don't know. And neither of us has any clue why he made that last-minute trip. He might have had a family emergency."

"Then why didn't he say that?" Julie pulled herself together. "Anyway, now you know. Can we drop the subject?"

"Sure. At least we know the food will be good if Carl Logan's the chef for the weekend." I slipped my arm through hers, and we headed down to dinner.

At the bottom of the staircase, a guy I recognized from the Whisper Island Hotel ushered us in the direction of oak-paneled door. "The Huffingtons are having pre-dinner drinks in the drawing room."

"The drawing room?" Julie giggled. "Have we walked onto the set of a British period drama?"

"Don't make me laugh," I whispered. "Helen Huffington reminds me of the Dowager Countess from *Downton Abbey*."

Apart from Günter and Reynolds, everyone was already there and supplied with drinks. I surveyed the crowd. Candace sat primly on an uncomfortable-looking antique sofa, clutching her cocktail glass as though her life depended on it. Beside her, Amb appeared to be equally tense, with a half-empty Old Fashioned in his hand. A little girl played on the rug in front of the fireplace, next to an armchair that had been claimed by Noreen. The child glanced up when Julie and I came in and looked at us with open curiosity.

"Hi," I said, walking over to join her. "I'm Maggie, and this is my cousin Julie."

"I'm Hailey." Her voice was low and shy. "You've got pretty hair, Maggie."

"Why thank you, Miss Hailey. So do you. I always wanted nice, straight hair when I was a kid." I turned my attention to her doll. "Who's this?"

The little girl preened under our attention. "Her name's Lucy today, but that might change. She was Sophie yesterday. I like trying out new names."

"Very sensible," I said. "It's smart to keep your options open."

At the same moment that a waiter served me and Julie martinis, Reynolds walked into the room, devil-ishly handsome in a suit and tie. My heart performed a flip-flop. I dragged my attention away from Reynolds to his companion.

I slow-blinked. *Well, heck.* The man standing beside Reynolds was tall, blond, and clean-shaven with a powerful build that was shown off to advantage by his well-cut suit.

"Oh my goodness," Julie gasped. "It's Günter."

"Yeah—minus the beard." I cast a sly look at my cousin's shocked face. "He scrubs up nicely."

"He certainly does," Noreen added. "Even better than I'd expected."

Günter crossed the room and joined us by the fireplace. "Hey, ladies. You all look lovely."

I suppressed a smile. Noreen and I might be dressed in out best clothes, but Günter had eyes only for my cousin.

"You shaved," she stuttered. "And you cut your hair."

"Of course." He flashed her a mischievous smile. "You told me you didn't like guys with beards."

"I wasn't serious." She paused. "Well, not really. Facial hair wouldn't be a deal-breaker. For the right guy."

Günter took her hand in his. "I was planning on shaving it off anyway. It's too hot for a beard."

Julie stared up at him, her expression dazed.

Noreen and I took the unspoken hint and left the two lovebirds alone.

"Would you like a glass of lemonade?" Noreen asked Hailey.

The little girl nodded. "Yes, please."

While my aunt and Hailey went in search of lemonade, I checked out a bookcase. Reynolds came up beside me. "You look beautiful tonight, Maggie."

His words flustered me. "You must have seen this dress a hundred times by now."

"You wear it better each time." He grinned and slipped his arm through mine. "Let's get you a drink."

We strolled over to one of the waiters and secured Reynolds a whiskey. "Can you get me talking to Helen?" he asked, his glass at his lips. "I managed to chat with Huff on the walk back, but I haven't had a chance to corner his mother yet."

"Sure." I cast an eye around the room. Huff was by the patio doors, engaged in a heated conversation with Doug. Helen was chatting to Martha on the sofa opposite Candace and Amb.

Dragging Reynolds in my wake, I marched us up to them and smiled at Helen. "Thank you so much for arranging this trip. I'd forgotten how gorgeous Gull Island is."

"Well, you know, I barely remembered the place," the older lady said. "I'm not sure if I ever came out here as a girl. Of course, back then, it was run-down and isolated with just a few stubborn residents clinging on to their land."

Martha checked her watch and stood abruptly, almost spilling her martini glass. "So sorry. I must check on dinner."

"There aren't many permanent residents today," I said to Helen after her granddaughter's departure. "The numbers swell in the summer, but not to the extent of Whisper Island's. Most visitors to Gull Island are day-trippers."

"Very true." Helen's attention shifted to Reynolds.

"And what do you do, young man? Are you in business?"

Reynolds laughed. "I'm certainly kept busy. No, the businessperson in my family is my mother, but on a less grand scale than you. She runs a cocktail bar in Dublin. She made sure we learned the value of hard work."

Very cleverly done. He'd succeeded in diverting the conversation away from his profession without resorting to lying.

"Instilling a healthy work ethic in children is important." Helen's expression grew serious. "I grew up on a farm, and helping out was expected of us from an early age. I hated the work, and I couldn't wait to escape the island, but I've always been grateful for the lessons I learned while growing up." Whether by accident or design, Helen's gaze drifted over her son and grandchildren. "Growing up rich isn't all it's cracked up to be. Unless you earn your money through hard work, it's hard to appreciate the true value of a dollar."

"That's what my mum says," Reynolds said cheerfully. "Speaking of my mum, do you have many family left on Whisper Island?"

For the briefest of instants, Helen's eyes hardened, but then she was all smiles again. "No. I moved away when I was very young. Did Maggie tell you that her grandmother was my dearest friend?"

"Yes. She mentioned that." Reynolds slid a glance in my direction.

"Jimmy Wright was Helen's nephew," I said, picking up his silent message. "Such a dreadful thing to happen."

Helen crossed her legs at the ankles. "Yes, indeed. Very sad."

"I suppose the police had to question you," I said casually. "They've been talking to everyone with the vaguest connection to Jimmy."

Helen's benign smile gave nothing away. "Having found the body, I suppose you had to answer quite a few questions. How distressing for you."

*Well played, Helen.*

"I found Jimmy's body, but I had a rock-hard alibi for the time of his death. I was at the café that day until seven, and the doctor estimated that Jimmy was killed at some point between four and five."

"Which day was that?" Helen's expression was vague, but I didn't buy her confusion for a second.

"Wednesday," I supplied. "The day before the rest of your family arrived."

"Oh, yes. I remember now. That dreadful policeman asked me all about it." She shuddered. "He had dandruff all over his shoulders, and I'm sure I picked up a whiff of alcohol on his breath."

The dandruff was accurate, but in spite of my aversion to the odious Sergeant O'Shea, I'd never known him to drink on duty. Why would Helen invent that detail? Unless she wished to discredit him... "It was just you and Huff here on Wednesday, right?"

She inclined her neck in a regal nod. "Yes. My

nurse, Miss Dobbs, traveled with me, as did Huff's valet. Everyone else arrived on Thursday morning. I probably should have taken the time to visit poor Jimmy, but we weren't close. How could I have known he'd die so soon?"

"No one could have known." Except, perhaps, Jimmy's murderer. "I hope at least you were able to enjoy your days on the island before everyone arrived. I know how hectic it gets with family around."

"We played golf. I can't manage to play as many holes as I used to, but it's a hobby I have in common with my son."

Over in the corner, Doug moved away from his father, leaving Huff glaring after him.

Reynolds drained his glass. "I'm going to get a refill. Can I get either of you ladies anything?"

"No, thank you," Helen said with a smile. "One gin and tonic is quite enough for me."

I held up my barely touched martini glass. "I'm good, too, thanks."

Reynolds nodded to me and ambled over to the drinks table. In the corner of my eye, I saw him edge closer to Huff. How was he planning to get Huff to talk about Jimmy Wright? Whisper Island was a small place. Sooner or later, one of the waitstaff was bound to let Reynolds's identity slip.

At that instant, the gong sounded.

Helen got stiffly to her feet with the aid of her cane. "Will you walk in to dinner with me, dear?"

"Of course."

Helen leaned heavily against me, playing the role of the frail old lady who might be at her last gasp at any moment.

Old she might be, but I wasn't falling for her act. Helen Huffington knew something about Jimmy Wright's death. And the only reason I could think of for her to hold back info was to protect her son.

## 12

DINNER with the Huffingtons proved to be as tense as lunch had been relaxed. Huff's presence created a notable strain on all the younger members of his family. Only Helen appeared to be impervious to the stormy atmosphere.

Beside me, Reynolds exuded an easygoing appearance, but I wasn't fooled. He was taking in every nuance of every conversation and storing the relevant bits.

As the meal progressed, so did Huff's wine consumption. By the time the main course arrived, he'd downed at least four large glasses of wine on top of the cocktail he'd had earlier, and his comments increased in belligerence.

"Huff has quite an impact on his family," Reynolds murmured to me under his breath.

"That's putting it mildly. They're terrified of him."

As if to prove my point, Hailey's elbow hit off her

lemonade glass, sending it flying. A horrified silence descended over the company as everyone waited for the patriarch's reaction.

"Clumsy child," Huff snarled. "You're as awkward as your father. Rosie never could walk two feet without knocking something over. And as for running—" he snorted, "—more like an elephant careening."

The little girl burst into tears.

Martha stroked her niece's hair back from her tear-stained face. "Never mind, sweetheart. We'll clean it up."

"If you're so fond of the kid, why don't you have one of your own?" Huff took another slug from his wine glass. "Assuming you can find a guy blind enough to take you."

Martha didn't respond to her father's jibe, but her shoulders tensed. "Come on, Hailey. We'll get you changed into a clean dress."

"Leave this table, and you can stay gone," Huff snarled. "If the girl has no table manners, she deserves to spend the rest of the meal in wet clothes."

Martha's hand tensed on Hailey's back, but she acted as though her father hadn't spoken.

"Don't be silly, Huff." Helen addressed her grand-daughter. "Get Hailey changed and into bed, Martha. Then you come straight back down here, understand?"

Martha nodded and murmured reassurances to her niece until they were out of the dining room.

"Was that necessary, Dad?" Amb's thin face bore the signs of a man struggling to keep his emotions in check. "Hailey's only five."

"Which is why I keep saying she has no place at a dinner party. When I was a kid, I took all my meals in the nursery."

"Times have changed, dear," Helen said mildly. "Your father insisted on separating children and adults at mealtimes. Frankly, I prefer the modern approach."

"Well, I don't. Not when I'm footing the bill."

Helen took a delicate sip from her wine glass. "Technically, dear, *I'm* footing the bill for this weekend. I had my secretary arrange everything."

I smothered a smile at the sight of Huff's gaping mouth.

He caught my eye and glared at me. "What are you looking at?" he growled.

I cocked my head to one side and gave him a critical once-over. "I haven't decided yet. I'm debating between Homo erectus and Neanderthal."

Huff's visage developed a purple hue, and his eyes bulged out of their sockets.

"What do you think, Liam?" I pointed to the painting behind Huff's head. "Which species is that?"

Reynolds didn't miss a beat. "Homo erectus. The remains are in a museum in Dublin."

Huff whipped around and stared at the painting of an archaeological dig that had occurred on Gull

Island during the nineteenth century. He jerked back to glare at me, his eyes narrowed in suspicion.

"Is that the archaeological site we passed on our walk today?" Candace asked. "I find history fascinating."

"Yes," I said. "There have been several digs on the island over the years, but Julie would probably know more about that than me."

While Julie engaged Candace in a discussion about the history of Gull Island, Liam whispered to me, "Naughty, naughty."

"The dude deserved it," I whispered back. "He's a boor."

"Agreed, but tread carefully. For all we know, he's a boor with a lethal temper."

Martha slipped back into the dining room in time for dessert. After we'd finished Carl's delicious white and milk chocolate mousse, Huff stood abruptly and raised his wine glass to us. "Now that we're all gathered together, I have an announcement to make."

"An announcement?" Amb stared at his father blankly. "Is this about the business?"

"Yes," Huff said smugly, "and no."

Amb opened and closed his mouth, fishlike.

"Surely anything pertaining to the family would be best left for a time when we don't have guests?" Candace fiddled with her napkin, her knuckles turning white. "We don't want to bore them with our private affairs."

"Family?" Huff snorted. "You're not my flesh and

blood. You're just married to my son. Don't tell me what to do. Everything you own was bought with my money, right down to the fertility treatments you needed to have the kid."

Candace blanched. She stood, swayed in place, and then staggered out of the room. Julie tossed her napkin on the table and ran after her. The rest of us remained seated, too stunned to move.

"What did I tell you, Rosie?" Huff demanded of his eldest son with an air of triumph. "That woman has no backbone."

Amb's pale face was chalky white. His mouth twitched as though it longed to form words its owner would never utter.

I clapped, long and slow. "That's quite a performance. Pity none of us thought to film it. It would have made a worthy addition to your tantrum collection on YouTube."

Huff turned his steely gaze on me. "How dare you criticize me in my own home?"

"Marley House belongs to the state," I pointed out. "You've just rented it for the weekend."

Huff's nostrils flared. "You're a *guest* at my dinner table. How dare you speak to me like that?"

"I'm a guest against my better judgment. I came for your mother's sake."

"And I'm delighted you did, dear." Helen cast a benevolent look in her son's direction. "It's important to me that my guests feel welcome."

"I feel about as welcome as a dose of the clap, but

the last ferry to Whisper Island left an hour ago. Like it or not, we're stuck with each other until the morning."

The struggle to rein in his temper was visible on Huff's alcohol-flushed face. "If you're finished insulting me, I have an announcement to make." He dragged his gaze away from me and put a hand on Brandi's shoulder. "As I was saying before I was so rudely interrupted, I have something important to tell you. Brandi is expecting our first child together, and the doctor says it's a boy."

A stunned silence fell over the table.

Huff smirked and let the significance of this information settle before continuing. "So I'll be making some changes. For years, I've said I'd leave the majority share of Huffington Enterprises to the son who proved himself the most business savvy. Neither Rosie nor Doug have shown any aptitude for running a business."

"That's not f—" Amb began, but his father's quelling look cut his sentence short.

"I've decided to leave the majority share to my son with Brandi. I figure I've got nothing to lose. This baby might be my last son, and seeing as you two are pretty much useless, I'm betting on the unknown quantity."

Doug slammed his glass down on the table. "This is crazy, Dad. Brandi's baby won't come of age for nearly twenty years."

"I'm not planning on dying any time soon," Huff

said. "And I have no problem with you and Rosie playing a role in the business until then—under the supervision of managers of my choosing."

"You can't disinherit us," Amb said, his Adam's apple working overtime. "I've dedicated my entire career to Huffington Enterprises."

"I never said I was disinheriting you, boy. You'll still get a lump sum when I die, same as your brother and sister."

"But the real money lies in the business," Amb protested. "You know that."

"Sure it does. But only if the business is run by someone who knows what he's doing." Huff sloshed more wine into his glass and glared at his eldest son. "We've already established that that someone isn't you."

Amb pushed back his chair and leaped to his feet, swaying unsteadily in an unconscious imitation of his wife moments ago. His face bore the signs of a man under considerable strain. "Please excuse me, Grandma. I'm going to see how Candace and Hailey are."

*About time,* I thought.

"Of course, dear," Helen said. "I'll see you in the morning."

Amb nodded stiffly and strode out of the room. If the guy had any sense, he'd pack up and leave first thing.

Courtesy of Huff's dramatic announcement, we were a subdued bunch when we trooped back to the drawing room for an after-dinner drink. Only Huff and Brandi were in a good mood. He appeared to be very pleased with the mayhem he'd wrought, and Brandi's expression was smug.

Amb and Candace didn't put in a reappearance. Doug stared moodily out the window and displayed none of his usual practiced charms. Martha wore the same worried expression she'd had all evening. Even Helen's armor of controlled blandness displayed dents. Her outward appearance was calm and friendly, but every once in a while, I caught her sliding an inscrutable look at her son. Somehow, I didn't get the impression that Huff had run his plans for the business by his mother before making his dramatic announcement.

The Whisper Island contingent didn't linger, and we soon made our respective excuses and headed to bed.

"Do you know how much control Helen has over Huffington Enterprises?" I whispered to Reynolds as we ascended the stairs.

"I believe she has a seat on the board of directors," he said, "but she handed over the reins to Huff more than twenty years ago. He's the face of Huffington Enterprises now."

"Did you get any info out of him about Jimmy Wright?"

Reynolds grimaced. "Nothing of use. Huff kept changing the subject."

"Much as I despise the guy, I'm going to tackle him about Jimmy in the morning."

We reached the top of the stairs a moment after Noreen.

"My room's that way." My aunt pointed in the opposite direction to where our rooms were located.

"Night, Noreen," I said. "Sleep well."

Reynolds and I ambled down the corridor. Julie and Günter took a very long time to climb the stairs, and Reynolds and I lingered in front of our respective bedroom doors while we waited for our roommates to reach us.

Under the dim light of the hall, his hair appeared darker than it was in daylight, and the shadows made him appear mysterious.

"Why are you smiling?" he asked in a teasing tone. "Are you regretting our sleeping arrangements?"

I laughed. "Nice try. No, I'm perfectly happy sharing with Julie."

"Why do I sense an unspoken 'but' in that sentence?"

"But I wouldn't say no to a goodnight kiss." The words were out of my mouth before I had time to register their significance.

Chuckling, Reynolds bent down and claimed my mouth with his. This time, the kiss was slow and deliberate, leaving me breathless and flustered when he stepped back. "Goodnight, Maggie."

And then he was gone, leaving me alone in the dark hallway, my lips still tingling from his touch.

# 13
***

In spite of my plan to interrogate Julie about Günter, she didn't come back to our room immediately, and I fell asleep within seconds of my head hitting the pillow. I was dreaming about rakes and cats and mankinis when a noise jerked me awake.

"What was that?" I sat bolt upright in our bed. "Did you hear a splash?"

Beside me, Julie turned to her other side. "Dunno," she murmured. "Maybe." And then she yawned and drifted back to sleep.

For several long seconds, I debated the wisdom of going downstairs on my own to investigate. Taking a deep breath, I threw off the bedcover and located my slippers. I might as well check out what had caused the sound. I'd never go back to sleep until I did. Before I left the room, I grabbed the small flashlight I always carried with me in my purse and eased the door shut behind me.

The full moon cast an eerie blue-gray light down the hallway. I headed for the main staircase, switching on my flashlight to make sure I didn't fall and break my neck. We'd had enough drama over the last few days without me causing additional chaos.

I descended with caution, my senses dulled from lack of sleep. When I reached the bottom step without incident, I exhaled in relief. I cast the flashlight around the entrance hall. Nothing appeared to be out of place, and I judged this room not to be the source of the noise.

The commotion I'd heard had sounded like a splash. Could someone or something have fallen into the fountain? Wait...hadn't Noreen mentioned the house having a pool? We hadn't had a chance to tour the house earlier. Well, now was as good a time as ever. I steeled myself and took a step forward.

On the other side of the hall, the suits of armor loomed menacingly in the darkness. When the visor of one appeared to move, my heart leaped in my chest. I gave myself a mental shaking. I was letting the tension in the house get under my skin. Ghosts didn't exist.

I tiptoed toward the side of the house where I thought the splash had occurred. In the next instant, one of the suits of armor fell to the ground with a monumental crash. I leaped back and let out a screech. Blood roared in my ears. With shaking hands, I shone the flashlight over the debris.

Bits of old steel lay strewn across the floor. Inside

the visored helmet, a moan escaped. I shone the light on it. The visor shot up, and a pair of familiar pale blue eyes peered out. "Maggie?"

"*Lenny*? What the heck are you doing here?"

My friend pulled off the helmet and grinned up at me. "Carl was short-staffed and asked me to help out in the kitchen. I was hoping I'd run into you earlier, but my brother's a slave-driver. What's all this about you and the sarge getting it on?"

"Sergeant Reynolds and I are not 'getting it on,'" I said primly. "And please don't call him sarge around here. He's my fake date for the weekend—I'm helping him with a case."

Lenny roared with laughter. "So that's what they're calling it these days. Can you give me a hand up? I'm having issues standing."

I hauled him to his feet. He swayed under the unfamiliar weight of the armor but managed to stay upright.

"What are you doing in that armor?" I demanded.

"I thought I'd clank into the kitchen and scare Carl." Lenny raised one metal arm. "Problem is, I can't move in this thing. I have no idea how people went into battle wearing this clobber."

"Maggie?"

I whipped around at the sound of Reynolds's voice. He appeared at the foot of the stairs, fully dressed and wide-awake. I tugged at the short hem of the oversized T-shirt that served as my nightgown, but Reynolds's attention was fixed on Lenny.

"What on earth?" He raised a hand. "No, don't tell me. If it involves breaking and entering, I'd have to arrest you, and I don't have time to make two arrests in one night."

I bounced from foot to foot. "You have concrete evidence?"

Reynolds slid a glance at my friend and shot me a warning look.

I rolled my eyes. "Oh, come on. If you're about to make an arrest, Lenny'll know. Besides, you'll need backup."

His lips twitched. "An eejit in medieval armor wasn't quite what I had in mind."

"Who are you calling an eejit?" Lenny raised an arm, and part of the armor fell to the ground with a crash.

I winced. "Okay, so Lenny's not exactly going to help make your approach subtle, but I'm willing to help."

"Hey, you're not leaving me out of the action." My friend took a cautious step forward and sent a metal hand flying.

Reynolds squeezed his eyes shut. "This is going to be a disaster. I need the pair of you to be quiet. I've called the mainland for help, and Günter's agreed to back me up in the meantime."

"Did the call just come in?" I asked, lowering my voice to a whisper.

"An email confirming what we discussed earlier."

Lenny looked from me to Reynolds. "Come on, man. Don't leave me hanging. Who are you arresting?"

Reynolds was saved from answering when Günter appeared at the foot of the stairs, closely followed by Julie.

My cousin shivered and pulled her nightgown close. "I heard you leave, Maggie. And when I got up to follow you, I found Günter sneaking about."

Günter grinned. "I wasn't sneaking about. I told you, Reynolds asked me to help him with something."

"Well, I want to know what that something is," she said, stifling a yawn. "I always miss out on the fun."

Günter's gaze moved to the suit of armor. "Hey, Lenny. Nice outfit."

"Dude," Lenny exclaimed, "you lost your fuzz."

Lenny fell into step with Julie and Günter, and I sidled over to Reynolds. "What's happened?" I whispered.

He lowered his voice to match mine. "My contacts in the U.S. came through with an excellent motive for Huff to want Jimmy Wright dead, and forensics found a fingerprint on the rake. It's Huff's. I'm hoping the amount of alcohol he consumed tonight will make him come quietly." Reynolds looked around him. "Do you have any idea which room is his? Martha mentioned he was sleeping on the ground floor when she showed me to my room earlier."

"I believe the family rooms are that way." I pointed to the corridor that led to the rooms in the west wing. "But I don't know which one he and Brandi are in."

"Let's go and find out."

Reynolds strode across the hall, and I jogged to keep pace. Julie and Günter followed close behind, and Lenny brought up the rear, clanking over the stone flooring.

"What brought you downstairs, Maggie?" Reynolds asked. "Couldn't sleep?"

I shook my head. "I heard a noise below my window. Like a splash?"

Reynolds jerked to a halt. "Our room overlooks the swimming pool, and your room is next door."

"Did you or Günter hear anything?"

He shook his head. "It must have happened after we went downstairs, and before Günter went back up to get his Swiss Army knife."

"I was on my way to investigate when Lenny fell at my feet, and you arrived. Want to check out the pool before we tackle Huff?"

"Yeah." Reynolds spoke over his shoulder to the others. "Anyone know how to get to the swimming pool?"

"I saw it on a school tour." Julie pivoted and changed direction. "We need to cut back through the main hall."

Lenny groaned. "Ah, no. Turning this armor isn't easy."

"You should have thought of that before you put it on," I regarded the pieces of metal still strapped to my friend's body. "I have no idea how you managed to get into it."

Günter and Reynolds helped Lenny to turn and propelled him into forward motion. We retraced our steps and crossed the hall. Julie stopped in front of a tapestry and pulled it to the side to reveal a wooden door.

Reynolds tried the handle and looked at me sharply. "It's unlocked."

"The side gate was unlocked, too, remember?" Despite my words, a shiver snaked down my spine, and it wasn't from the chill of the hall.

"Maybe someone wanted to go for a midnight swim," Julie said. "For all we know, we could be interrupting a romantic interlude."

I frowned. "I guess, but something doesn't feel right."

Outside, dark branches swayed in the breeze, and a poolside umbrella that had been left open flapped in a rhythmic beat. In the cool night, I was acutely aware of my thin cotton T-shirt. I wrapped my arms around my body in a futile effort to ward off the chill.

All thoughts of the cold froze the instant I looked in the swimming pool.

My cousin was the first to react. Julie's high-pitched scream jolted me to my senses, and it appeared to have a similar effect on Reynolds. He and

I raced to the side of the pool, and Lenny clanked after us.

Huff Huffington lay face down in the center of the swimming pool. Floating beside him was a plugged-in hedge trimmer.

"Whoa," Lenny said in awe. "Dude's as fried as his chicken balls."

I tasted bile and swallowed hard. "Sorry, Liam. Looks like you solved one murder case only to open another."

## 14

———

IT WAS eleven o'clock in the morning by the time Reynolds and the forensics team had finished examining the crime scene. I buzzed with impatience to know all the details. Being kept out of the loop sucked. Yeah, it wasn't my case. I had no right to expect special treatment from Reynolds, but, man, it was frustrating.

I scanned the faces of the subdued gathering in the morning room. Whoever killed Huff was in this room. Yes, there was hired staff from the hotel to question, as well as Huff and Helen's employees who'd accompanied them to Gull Island. Despite Huff's obnoxious behavior toward Felicity yesterday, the people with the most compelling motives to murder Huff were Huff's own family.

The door to the morning room swung open. Reynolds marched in with a purposeful spring to his step. One of Whisper Island's two reserve policemen trailed behind his boss. Reynolds regarded the gathered company coolly. "Thank you for your patience. Reserve Garda Timms and I would like to ask each of you a few questions." He focused on Helen. "Which room should we use for that, Mrs. Huffington?"

She regarded him with a frosty expression. "So you're a policeman, huh? You didn't let that slip last night."

"Didn't I mention it?" His expression remained bland. "I live at Shamrock Cottages. One of your young relatives must have seen me in my uniform."

I swallowed a laugh. Reynolds had been careful to ensure that that didn't happen.

"No, they did not." Helen turned accusing eyes on me. "And you didn't mention it, either."

"You didn't ask me what Liam did for a living," I pointed out. "It's fortunate that he's here to handle the case. He'll make sure Huff's killer is caught."

"Killer? Couldn't my son's death have been a terrible accident?" Helen pulled her shawl tight around her shoulders. "Maybe he slipped and fell."

"While holding a plugged-in power tool?" I shook my head. "It doesn't seem likely."

"Neither does my son being murdered," the old lady snapped. "Who would want to hurt him?"

*How about his entire family, except maybe you and Brandi?* I looked at Reynolds for assistance.

He didn't miss a beat. "If you don't think your son was murdered, what about suicide?"

Helen's incredulous expression spoke volumes.

"My son was hardly the suicidal type. I doubt he suffered a day of depression his entire life."

"I'll bet he caused a few, though." The words were out of my mouth before I could engage my internal filter.

Reynolds shot me a warning look, but Helen chose to ignore my faux pas. "Suicide is out of the question," she said in a tone of steel, "and so is murder."

"Mrs. Huffington, I understand that this is difficult for you, but your son's death was not an accident. That leaves murder and suicide." Reynolds's smile was tight. "You should know that I was on my way to arrest Huff for the murder of Jimmy Wright."

A collective gasp resounded around the gathered members of the Huffington clan.

Helen cast Reynolds a venomous glare. "My son wouldn't harm a fly."

So she was annoyed by the allegation, but not surprised. This intrigued me.

"Come on, Grandma," Martha said. "Dad had a terrible temper. Why do you think Mom left him? He'd be the type to fly into a rage and kill someone."

This was the most I'd heard her utter since we'd met. I took another look at Huff's only daughter. In contrast to the rest of her family, Martha appeared to have blossomed since receiving the news of her father's death. Even her cherry-patterned dress was cheerier than the drab hues she'd chosen on previous days. Could she have snapped and murdered him?

"If Dad knew he was on the verge of being arrested, doesn't that point to suicide?" Amb's voice was unnaturally high. "Maybe he wanted to spare the family the humiliation of a trial."

"I don't see how taking himself out spares you guys humiliation," I said. "It'll be all over the media regardless."

"I need to talk to everyone who was in the house when Mr. Huffington died." Reynolds focused on Amb. "Let's start with you."

The man paled under Reynolds's scrutiny. "Okay. It's no secret my father wasn't a popular man, but none of us would have killed him."

"In that case, you have nothing to fear." Reynolds motioned for Amb to follow him. To the rest of us, he said, "I'll send Garda Timms in to collect each of you in turn."

After Amb had trooped out of the room with the policemen, Helen struggled to her feet and leaned heavily on her cane. She'd aged over the last few hours and looked every second of her eighty-four years. "Maggie, may I have a word with you in private?"

I blinked in surprise. "Okay."

She led me to a sofa at the far end of the room, where we wouldn't be overheard. She eased herself onto the sofa, wincing from the effort. "I'd like to ask you a favor."

I took a seat beside her on the sofa. "Sure, ask away. What can I do to help?"

"You're a private investigator. I want you to look into the false allegation Sergeant Reynolds made against my son." Helen clasped her hands in her lap. Grief was etched in every line on her face. "I don't know why the police have accused Huff of this terrible crime, but I won't have his good name maligned."

Huff's good name? Either Helen was delusional, or she was deliberately obtuse.

"I'm sure the police will tell you why they think Huff was responsible for Jimmy's death. Just because Huff is dead doesn't mean the case on Jimmy Wright's murder is closed."

Helen's eyelids drooped. "Despite his sometimes difficult behavior, I can't believe my son would take another man's life. Especially not Jimmy's. They were friends."

"If that was the case, why did you give me the impression you didn't know Jimmy?"

Helen's gaze darted to the left. "We had a falling out many years ago. I hadn't seen my nephew in thirty years."

I weighed my next words with care. "If I'm to investigate on your behalf, I need you to be honest with me, and you haven't been so far. I understand that Jimmy worked for your company for several years and that you paid for his college education." I leaned forward. "Why did you try to conceal that information?"

"Perhaps I should have been more open, but I

didn't want to discuss the matter so soon after learning about Jimmy's death, especially with a stranger." Helen sighed. "No offense, dear, but we barely know each other."

The woman had a point, but I couldn't shake the feeling that she was deflecting again.

"My relationship with my nephew was complicated," Helen continued. "I regret that we didn't part on good terms when he left America, but my son remained in touch with him sporadically over the years. I believe they were involved in a business venture together."

"Do you mind sharing why you parted with Jimmy on bad terms?"

Helen stood and stretched, making her old bones creak. "Come have a walk with me around the gardens."

I glanced at the closed door. "Shouldn't we wait for Liam to question us first?"

"We should, but we won't." Helen grabbed her cane and hobbled toward the patio doors. "I'm eighty-four years old. I'm hardly about to make a run for it."

The lady had a valid point. I followed her out onto the patio, and we walked in the direction of the Japanese garden.

Helen leaned heavily on her cane, cementing my impression that she'd aged overnight. "I can guess why your Sergeant Reynolds thinks my son killed Jimmy Wright."

I waited for her to continue, clamping down on my eagerness to hear the whole story. We had walked another few feet before Helen picked up where she'd left off.

"My son had a difficult first marriage. Suzanne came from a different background than ours. Theirs was a love match, but the affection soon fizzled due to Huff working long hours and traveling so frequently." Helen paused at the entrance to the Japanese garden and ascended the steps up to the pagoda. She eased herself onto the wooden bench, wincing in pain. "At this time, my nephew Jimmy was working for the company. He was a handsome lad in his youth, and he and Suzanne became great friends. And then it became more than friends. I tried to turn a blind eye. No marriage is perfect, and my son was no saint. But when Suzanne fell pregnant, I couldn't keep silent any longer. I confronted her, and she crumpled. She said she wasn't sure who was the father of her baby. She begged me not to tell Huff. I agreed on the conditions that Jimmy left and went back to Ireland, and Suzanne made an effort to be a good wife to my son."

"Did your ultimatum work?"

"For a while." Helen shifted her weight on the bench and stared out at the flowers floating down the slow-flowing stream. "When Rosie was born, I knew at once he must be Jimmy's child, but I loved that little boy from the instant I clapped eyes on him. I don't care if he's not my biological grandson. I love him just as much as his brother and sister."

"Did Huff find out about Suzanne and Jimmy?"

"Not immediately. I'm not sure how he discovered that Rosie wasn't his son, but at some point in the last eighteen months, his attitude toward him changed. He'd always been hard on the boy but regarded him as his son and heir. A couple of years ago, he flew to Ireland to conduct business dealings with the Greers. He chose to come to Whisper Island incognito and stayed at Jimmy's farm. I don't know what happened. Huff persuaded Jimmy to invest in the hotel, and Jimmy had no reason not to trust his cousin."

"Did Huff take Jimmy's money as revenge?"

"I think so. That's the sort of revenge my son would engage in." Helen sighed. "For him, losing money was akin to losing face. To be stripped of your life savings would be the ultimate humiliation."

"If Huff knew that Amb wasn't his biological son, why did he say nothing?"

"Huff would hate to be regarded as a cuckolded husband. He'd feel it would make him look foolish, and Huff could never abide being laughed at."

"So he cooked up a plan to rip off Jimmy, and more or less disinherit Amb the first chance he got."

"Exactly." Helen rose and leaned on her cane. "Now do you understand why I don't believe my son killed Jimmy? It wouldn't make sense. He'd already exercised his revenge. Why would he risk going to jail for murder?"

"I don't see how I can help, Helen. What can I do

to clear Huff's name if the evidence against him is compelling?"

"I don't expect you to work miracles. I'd just like you to take another look at the case and give me your honest conclusion."

"What if my conclusion is that your son was guilty?"

"Then I'll have to make my peace with it." Helen accepted my offer of support as we walked back toward the house, arm in arm. "I blame myself for his behavior. He was an only child, and not by choice. I always imagined, I'd have a large family, but Huff's birth was complicated. When the doctors told me I wouldn't have any more babies, I didn't believe them. But as the years passed and I didn't fall pregnant, I poured all my affection into Huff. I didn't realize it at the time, but I spoiled him horribly."

"Lots of parents spoil their kids," I said. "But kids grow into adults, and adults are responsible for their own behavior."

"You're right, of course. The logical side of me knows this, but the emotional side of me feels I failed him by not setting boundaries." She blinked back tears. "Now it's too late."

In that second, I made my decision. "All right. I'll take another look at the case." Reynolds would have a fit, but hopefully, he'd be too busy solving Huff's murder to worry about me taking another look at Jimmy's.

Helen squeezed my arm. "Thank you, Maggie.

Your grandmother would be so proud of the woman you've become."

When she left me standing on the patio, I stared after her retreating form. Helen Huffington didn't just enjoy the movies. She was an excellent actress. I'd just witnessed her in the role of grieving mama, which was doubtless accurate—up to a point. But I knew when someone was manipulating me. How much of the story she'd spun me was true? How many slivers of information had she conveniently left out? Regardless, I'd keep my promise. I'd take a fresh look at Jimmy Wright's murder and draw my own conclusions, even if my gut told me that Huff was guilty.

## 15

WHEN MY TURN TO be questioned by the police rolled around, I was surprised to find Reynolds alone in the library. I closed the door behind me and took a seat in the leather armchair opposite his.

"Where's Timms?" I asked. "I thought he was in here taking notes."

"He's on an errand. When that's done, he'll talk to Carl Logan and his staff." Reynolds rubbed his eyes and allowed the tiredness to show through his professional demeanor. "Apart from Carl and Lenny, they all stayed overnight at a hostel in the village, but they still need to be questioned."

"I doubt Carl, Lenny, or anyone outside the family is the killer."

"I agree, but I have to make sure." He flipped through the papers on the desk. "Besides, I have to rule out an intruder as the culprit."

This made me laugh. "You don't seriously believe

that somebody traveled all the way to Gull Island just to bump off Huff? That's extreme, even for the most disgruntled of business associates."

"True, but you know how this works, Maggie. I have to keep an open mind. My gut tells me Huff Huffington was killed by a member of his family, but a hunch is useless without proof."

"Once you've finished eliminating outsiders, you're going to be left with a substantial list of people who had a motive, the means, and the opportunity. I don't envy you the job of sifting through that bunch of suspects."

"Tell me something I don't know." Reynolds reached for his coffee cup and took a gulp. "Let's go over your statement again."

I ran through the events of last night from the time the noise had jolted me awake to the point at which Reynolds had entered the scene. "You showed up pretty soon after I'd gone downstairs, and the only person I'd encountered before you arrived was Lenny."

A smile cracked through his serious expression. "If anyone else had donned that suit of armor, they'd be high on my list of suspects."

"Even if Lenny wanted to kill Huff, he knows electronics. There's no way he'd wear a metal suit of armor to throw an electrical appliance into the water. He's not suicidal."

"He could have done it before he got into the armor," Reynolds pointed out.

"Would Lenny have had time to run back from the pool area and put it on before I came downstairs? Less than five minutes passed between the splash and Lenny falling over in the main hall. How could he—"

An almighty crash interrupted my train of thought.

"That'll be Timms," Reynolds said dryly. "Want to see how much of a mess he's made?" With these cryptic words, he stood and strode toward the library door. After a second of bewildered inactivity, I bolted after him.

Out in the main hall, Reserve Garda Timms lay on the stone floor, moaning and surrounded by pieces of metal armor. He'd managed to get the helmet on, but the visor had slammed shut, leaving Timms gasping for air.

The commotion had attracted the group from the morning room, all of whom were staring at the dented armor on the floor.

"What on earth are you doing?" Helen demanded, brandishing her cane like a weapon. "Are you trying to destroy the house?"

"Just a hunch I had," Reynolds said easily and hauled Timms to his feet. "And I have a feeling Timms here proved it beyond a reasonable doubt."

Günter ambled over and took in the destruction with a jaundiced gaze. "You should have picked a helmet with a battle visor," he said to Timms. "This one is designed for jousting. Harder to see and breathe. It shouldn't be paired with this suit of armor. Someone made a mistake."

"Never mind historical accuracy," Reynolds said, unfazed by the chaos around him. "Help me get Timms out of this helmet."

Günter held Timms still while Reynolds pulled off the man's helmet.

"What's the verdict?" Reynolds asked his gasping underling.

"There's no way, Sarge," Timms said, wiping sweat from his brow. "Even if Lenny knew what he was doing, I can't see anyone getting into this clobber in less than five minutes."

Günter snorted. "Even with help, it took me close to half an hour."

"Am I the only person in the house who hasn't attempted to get into a suit of armor?" I asked. "Is this a European thing?"

"I took part in battle reenactments back in Germany," Günter explained as though this were an everyday occurrence, "and the armor we wore was similar to these suits."

"Would you mind helping Timms clean up the mess?" Reynolds asked Günter.

"Sure." Günter gave the suit a disapproving frown. "Even if the bits don't match. When we get back to Whisper Island, I'm contacting the museum."

"You do that," Reynolds said in a soothing voice and ushered me back into the library. After he'd reclaimed his seat behind the large wooden desk, he said, "Timms's experiment rules Lenny out."

"And you can probably scratch Brandi off your list of suspects," I added. "She had more to lose from Huff's death than gain. If he'd lived and changed his will to include the terms he mentioned last night, her baby would have benefited enormously."

"On the surface, yes, but we don't yet know the exact contents of either the will Huff intended to make or the current one. Maybe Brandi was sick of her domineering husband. She'd seen how he treated his existing children. Maybe she didn't want that future for her baby. What did she care that her son stood to inherit the majority share in a business that may or may not exist in eighteen years? Perhaps she wanted money now."

"These are all valid points," I conceded, "but we can argue that Amb and Doug stood to lose the most if their father changed his will. I don't know about Martha. I don't get the impression that she plays a role in Huffington Enterprises."

"What about Candace? She strikes me as a woman with a temper when riled."

I considered Candace for a moment. "She's uptight and snobby, but devoted to Amb and Hailey."

"In other words, she'd do anything to protect them," Reynolds said.

"But murder?" I frowned. "Huff wasn't threatening her family with physical harm. Killing him is an extreme reaction."

"Murder is always extreme," Reynolds pointed out. "It would depend on how badly Candace and Amb would be affected financially by the new will. From what Huff said at the dinner table, the change seems to mean a demotion for Amb. Isn't he the vice president at the moment?"

"I haven't a clue how their company is structured, but you could be right. Huff mentioned Doug and Amb working for the company but not running it. Doug said he doesn't currently hold a position with the company, so that would be new. Amb does work for Huffington Enterprises. The terms of the new will could have been synonymous with a demotion—and a pay cut."

"I'm running financial checks on all of Huff's heirs," Reynolds said. "So far, all I know is that Doug Huffington is a frequent visitor to Vegas casinos, but that doesn't necessarily mean he's in debt."

I appreciated Reynolds trusting me with this information. He'd trusted me with insider info during a previous investigation, and I'd screwed up by withholding information from him. I wouldn't make that mistake again. "Liam, there's something you should know. Helen has asked me to look into Jimmy Wright's murder. She'd like me to prove that her son was innocent."

Reynolds stared at me, incredulity written all over his face in flashing neon letters. "You can't be serious, Maggie. The case against Huff is watertight."

"Maybe it is, but I've promised her I'll take a look.

At the very least, it might help me discover what it is that she's holding back. I can't put my finger on it, but I know she was deliberately steering me in a certain direction. Why and where, I don't know." A thought occurred to me. "Did your tech guys manage to track down the woman Jimmy had arranged to meet on the day of his death?"

Reynolds shook his head. "We've questioned two women he met on kink dating sites, but both have cast-iron alibis for the day of the murder. There's no way they could have been on Whisper Island at the time Lenny says he saw the half-naked woman."

I turned this info over in my mind. "Thanks. I'll see if Lenny can help me track her down. Could you write down their profile names so we can rule them out?"

"Okay, but I'm not giving you their real names."

"I didn't expect you to." If necessary, Lenny should be able to find that out, but I refrained from mentioning that tidbit to Reynolds.

The policeman scribbled on a piece of paper and handed it to me. I took the proffered sheet gingerly. It listed the profile names Lenny had tracked down before. "Did you ever find the woman's clothes?"

"No. If she witnessed the murder, or found the body after and fled, her clothes should have been somewhere on Wright's property."

"It's a puzzle, all right."

"You're wasting your time trying to prove Huff's

innocence, but if Helen's paying you, go for it. But keep me posted, yeah? If you play fair with me, I might let you see some info on this murder investigation, but only if the information exchange is a two-way street."

"Okay." I stretched out my hand. "It's a deal."

The gong sounded, and Reynolds looked at his watch. "Time for lunch. I need to go into the village and ask if anyone saw or spoke to Huff yesterday. Want to meet for a walk later? I'd appreciate someone to bounce ideas off of, and Timms isn't the right person for the job."

My chest swelled with joy at being asked to help. "Sure. How long will we all have to stay on the island?"

"I've spoken to the district superintendent," he said. "He's fine with us returning to Whisper Island this evening. The younger Huffingtons may need to change their travel plans, though."

"When were they supposed to leave Whisper Island? Helen mentioned something about them traveling around the country."

"That's correct. Brandi and Helen's rooms are booked at the hotel for another two weeks, but the others were due to leave next Wednesday. Unless I have someone in custody by then, I'll have to ask them to stay a while longer."

I raised my eyebrows. "They won't like that."

"No. Amb's already started throwing his weight around." Reynolds led me out of the room and paused in front of the dining room. "Meet at three outside O'Dwyer's Pub in the village?"

"Sounds good. I'll see you then."

After Liam had left to question the locals, I took a deep breath. Time to start my covert investigation into Huff's death while giving Helen the impression I was concentrating my efforts on Jimmy's murder. And I knew just the person who could help.

## 16

AFTER LUNCH, I went in search of Lenny. I found him in the kitchen, loading plates into an industrial-sized dishwasher. His bored stance vanished the instant he spotted me. "Hey, Maggie. How's it hanging?"

"At the rate my day is going, backward." I gave Lenny's brother Carl my most ingratiating smile. "Can I borrow Lenny for a while? Mrs. Huffington needs his help."

Carl, who was concentrating on a list of ingredients, barely glanced my way. "Sure," he said vaguely. "We're nearly finished here anyway."

"Great. The food was awesome by the way."

This snagged his attention. "Hey, Maggie, I heard Paddy Driscoll hired you to look for that sheep."

"Yeah." I eyed him curiously. "Why? Do you remember something about Nancy's disappearance? You must have been a kid at the time."

"I remember hearing people talk about it." An

emotion flickered over his face too fast for me to pinpoint. "They all thought Paddy was crazy to care so much about a missing sheep."

"You didn't think he was crazy?" I prompted.

Carl averted his gaze. "No."

I hesitated for a second. "Carl, do you know what happened to Nancy?"

A flush darkened his tanned cheeks. "No. Why should I? You'd better have that chat with Lenny. I need him back in the kitchen in fifteen minutes."

"Got it."

I grabbed Lenny's arm and dragged him outside into the gardens. We collided with the young uniformed policeman guarding the back door.

"Names?" he demanded. "I have orders not to let anyone out."

"Maggie Doyle and Lenny Logan." I eyed his insignia. "Are you part of the backup from the mainland?"

"Yeah. Just here for the day." The guy consulted a printed list. "Okay, you're on the list of people who can leave the house, but you need to inform me if you want to go beyond the grounds."

"Sure. I'm due to meet Sergeant Reynolds in the village at three, but I have no plans to leave Marley House before then."

"Fair enough." The man cast his gaze toward the dark clouds above. "Rain's forecast. You're going to get soaked."

"Rain's always forecast in Ireland," I said with a laugh. "We'll take our chances."

Once the policeman was satisfied that letting Lenny and me out of his sight wouldn't cost him his job, we skedaddled and headed in the direction of the Japanese garden.

"What's going on, Maggie? Why did you tell Carl that Helen Huffington needed my help?"

"She does, even if she doesn't know it." A fat raindrop hit my nose. "Quick. Let's find shelter before the downpour hits."

We took the steps up to the Japanese garden two at a time and made a beeline for the pagoda.

"So," Lenny began once we were settled on the wooden bench. "Spill. What's going on?"

I gave him a brief summary of my morning, leaving out any confidential information that Reynolds had shared with me. "Basically, I need your help in tracking down the woman Jimmy Wright had arranged to meet on the day of his murder."

"You don't seriously believe Huff was innocent? From what Reynolds said last night, he has hard evidence to back up his theory."

"Heck no. Huff killed Jimmy." I leaned back on the bench and stared out at the raindrops dancing off the stream. "Something doesn't add up. First, why does Helen seem more concerned with clearing Huff's name than in solving his murder? Second, what happened to the clothes of the woman you saw?"

"No clue. Pity she hasn't come forward to give her story to the police."

"Yeah, but if she was cheating on her partner with Jimmy, she wouldn't want to be called as a witness in a court case."

"True, but this is murder," Lenny said. "Would you keep your mouth shut over something that serious?"

"No, but you'd be surprised at how people justify their decision not to do the right thing."

"Speaking of doing the right thing…" Lenny gave me a long look. "Timms questioned the kitchen staff about our movements on the night of the murder. Timms is a good guy, but he doesn't always ask the right questions, you know?"

I did know. And so did Reynolds. "What did Timms not ask?"

"After Timms had gone, the Whisper Island Hotel staff got talking. Carl let slip that Helen and Huff and arrived at the hotel on Monday with an entourage of six employees."

"Six?" I frowned, mentally checking Felicity, the valet, and Helen's nurse off my list. "Are the other three still on Whisper Island?"

"That's where it gets weird." Lenny frowned. "Apparently, there was a fight on Wednesday evening, and Huff sent three of their staff back to the mainland on the last ferry."

I straightened, my detective instincts on full alert. "What sort of a fight?"

"Carl doesn't know. He's dating one of the maids. Do you remember Carol?"

I cast my mind back to my time working as an undercover maid at the hotel. "Short dark hair with an elfin face?"

My friend nodded. "That's the one. Anyway, she said that two of the women left in tears and the guy—some sort of manservant—was livid."

"So Huff fired his manservant and two female employees within hours of Jimmy Wright's murder?" I contemplated this new fact for a moment. "We need to find out who they were, where they went, and why they were fired."

"Coaxing people to bare their souls is more your strength than mine," Lenny said with a grin. "Why don't you head over to the hotel tomorrow? I'll give Carl a heads-up, and maybe he can ask around, find out whose the best person to talk to. At the very least, he can arrange for you to meet Carol."

"Thanks. That would be great. Give Carl my number, and he can text me with the details. My shift at the café ends at four. I can talk to Carol any time after that. Meanwhile, could you do some more digging on Jimmy's dating profiles?"

"Sure."

I pulled the piece of paper Reynolds had given me out of my jeans pocket and handed it to Lenny. "The police tracked down the two profile users you found on Jimmy's kink dating sites."

Lenny perked up. "And?"

I sighed. "According to Reynolds, both women have alibis for the day of the murder and couldn't have been on Whisper Island. Do you think you could find more women he was in touch with?"

Lenny frowned. "Maybe, but these two were his most recent contacts. Is Reynolds certain about their alibis?"

"He seemed confident, but I didn't press him on the issue."

Lenny pocketed the piece of paper. "Okay. When I get home tonight, I'll try again. So far, I only looked at the dating sites you spotted in Jimmy's search history. I'll cast the net wider this time and look at other dating sites."

"Thanks, Lenny. I'll pay you for your time, of course."

"We'll sort that out later." He grinned. "I'm just glad to have something more interesting to do on a Sunday night than watch *Magnum, P.I.* reruns with Granddad."

"Hey, I loved Magnum as a kid."

"So did I, but I've seen all the episodes several times at this stage. I'd rather do some live P.I. work." Lenny checked the time. "I'd better get back and help Carl and the others pack up our stuff."

"Are you catching the ferry back to Whisper Island?"

"Yeah. Reynolds said we could take the six o'clock connection. How are you guys getting back?"

"I don't know yet. The Huffingtons have hired a

boat, but I'm going to suggest to Julie and Noreen that we catch the ferry. Frankly, I'm sick of being stuck with the Huffingtons and their family tensions."

"Don't you want to observe them in case they let something interesting slip?" Lenny's smile was teasing.

"Ugh. After a weekend cooped up with them, I'm done observing them. And they're not stupid. They won't let anything about Huff's murder slip in front of me."

"Okay. Let me do some digging tonight. I'll call you if I find anything urgent. Otherwise, I'll swing by the café tomorrow morning."

"Okay."

We left the pagoda and hurried back to the house. The rain had lightened in intensity, but my shirt was damp by the time we got inside. Lenny and I parted in the kitchen, and I ran upstairs to get changed.

When I entered our room, Julie was lying on the bed with her digital reader. She sat up when she saw me. "Where have you been? Günter and I were worried."

I was sorely tempted to tease her about her use of "Günter and I," but her tense expression told me this wasn't the moment for levity. "What's happened?" I asked, reaching into my backpack for a dry top.

"Do you mean apart from being stuck in a house with a murderer?"

"Yeah, that part's not so cool." I pulled on the dry T-shirt and flopped onto the bed beside her. "Sorry for abandoning you, but I needed to talk to Lenny."

"How's he coping?"

"Oh, you know Lenny. Taking the whole situation in his stride."

"I guess you two are used to finding dead people at this point." Julie wrapped her arms around herself. "Seeing Huff floating in that pool…it was horrible."

"Have you been up here all afternoon?"

My cousin shook her head. "No, Günter and I went out for a walk, but then we got caught in the downpour and came back to change."

"We must have just missed each other. Lenny and I went into the gardens as it was starting to rain." I rolled onto my stomach and propped myself up on my elbows. "So, tell me…are you and Günter an item?"

Julie's freckled cheeks turned a charming shade of pink. "Maybe? He kissed me last night before I came up to bed, and again out in the gardens."

"Well, now. Your mother will be pleased."

My cousin cast her eyes heavenward. "Don't remind me. She'll gloat. I'd like to keep this under wraps for a while if I can."

"Philomena won't hear about it from me, but there's no way Noreen will keep quiet."

"Tell me about it. I'm hoping to persuade her to give me a couple of weeks of privacy before she blabs to Mum."

"Noreen is a terrible liar. Philomena will have the whole story out of her within thirty seconds. So…" I grinned slyly, "...did Günter's new clean-shaven look make the difference?"

"He looks better without the beard, but I'm not that shallow. After the way he supported me last night, I'd have kissed him with or without the beard."

"Ah." I laughed. "I noticed it took you a while to return to our room after we discovered the body."

"I know Huff was an awful man, but what a way to go." Julie paled and dropped her voice to a whisper. "Which of them do you think did it? My money's on Martha."

"Why do you say that?" I asked, my ears pricking up. "Did you overhear something?"

"No, but yesterday evening, just before we went down for cocktails, I was standing at the window—" she pointed to the window nearest our bed, "—and I saw Martha go out into the gardens and talk to one of the gardeners. The guy was holding a pair of plug-in hedge trimmers, and he was using them to trim the greenery around the pool."

"Did you see where he put the power tool when he was finished using it?"

Julie shook her head. "No. I got distracted getting ready and worrying about my appearance. All I know is that I saw a gardener holding a tool like the one in the pool with Huff, and Martha also knew it existed."

I cast my mind back to my arrival at Marley House yesterday. "Reynolds and I passed gardeners trimming the maze," I said. "I'm trying to remember if they had plugged-in power tools or the cordless variety. I should ask Reynolds if he's spoken to the gardeners yet."

"Günter heard the gardeners are all local men. Reynolds will probably talk to them this afternoon in the village."

"Speaking of Reynolds, I'm due to meet him to go for a walk."

My cousin perked up. "A walk outside Marley House and its gardens?"

"Yes," I began slowly, "but…"

Julie leaped off the bed. "Fantastic. I can't wait to get out of here, and the next ferry doesn't leave until six. If Reynolds is with us, he can hardly object to us leaving the property."

I swallowed a sigh. I'd been looking forward to pumping Reynolds for information, but my cousin was anxious to escape what had turned into a house of horrors. I didn't have the heart to snub her. "We'd better see if Noreen wants to tag along."

"No point. She's playing bridge with the Huffing-tons." My cousin shivered and wrapped her arms around her body. "They asked Günter and me to join them, but they're the last people I feel like hanging out with today."

"Why don't you ask Günter to join us?" With him along to distract her, I might still manage to get some alone time with Liam.

"Sure." Julie pulled on a long-sleeved top and tied her hair into a loose ponytail. "Meet downstairs in five minutes?"

"Deal. And don't forget your rain jacket. More rain is forecast."

"Ugh." My cousin screwed up her nose. "That fits right in with the whole ambiance of the weekend."

"True, that." I grabbed my own raincoat from the dressing table chair and made for the door. "See you in five."

## 17

DESPITE THE DARK clouds that obscured the afternoon sun, our walk was glorious. After we'd met Reynolds outside O'Dwyer's Pub as arranged, we walked through Gull Island's only village and onward to a rocky trail on the northern side of the island.

Today's walk meandered in the opposite direction of yesterday's hike. Our goal was to reach the old lighthouse that perched on the top of a cliff and looked out over the Atlantic.

"This walk is popular with tourists," Julie informed us, proudly holding up a slim guidebook. "It's less steep than the trails up to the monastery but offers similarly spectacular views. I came up here last summer with a tour organized by the Whisper Island Ramblers."

We passed several groups of tourists on our way up the rocky path. While this route was less steep than yesterday's, it was also narrower and closer to the edge of the cliff. I watched my step and stayed as close to the safe edge of the path as possible.

When we reached the top, I inhaled deeply, relishing the rain-rinsed fresh air. "You didn't exaggerate about the view."

My cousin shielded her eyes from a sudden burst of sunlight through the cloud cover. "The view's even better from the top of the lighthouse. Want to race me to the top, Günter?"

The German grinned. "Okay, but I will win."

"Not if I can help it." Julie took off at a sprint, and Günter soon caught up with her.

Reynolds and I hung back in a tacit acknowledgment that this was our opportunity to talk. He put his arm around my waist and led me toward a stone slab that served as a bench. Under the thin material of my jacket and T-shirt, my skin was hyperaware of his touch. "We don't need to pretend anymore," I reminded him.

His wolfish grin made my heart skip a beat. "Who said anything about pretending?"

"I—" I swallowed hard, too stunned to form a coherent sentence. I clasped my shaky hands in my lap. I'd expected this. Of course I had. So why had his words sent my emotions into a tailspin?

He leaned in and brushed his lips against my cheek, sending my already rapid heartbeat into overdrive. "We can talk about us once we get our respective investigations wrapped up. Sound good?"

I jerked my neck in agreement. "Okay."

At the rate my progress into the sheep's disappearance was going, my divorce would be through by the time Reynolds and I had that conversation.

"On a more serious note," he said, "I'd like to run my afternoon interviews by you."

"Sure." I sat beside him, eager to hear what he'd discovered.

As if he could read my thoughts, Reynolds laughed. "Sorry to disappoint you, Maggie. No one knew anything of significance. I spoke to the two gardeners who worked at the house yesterday, and they were adamant that they'd locked the power tools into the shed where all the Marley House gardening equipment is stored."

"Who had access to a key to that shed?"

"No one in the house, but they didn't need a key. The shed was secured with a padlock. Whoever killed Huff broke the lock and stole one of the hedge trimmers."

"Julie says she saw Martha speaking to one of the gardeners yesterday," I said. "Do you have any idea what was said?"

"Yeah." Reynolds rubbed his jaw. "The guy she spoke to was Rob Hennessy. According to Hennessy, Martha Huffington asked him to finish work early because her father was disturbed by the noise of his hedge trimmer that close to the house. Hennessy was only too pleased to push off early, and he and his brother headed straight to O'Dwyer's Pub for their usual Saturday evening pub dinner."

"Martha knew the gardeners had hedge trimmers and where they were stored," I said. "Did the rest of the family know where the shed was located? I don't remember passing it in the gardens."

"We did, actually. Do you remember the grass-covered little house next to the greenhouse?"

I nodded. "I remember admiring it yesterday."

"That's the shed."

I whistled. "It's fancier than any shed I've ever seen."

"I believe it used to be the live-in gardener's house back in the day. At any rate, the Huffington family arrived at Marley House yesterday morning. Martha's brothers and sister-in-law had plenty of time to explore the grounds and see the Hennessy brothers at work. In theory, they all could have seen the shed."

I cast my mind back to yesterday's events. "What about Felicity, the girl Huff yelled at yesterday for not reading his mind? And didn't Huff have a valet?"

"Huff's personal assistant has taken to her bed with a nervous collapse." Reynolds looked amused. "I couldn't get much sense out of her, but her records check out, and she hadn't been in Huff's employ long."

"Long enough for him to treat her badly," I pointed out. "Could she have killed her employer in a fit of rage?"

He shrugged. "I haven't crossed her off my list, but Huff's relatives had stronger motives for wanting him dead."

"What did the valet have to say about his boss?"

Reynolds laughed. "Nothing positive. He's not pleased that he's out of a job, but he's not exactly in mourning. Ditto Helen's nurse. Did you have any luck with your line of inquiry?"

"I don't have a line, unfortunately. As long as I'm stuck on Gull Island, I can't do much to investigate Jimmy Wright's death. My progress so far has consisted of asking Lenny to take another look online." The mention of Lenny jogged a memory. "Did you know Huff fired three of his employees on the night Jimmy Wright was murdered? Carl Logan's girlfriend is a maid at the hotel, and she overheard a fight."

Reynolds's intelligent eyes grew contemplative. "I didn't know that. Thanks for sharing. I'll check it out."

Hopefully, not before I'd had a chance to talk to Carol. Sharing was all well and good, but I had to earn a crust. I wasn't going to spill my entire agenda to Reynolds.

"Are you thinking about who killed Huff?" He asked, misinterpreting my expression.

"Hmm?" I mulled over the question for a bit before answering. "At the moment, Martha is at the top of my list, with Candace a close second."

"Candace?" He looked at me in surprise. "What makes you suspect her?"

"For a start, she's fiercely protective of her husband and daughter, and she hates the fact that

Huff treated them badly. She confided in me yesterday that she'd leave Amb if he didn't start standing up to his father."

"I wonder if she shared these thoughts with her husband," Reynolds mused. "If she had, it might point to him having a strong motive to do away with the man."

"Yesterday? I don't know, but I got the impression it was an ongoing issue between them rather than a new revelation on her part." I removed my water bottle from my backpack and took a sip, turning ideas over in my mind. "Do you know what will happen to Huff's estate now that he died before he could change his will?"

"I spoke to Huff's lawyer an hour ago. The current status quo is an equal division of his private assets between all his children. That'll include Brandi's baby. As for Huffington Enterprises, ownership will be divided between his sons."

"Which will once again include Brandi's child," I said, "but exclude Martha."

"Exactly."

I sighed. "There goes my pet theory. From what you've said, it sounds like Martha's position wouldn't have changed under the terms of the new will, so why would she have wanted to kill her father? I mean, yeah, he was horrible to her, but why pick last night?"

"To stand up for her brothers?" Reynolds shook his head. "As theories go, it's weak, I know. My money is still on the brothers, either one or both of them."

My head jerked to attention. "Do you have reason to believe two people were involved in the murder?"

"No, but equally, I have no reason to blindly assume only one other person was present when Huff died. We have no prints and no obvious DNA evidence. I'm waiting for forensics to give me their full report, but the preliminary report contains nothing of use in terms of ruling in or out suspects."

A flash of Julie's bright pink rain jacket attracted my attention. My cousin and Günter were on the top landing of the lighthouse. I nudged Reynolds. "I guess we'd better get moving if we want to see the view from the top."

We walked back to the lighthouse, but Reynolds lingered in front of the door. "Thanks for listening, Maggie. I appreciate having someone with your mind for detection to share ideas with."

"You know I'm always happy to discuss murder," I said and opened the door that led to the staircase. "Do you have any idea how long you'll have to put up with O'Shea?"

When Reynolds had been appointed to Whisper Island Garda Station, it was ostensibly to help Sergeant O'Shea "transition to retirement." Five months later, O'Shea was showing no signs of leaving.

"Your presence has had a positive effect on his work ethic," I remarked. "I'll bet O'Shea's worked more hours since you arrived than he had for the previous thirty-five years. Unfortunately, that's not saying much."

"The trouble is you and your collection of dead bodies." At my outraged squawk, he laughed. "I'm teasing you, but only partly. We've been kept busy over these last few months. With only two part-time reservists, I can't manage on my own."

I turned to look back at him. "Why won't the district superintendent hire someone new?"

"I've asked, and he's put in the paperwork, but these things take time."

"I'll keep my fingers crossed that he finds someone soon."

Julie, Günter, Reynolds, and I stayed on the top landing of the lighthouse as long as we dared. All too soon, it was time for us to return to Marley House to collect our things and catch the ferry back to Whisper Island.

On the way back, Julie, who'd taken everything she owned with her to Gull Island except a backpack, tied her pink rain poncho around her waist. She and Günter stayed a little ahead of Reynolds and me, talking earnestly.

Reynolds and I parted in the gardens. "I need to check the shed again," he said, toying with my hair. "Can I call over to your house when I get back later?"

"Sure," I whispered, feeling my breath catch at the back of my throat. We needed to talk about our not-quite-fake date this weekend, and what to do next, but the gardens of Marley House weren't the place for that conversation.

He brushed his lips against my cheek. "Thanks

again, Maggie. Have a safe trip home."

"You, too." I ran back to the house, not able to stop the wide grin on my face. At the fountain in front of the house, I ran into Julie—literally. "Whoa. What's the hurry?"

"I must have dropped my rain jacket," she said, flustered. "Günter and I, well…" she trailed off.

"You were kissing," I finished, enjoying the pink flush on her cheeks.

"Yes, and my jacket must have fallen off."

A raindrop fell onto my palm. "Go back inside. I'll go and look for your jacket. There's no point in you getting soaked."

"Are you sure? Günter would have gone, but Carl Logan asked him to help load the van."

"No prob. Any idea where you were when you lost it?"

My cousin frowned. "I'm not sure. Somewhere around the Japanese garden?"

"Don't worry. I'm on it."

I jogged back the way I'd come and reached the Japanese garden within a few minutes. If Julie had been making out with Günter, the most likely place to look would be the pagoda.

I walked up the stone steps that ran parallel to the stream.

And froze.

A prone form lay face down in the stream, a pool of red seeping from his head. It was Sergeant Reynolds.

## 18

For a second, I froze, and then an adrenaline rush kicked in. I raced over to the stream, my blood ringing in my ears. I looped my arms around Reynolds's chest and hauled him out of the water. By the time I got him onto the grass, I was out of breath. The guy was no lightweight. I rolled him onto his back and checked his pulse and breathing. Both were present, if not satisfactory.

All of a sudden, Reynolds made a gurgling noise. I rolled him onto his side an instant before he heaved up half the contents of the stream.

He moaned and stared at me through dazed eyes. "What hap—"

And then he passed out.

My stomach lurched. I didn't know much about head injuries, but I knew enough to recognize the signs of a concussion. "Liam?" I shook him gently. "Wake up."

But he was out cold. I eased his head back onto the ground, careful to position him on the non-injured side. The gash on the right side of his head oozed with warm blood that trickled through my shaking fingers. I needed someone with more medical knowledge than I possessed to assess the situation. Thankfully, just such a person was staying at Marley House. I whipped my phone from my pocket and called Günter.

"I need your paramedic skills," I said the instant he picked up. "Someone attacked Liam. We're in the Japanese garden. And rustle up a first aid kit if you can."

Günter, to his credit, didn't waste time asking questions. "I'm on it."

A few tense minutes later, Julie's new beau ran up the steps to the Japanese garden, closely followed by Lenny and Carl. I exhaled in relief at the sight of the sturdy first aid box in Carl's hand.

"I always carry basic first aid supplies with me," Günter said in response to my questioning look, "but Carl's supplies truck comes equipped with a big box."

"We need to be prepared for first aid emergencies in the kitchen," Carl explained while Günter kneeled down to examine Reynolds. "Burns, cuts, that sort of thing. They're a professional hazard."

Lenny took a step closer to Reynolds's still form. "Whoa. Dude's got an almighty gash on his head. Are you hurt, Maggie?"

I took a shuddery breath and shook my head. "I wasn't here when Liam was attacked. Someone must have snuck up behind him and hit him over the head." My voice cracked, and hot tears stung my eyes. "And then they left him face down in the stream to drown."

Lenny and Carl stared at me, wearing matching expressions of horror.

"Do you think it was the same person who killed Huff?" Carl asked me, scratching his neat goatee. "I mean, how many killers can there be on Gull Island?"

"My guess is that whoever killed Huff tried to kill Reynolds." A muscle in my jaw flexed, and my fingers curled into fists. "When I find out who did this, I'll make sure they pay."

"But why attack Reynolds?" Lenny scratched his scraggly beard in an unconscious imitation of his brother. "Unlike Jimmy, Reynolds has no connection to the Huffington family."

"When I left him, Reynolds intended to head in the direction of the shed," I said. "That's way over on the opposite side of the gardens. There has to be a reason he retraced his steps and ended up here."

"Maybe he saw something," Lenny said excitedly. "And went to investigate."

"More like saw *someone*. And that person didn't appreciate Reynolds's interest in him or her."

Günter, still examining Reynolds's still form, looked up. "He has a concussion. No telling how bad it is until he comes round. I'm calling an air ambulance to take him to the hospital in Galway."

"Thanks, Günter." I wrapped my arms around my body to stop my shivering. Now that the adrenaline had worn off, the shock was setting in.

Lenny put his arm around my shoulders. "You need to get indoors. Have a shot of whiskey."

"No," I said through chattering teeth. "I'm not leaving before the air ambulance gets here."

Carl took a hip flask out of his jacket pocket. "Try this. Granddad's poteen is my go-to cure-all."

Gerry Logan, a regular at the Movie Theater Café, was notorious for making moonshine strong enough to strip paint. I took the hip flask from Carl and drank deep, relishing the burn as the coarse alcohol snaked down my throat.

"Is Timms still on the island?" I asked when the poteen had worked its magic. "I guess he's in charge until O'Shea takes over." The notion of Sergeant O'Shea heading two murder investigations as well as an attempted murder made my blood run cold.

"I play hurling with Timms. I'll give him a call." Carl pulled out his phone and hit a number. "Hey, T. We need you in the Japanese garden. Reynolds got hit over the head. Yeah. Lots of blood. Okay, thanks." To us, he said, "Timms is on his way."

The wait for the air ambulance seemed to take forever. I sat next to Reynolds, whom Günter had made as comfortable as possible under the circumstances. My heart pounded against my ribs. I dragged air into my lungs and forced myself to stay calm. "Liam?" My voice shook with emotion. "Please wake up."

He groaned, and his eyes fluttered open, unfocused at first, then looking at me. He managed a weak smile. "Hey, gorgeous. Why are you here?"

I exhaled the breath I hadn't realized I'd been holding. He'd never referred to me as 'gorgeous' before. That must have been some blow to the head. I touched his cheek and whispered, "Thank goodness."

"What happened?" he murmured. "Why does my head hurt?"

"You were attacked. Someone hit you over the head."

"I want to go back to sleep," Liam murmured, not appearing to absorb what I'd just told him.

"That's a bad idea," Günter said. "You need to stay awake."

I squeezed Reynolds's hand. "You're going to the hospital to get your head checked."

He laughed. "I can't go to the hospital. I'm working. Have to…" He trailed off in confusion. "I can't remember, but I know I have to do something."

"What do you remember before you were hit on the head?"

"We went to see the lighthouse." He scrunched up his forehead in an obvious effort to concentrate. "Julie was there. And Günter."

"What about after we returned to Marley House?" I prompted. "When I left you in the gardens, you said you wanted to take another look at the shed."

He stared at me blankly. "I don't know. Did it have something to do with Huff's murder?"

"Yes. You wanted to make sure you hadn't missed something in or around the area of the shed, but I don't think you ever got there. For some reason, you changed your mind and went back in the direction of the Japanese garden. Do you have any idea what prompted you to come back here?"

He shook his head and winced. "Ouch. Moving doesn't seem to agree with me."

I took his hand in mine. It was colder than usual, and he was pale as snow. "Stay still. I can hear the helicopter approaching."

Sure enough, the sound of the chopper roared overhead. Within a couple of minutes, the para-medics arrived on the scene and took over. After a cursory examination, Reynolds was heaved onto a stretcher and carried out of Marley House's gardens via the side gate Reynolds and I had used the day before.

I lost my battle against the tears. Warm, fat drops coursed down my face. Lenny put a comforting arm around my shoulders and handed me a tissue to wipe my eyes. "He's tough, Maggie. He'll be okay."

I wiped at my tears and forced a smile. "I know he's tough. I just…I just don't want anything to happen to him."

Lenny squeezed me tight. "He'll be fine. The paramedics know what they're doing."

"With Reynolds in the hospital, it's up to us now," I said under my breath so the others wouldn't overhear. "We'll have to find the killer."

My friend's face lit up. "Awesome. I'm totally up for that."

"It's not going to be easy," I cautioned. "I can already predict that Sergeant O'Shea will persuade the district superintendent to put him in charge while Reynolds is out of commission, and O'Shea will not appreciate us interfering in his investigations."

Lenny grinned down at me. "Since when has that ever stopped you, Maggie?"

"Never," I conceded, "but there's no way I can juggle Paddy's missing sheep and two murder investigations on my own. Are you sure you want to get involved? O'Shea will be furious."

Lenny roared with laughter. "Bring it on. The man's an eejit. If we leave it up to him, neither case will be solved. Paddy's sheep has been missing for twenty-two years. He'll just have to wait a little longer for answers."

"Assuming we'll ever be able to provide them." I shook my head. "Jimmy Wright was my only lead there, and he's dead. And now the man who killed him is also dead."

"You don't think there could be one killer and not two? What if the same person who killed Jimmy also killed Huff?"

I shook my head. "I don't think so. According to Reynolds, Huff's fingerprint was found on the rake. He'd tried to rub it clean but missed a spot. The case against Huff seems pretty clear. Unfortunately, we're no closer to figuring out who bumped him off."

## 19

THANKS to the drama surrounding the attack on Reynolds, we missed the last ferry back to Whisper Island. Reserve Garda Timms arranged for his brother-in-law to collect us with his fishing boat, and Julie, Günter, Noreen, and I were back home by eight that evening.

After a night spent tossing and turning, I drove through the pouring rain and arrived at the Movie Theatre Café just in time to start my Monday morning shift. Inside the café, I peeled off my raincoat and hung it on the staff coat stand in the kitchen.

"Horrible weather," I said when I joined my aunt at the counter. "The poor tourists will be experiencing Irish rain at its finest."

"You look like I feel, love." Noreen shoved a double espresso across the polished chrome surface. "Get that down you."

I glanced over my shoulder at the table occupied

by a group of teenagers. "Shouldn't I take their order first?"

"No need. I let them in before our official opening time and took their order myself." My aunt gestured at a tray of coffees on the counter. "I still need to fix one more cappuccino. I'll make it while you drink your espresso."

Inhaling the comforting aroma of freshly ground coffee, I picked up my cup and took a sip. "Divine. I needed this. I had a rough night."

"Tell me about it." Noreen ground coffee beans and fetched a fresh carton of milk from the fridge. "What a weekend. I feel awful about what happened to Reynolds."

"If the attack on Reynolds was the worst part of the weekend, I take it you're not in mourning for Huff?" I asked, deadpan.

My aunt's disdainful expression was more eloquent than a thousand words. "Huff was an odious individual. While I wouldn't wish his fate on anyone, I'm more upset about the sergeant getting clobbered over the head. Have you heard how he's doing?"

"Yeah. Timms texted me late last night. Reynolds has a concussion, and he needed stitches for the wound on his head. He'll have to stay at the hospital for a few days, but he'll be okay." I sighed. "I'm sorry to love you and leave you, but I have to go to the station this morning to answer a few questions. As expected, Sergeant O'Shea's at the helm."

"I don't know what the district superintendent was

thinking," Noreen said, sprinkling a light dusting of cocoa powder onto the cappuccino. "He has to know O'Shea will make a mess of everything."

"According to Timms, Reynolds won't be back at work for at least a week. Someone has to take charge."

I placed the last cappuccino onto the tray with the rest of the order and carried it over to the group of teenagers huddled around the James Dean table. When I'd unburdened the tray of its load, I rejoined my aunt behind the counter.

She was flicking through a magazine and muttering about police incompetency, the idiocy of civil servants and, incongruously, current wedding dress trends. As we had no other customers yet, I fixed her a pot of tea and made another espresso for myself.

I picked up one of Noreen's bridal magazines. "Why the sudden interest in bridal attire? Has Paddy Driscoll finally proposed?"

"Even if he did, he's at least twenty years too late. No, I'm looking for ideas for Julie's wedding."

"Gosh, don't tell her you're looking at dresses. She'd be on the next ferry to the mainland and never come back."

Noreen's smile was smug. "Oh, no she wouldn't. Not when she has Günter to keep her occupied on Whisper Island."

Poor Julie. My aunts would have the dress and venue picked out before she and Günter had had a chance to go on their first official date. Time to coax Noreen's thoughts away from weddings.

"What's all this about you and Paddy twenty years ago?" I asked. "Were you guys an item?"

My aunt shrugged. "If he hadn't become obsessed with that blasted sheep, we might have made a go of it."

"The sheep? Were you dating at the time Nancy went missing?"

Noreen took a sip of her tea and seemed in no hurry to answer my question. "Off and on, but the time was never right. Maybe that was a sign we weren't a good fit. And once the sheep went missing, Paddy lost interest in everything except his obsession that Jimmy Wright was responsible."

"Why did he suspect Wright? Was he still mad that Wright had married his ex?"

"Mad about Sally?" Noreen raised an eyebrow. "Paddy was well rid of her. Jimmy, too, once she took off for new pastures."

"Was there another reason Paddy suspected Jimmy?"

Noreen considered this for a moment. "He said Jimmy had been annoying him about the border between the fields that divided their property. He claimed Paddy had put the fence half a meter onto his land, and Paddy said Jimmy was talking rubbish."

"Had Jimmy been known to be cruel to livestock?"

"Ah, no. Jimmy was a dote. If anything, Paddy is

the grumpier of the two, but neither of them would hurt an animal."

I shook my head. "It doesn't make sense."

"Not much does at the moment. Huff was a horrible man, but I don't understand why he'd want to kill Jimmy." At my look of surprise, my aunt laughed. "Helen told me that Huff was about to be arrested, but I'd already overheard Julie and Günter talking about it after you all found Huff's body."

"I don't understand Huff's motivation," I said, "but apart from Paddy, I haven't been able to find anyone else with a known grudge against Jimmy."

My aunt creased her forehead. "There was that argument Jimmy had with Noel Ahearn last summer, but I doubt their tiff escalated to murder."

"What happened?"

"Noel wanted to turn one of his fields into a fee-paying car park for tourists. As the field in question is right on the border between Noel's land and Jimmy's, Jimmy was furious. He wrote a blistering letter to the *Whisper Island Gazette* about the matter."

"Did Noel get his parking lot in the end?"

My aunt shook her head. "Jimmy wasn't the only person to object, and the planning permission wasn't granted."

"I'd like to track down Noel and ask him a few questions."

"You'll have to wait a couple of days. I know his wife, and she mentioned they were going to Lanzarote on their holidays. They won't be back until tomorrow evening. Oh, speaking of holidays…" My aunt bustled into the kitchen and returned with a large box, which she deposited onto the counter. "The tourist office gave me these brochures to give our customers. I thought we could make a nice display in front of the entrance. Would you take care of that before you go to the police station?"

"Sure." I selected a glossy brochure from the box, and my stomach lurched at the sight of a photo of Marley House, bringing back the horror of my weekend in its full Technicolor glory. "Didn't you find it weird that the Huffingtons opted to stay another night at Marley House?"

My aunt snorted. "They probably wanted to use the opportunity to get their stories straight before returning to Whisper Island."

I exhaled slowly and nodded. "That's exactly what I suspect. One of them has to be the killer."

Noreen shuddered and clutched her teacup to her chest. "Which means one of them hit Reynolds over the head. I'm going to need to distract myself with wedding dresses, or I'll never sleep tonight."

I glanced at my watch. "I'll get moving on the brochure display."

"When are you due to be quizzed at the station?"

"In twenty minutes. I have enough time to take care of the display first."

I took a selection of the tourist brochures and arranged them on the display stand, shifting the stand's position to attract the attention of both the customers entering and exiting the café. I stood back to admire my handiwork. Not bad.

The bell over the door jangled, heralding the arrival of more customers. Felicity, Huff's assistant, walked in, accompanied by a man in his forties and a woman pushing retirement age. Their raincoats were slick with rain. They barely glanced my way in their haste to divest themselves of their wet clothing.

My blood hummed with excitement. This was my chance to coax Felicity to talk about her murdered boss, but I had to approach her with caution. Even free from Huff's aggressive presence, his personal assistant exuded shyness. The last thing I wanted to do was come on strong and scare her into silence.

Jittery with impatience, I waited until Felicity and her friends were seated at the Marilyn Monroe table by the window. Plastering a smile on my tired face, I slipped my notepad and pen from my apron pocket and strolled over to their table.

"Good morning. Can I take your order, or would you like a moment to look at the menu?"

"Oh, I know what I want." The older woman tapped the menu. "We were here last Friday. I'd like one of your delicious berry scones with clotted cream."

"Excellent choice. The berry scones are my favorite. Would you like something to drink?"

"A pot of Earl Grey tea," the woman said with a decisive air.

"Earl Grey sounds good," Felicity said. "Make it a large pot, and I'll have a cup, too."

The man checked the coffee menu. "I'll have an espresso and a full Irish breakfast."

"Sure." I scribbled the order on my notepad and glanced at Felicity. "Oh, hi. I think I've seen you before."

The woman's eyes widened, and she blinked several times. And then she blushed. "Oh, right. At Marley House."

"Yeah. I was one of the Huffingtons' guests for the weekend."

"That's one weekend none of us will forget," the man said. "I'm George, by the way. I am—was— Huff's valet."

"And I'm Mary Ryan, Mrs. Huffington's nurse." The older woman's lined face grew grave. "Such an awful thing to happen."

"He was a difficult man," I ventured. "Given his lack of charm to his guests, I can't imagine he was easy to work for."

Felicity's smile was wry. "You saw how he treated me. Temper tantrums were the norm for him."

"You didn't have to deal with him at night when he'd had too much to drink," George interjected. "If he was difficult sober, he was a nightmare when drunk."

"Why on earth did you stay in his employ if he treated you so abominably?" I asked. "Surely no job is worth that sort of aggravation?"

"Employees rarely stuck with Huff for long," Felicity said. "I intended to quit the moment we got back to Boston, but I have no regrets about taking the job."

I raised an eyebrow. "You enjoyed being treated like dog excrement?"

The woman laughed. "Hardly. No, I did it for the money."

The valet nodded. "Ditto."

Correctly interpreting my incredulous expression, Felicity elaborated. "Huff was notorious for being obnoxious to his staff, but he paid well above the usual rate for our services. I knew what I was getting into when I accepted the job. I saw it as a way to pay off the remainder of my student loans, and it worked."

Despite the humiliating scene I'd witnessed on Saturday, her words sounded sincere. "What will you do now?"

The valet grinned at me. "That's what we've met to discuss. If I'm out of a job, I intend to make the most of my time in Ireland."

"So do I," Felicity said. "George and I plan to drive around the country for the next couple of weeks. The return tickets to Boston that Huff booked us are still valid. There's no reason not to enjoy our time in Ireland."

I turned my attention to the older lady. "What about you? Do you intend to travel while you're here?"

"Oh, no. Huff's death doesn't affect my job. I

won't desert Mrs. Huffington when she needs me most."

"Is it true that Huff fired half his staff last week?"

This elicited a peal of laughter from the table's occupants.

"He fired me every other day," Felicity said.

"And me more often," George added. "I didn't take him seriously."

"But isn't it true that three members of staff left?"

"Two," the valet corrected. "I was one of the people he fired that day, but I ignored him. As for Jill and Alexis, they'd intended to quit anyway. Last I heard, they were touring Ireland, just like Felicity and I intend to do."

Distant church bells chimed the hour. My heart leaped in my chest. Ten o'clock. I was late for my appointment at the police station.

"I'll go and fill your order," I said to Felicity and her friends. "If I don't see you before you leave Whisper Island, enjoy your trip."

I hurried back to the counter and handed Noreen their order. Then I grabbed my coat and my bag and waved at my aunt. "I need to get moving. I'm late."

"Deep breaths and don't lose your temper."

I grimaced. "I'll do my best, but I'm not looking forward to this interview."

"You'll be fine, love. Don't let O'Shea bully you. Just tell him what you saw and leave it at that."

## 20

Despite my best intentions to follow my aunt's advice, thirty seconds in the odious policeman's company had me imagining ways to wipe the smug smile off his florid face. Sixty painful minutes of questions had followed before I was finally allowed to read over my formal statement and sign the document.

Sergeant O'Shea leaned back in his cheap plastic chair and smirked. "Once again, Maggie Doyle is at the center of a crime. Why am I not surprised?"

"I'm hardly at the center. It seems to me that Huff Huffington is the link between the murders and the attack on Sergeant Reynolds."

"True, but Mr. Huffington is dead. You are not." These last words were delivered in a tone that indicated O'Shea was disappointed to find me still among the living.

I gritted my teeth but let it slide. "My continued existence doesn't make me responsible for two murders and an assault. Have you made progress on interviewing the Huffington family?"

The older policeman's nostrils flared. "What business is that of yours?"

"Well, let's see. I spent the weekend with them, and I found Huff's body. I'd say that gives me a vested interest in the case."

"I'll have none of your cheek," the man snapped. "The private investigator's license has gone to your head. You have no business poking your nose into police matters."

"Ah, but you see, that's where you're wrong." I flashed him a saccharine smile. "Helen Huffington has hired me to clear her son's name. The Jimmy Wright inquiry is very much my business."

O'Shea blanched before turning a shade of purple I'd last seen on Huff Huffington when he'd been about to chew out his hapless personal assistant. "I don't care what she's hired you to do. I don't want you anywhere near this station or its staff. Don't think I don't know about you interrogating Reserve Garda Timms on the boat last night. I got the whole story out of him this morning."

Poor old Timms. He was a nice guy, but not the brightest, and definitely not able to stand up for himself during one of O'Shea's temper tantrums. "I didn't need to interrogate Timms. I was on Gull Island with the Huffingtons all weekend. Timms doesn't know anything I don't."

Sergeant O'Shea sneered. "I suppose your boyfriend let you run the show. The Hennessy brothers said you were snooping around the gardens together just before Reynolds was attacked. Perhaps your amateur detective act panicked the killer into attacking the sergeant."

"I was a police officer for several years before I moved to Whisper Island," I pointed out, "and Reynolds was a detective for the Met. We're hardly amateurs."

"If the pair of you knew what you were doing, Reynolds wouldn't have gone and gotten himself knocked over the head. That would never have happened on my watch."

I rolled my eyes. "*You* wouldn't have noticed something suspicious and tried to follow it up."

"That's pure speculation. Until Reynolds has his wits about him, we don't know why he was in that part of the garden. Nothing he's said so far has made any sense."

Perhaps not to O'Shea. "I was with him yesterday. Maybe I can interpret what he's said."

The man's jowls wobbled, and he pointed a meaty finger at my chest. "This is police business. Keep your nose out of it."

*For crying out loud.* If this was an example of the rusty cogs in O'Shea's brain working overtime, they needed an antirust treatment. "If you were capable of deductive reasoning, you'd see that the only way he'd have deviated from his plan to visit the shed was if he'd had a sound need to go back the way we'd just come."

"How dare you insult me in my own station."

O'Shea pulled at his collar, making me wonder, (a.) if I was about to witness him having a coronary, and (b.) what I'd do if he did. It was time to wrap up this charming interlude.

"I have a job to do," I said firmly. "As do you. So I suggest we both let each other get back to our respective professions."

"I'm not finished with you yet, Miss Doyle."

"That's unfortunate because I'm finished with you." I pushed back my chair and stood. "I've given you my statement regarding the attack on Sergeant Reynolds. You have no right to yell at me for carrying out a job I'm licensed to perform. I wasn't obliged to tell you that Helen Huffington had hired me, but I extended you a professional courtesy."

This last part was baloney. I'd just wanted to tick him off and goad him into letting info slip. Which he had—I now knew I needed to track down the Hennessy brothers.

When I swanned out of the interrogation room, Timms was at the desk. He cast me an apologetic look. "Sorry, Maggie. I didn't say you were bothering me on the trip back from Gull Island. That was Sergeant O'Shea's interpretation."

"Don't worry about it." I darted a glance at the still-closed door of the interrogation room. "Any updates on Reynolds?"

"Nothing new."

"Has he asked to see me?" I adopted a love-struck mien and leaned forward. "Or said anything about me at all?"

Timms gave me a pitying look. "Sorry, Maggie. He said nothing that made sense while I was there. Just kept going on about the color pink."

My heart sank. Nothing of use, then. "He must have been thinking about my cousin's poncho. She lost it in the gardens yesterday."

Timms appeared relieved. "That must be it, then. I knew the sarge couldn't be losing the plot."

I flashed him an ingratiating smile. "Could you give me his room number? I'd like to visit him this afternoon."

"No can do," Timms said. "We're assuming Reynolds was attacked in the line of duty. He has a police presence outside his hospital room, and only family is allowed to visit."

Although not being able to visit him sucked, I was glad to hear Reynolds had protection. Anyone desperate enough to attack a police officer and leave him to drown was very dangerous indeed. Cornered rats usually were. And I was in no doubt that Reynolds had said or seen something to cause Huff's killer to panic.

I retrieved my raincoat from the waiting room stand. "Thanks for keeping me updated, Timms. I appreciate it."

"No worries. If I have any more news, I'll send you a message."

"Please do."

When I left the station, I pulled up my hood to fend off the heavy rain. As I walked back to my car, a thought struck me. How could Reynolds have known about Julie's missing rain poncho? He hadn't been with me when I'd offered to go back and look for it. Had his assailant been wearing it to conceal his or her identity?

We'd never managed to find Julie's poncho yesterday. With the stress of Reynolds's attack, I'd forgotten all about it. What I did know was that the poncho hadn't been in the Japanese garden, where Julie had assumed she'd lost it. Had someone used it to disguise themselves before attacking Reynolds? If so, they must have hidden it somewhere. A coat that color was hard to miss.

I sat in my car and drummed my fingers on the steering wheel, brooding over the matter. I slipped my phone out of my pocket and sent Reynolds a get-well-soon text. Then I went online and found the number for Hennessy's Garden Services.

A gruff voice answered on the third ring. "Rob Hennessy speaking."

"Hi, Mr. Hennessy. This is Maggie Doyle. I was one of the Huffingtons' guests this weekend."

The man grunted an acknowledgment. "I remember you."

I took a deep breath and plunged on. "My cousin

lost her raincoat somewhere in the gardens. It's a bright pink poncho. I was wondering if you'd found it anywhere."

"That Timms fella asked me the same thing," the man said with a snort. "We tore up the gardens looking for it, but no luck."

"Thanks. If you have time, would you mind having another look?"

"Why is this coat so important to you? Does it have something to do with Sergeant Reynolds being attacked."

"I'm not sure," I said, careful not to elaborate on my theory that the attacker had used it to disguise him or herself. "All the same, I'd appreciate it if you'd keep an eye out for the poncho.

"Why are you asking all these questions?" Hennessy demanded. "Why not leave it to the police?"

The question was direct, and I took the bait. "I'm a private investigator. I'm looking into the attack on Reynolds."

In my defense, both statements were true. If Rob Hennessy assumed I'd been hired to investigate the attack, all the better.

"I don't want to be rude, Ms. Doyle, but I need to get back to work. What do you want to know from me?"

"As far as I know, I was the last person to see Sergeant Reynolds before his attack. When I left him, I understood he wanted to take another look at the shed. Something must have happened to make him retrace his steps back to the Japanese garden. Did you see anyone in the gardens shortly before I raised the alarm?"

"Yeah. A whole bunch of people."

My ears pricked up. "Could you tell me who?"

"The Logans and that German guy were loading up Carl's van. I don't think they left their position in front of the house, though."

"Anyone else?" I prompted. "Maybe one of the Huffingtons?"

"Yeah. The daughter went for a walk with one of the sons."

So Martha had been in the gardens at the time of the attack, and so had either Doug or Amb. I needed to find out which one. "Do you know which brother?" I asked. "Doug is the taller of the two, and Amb is the one with the receding hairline."

"I have no idea. He and the girl were too far away, and they both held umbrellas."

"Thanks for your help, Mr. Hennessy. If you think of anything else that happened that day, anything at all that was out of the ordinary, would you please give me a call?"

"Well…" he hesitated for a moment. "There was one thing that struck me as odd, but it wasn't in the garden.

"Go on," I said, my heart rate picking up. "What happened?"

"The plant outside Mr. and Mrs. Huffington's bedroom. It's dead."

"What?" I asked, baffled and trying to connect this unexpected announcement to the weekend's dramatic events.

"Yeah. A lovely Peace Lily." The man sounded more regretful about the demise of the plant than he was about Mr. Huffington's untimely death.

"Peace lily…" I searched my memory for plant names. "That's a spathiphyllum, right?"

"Yeah. They're easy-to-care-for indoor plants."

"How did it die?"

"Someone dumped weed killer into its pot."

I wrinkled my brow. "Why would someone want to do that?"

"Beats me," Hennessy said with a growl. "I'd like to know why they mixed the weed killer with milk first."

I clutched the phone tighter. "Are you sure?"

"I'm positive. The soil stank of sour milk and weed killer. I keep a close eye on the supplies in the shed." Hennessy gave a derisive snort. "That O'Shea bloke didn't want to listen to me, but I'm telling you that the bottle of weed killer I opened on Saturday morning is half empty. Someone was messing around with more than power tools in that shed."

"Sergeant O'Shea wasn't interested in hearing about this?"

Hennessy's laugh was bitter. "Heck, no. He said it was irrelevant to the case. Maybe it is, and maybe it isn't, but I've never seen such strange goings on at Marley House in all my years working there. Seems strange if it was just a coincidence."

I agreed, but I couldn't yet make the poisoned plant fit into the weekend's events. "Thanks for your time, Mr. Hennessy. I appreciate your candor."

"No problem. Good luck with your case."

After I'd disconnected, I mulled over what the gardener had told me. The dead plant hadn't raised any alarm bells until Hennessy mentioned it had been mixed with milk. Had Huff's killer intended to use poisoned milk as a backup plan? But why throw it in the plant's pot? Why not wash it down the sink? Had they been interrupted on their way to Huff's room and panicked?

The church bells chimed the hour, jolting me back to the present. It was time for me to get back to the café to help Noreen with the lunchtime rush. I turned my key in the ignition and started the car's engine. I had no idea how the weed killer tied in with the case, but my instinct told me it did. The challenge was figuring out *how*.

## 21

AFTER MY MONDAY shift at the Movie Theater Café had ended, I drove to the Whisper Island Hotel. Carl Logan had arranged for Lenny and me to meet Carol, the maid who'd overheard Huff's fight with his staff. After my conversation with Felicity and her friends this morning, I was inclined to think that the staff angle was a dead end, but my police training had taught me to look at every angle in an investigation.

When I got to the hotel, Lenny was waiting for me in the bustling lobby, bouncing from foot to foot. I maneuvered my way through the crowd, and he greeted me with a broad grin. "Hey, Maggie. Ready to play Scully to my Mulder?"

Personally, I felt he was more Shaggy to my Scooby-Doo, but whatever. "Sorry to disappoint you, Lenny. Aliens played no role in Huff and Jimmy's murders."

"Whatever about Jimmy, I doubt aliens would want Huff," he said. "I'm sure they have better taste."

"I'll take your word for it," I said dryly. "You're the UFO expert."

Lenny glanced at his watch. "We're kinda early. Carl said Carol didn't finish work until five. Want to grab a coffee in the hotel café while we wait?"

After a day fueled by espresso, I was all coffeed out, but I nodded. "Sure—if we can find a seat."

Although the café was as busy as the lobby, we got lucky and scored the last table on the terrace. Out of habit, I cast my gaze over the customers. And sucked in a breath. Martha Huffington sat at a table on her own, a digital reader in one hand and an iced coffee in the other. I checked the time. We still had twenty minutes before we could meet Carol.

I leaned across the table and lowered my voice. "Is it okay if I go talk to Martha? I'd like the chance to speak to her on her own."

"Smart. Go ahead. If you're still with her when we're due to see Carol, I'll go on my own."

I bit my lip. "Are you sure? You know what to ask her, right?"

"I got this, Maggie," he said, his expression uncharacteristically serious. "If I want to be your assistant full-time, I've got to get used to interviewing people."

He had a point. I got to my feet. "Okay. Text me when you're finished."

Lenny gave me a mock salute. "Yes, boss."

I strolled over to Martha's table. She was engrossed in her book and didn't notice my approach. "Hey, Martha."

Startled, the woman jerked to attention. "Oh, hi."

I gestured to the free seat at her table. "Do you mind if I join you?"

"Uh, sure." She blinked owlishly and regarded me as though she were a cornered mouse.

I sat and pointed at her digital reader. "What are you reading?"

"A guide to Venice." Her voice was barely audible. "I'd like to visit Italy now that…" She trailed off, but I caught her drift.

"You mean now that your father is dead," I said gently.

"Yes." Martha swallowed and put her reading device into her bag. "Dad wasn't keen on the idea of me traveling alone."

"You're an adult," I pointed out with a touch of exasperation. "Why didn't you just go?"

The woman splayed her fingers on the tabletop and stared at her hands. "It seems strange to you, I know, but Dad was very protective of me."

"Controlling" was the word I'd have chosen, but I didn't quibble. "Now that's he's gone, you can go wherever you like."

"I guess so. I mean, it'll take a while for my inheritance to come through, but the bank is willing to offer me a short-term loan." She looked me straight in the eye and held my gaze for the first time since we'd met.

"I intend to take them up on that offer. I'm not flying back to Boston with the others. I'll tour Ireland and fly to Italy after."

"Good for you," I said and meant it. After years of belittlement, Martha deserved some fun.

A wry smile tugged at the corners of the woman's mouth. "Aren't you shocked that I'm not going back for Huff's funeral?"

"It's not my place to judge. You've got to do what's best for you."

These words appeared to relax her. "My brothers aren't happy, but Candace has been wonderful. She had traveled all over Europe before she married Amb. She was an art talent scout, you know."

I hadn't known. "Did she give up her job after she married your brother?"

"Yes, but not immediately. As Dad so rudely pointed out in front of everyone, she and Amb had trouble having kids. In the end, they resorted to IVF treatments, and all the appointments made the constant travel difficult. Once Hailey was born, Candace didn't want to be away from the baby."

"You're very fond of Hailey, aren't you?"

Martha's expression softened. "I adore her. I'd never considered myself a baby person until she was born."

"Listen, Martha…could I, well, may I ask you a couple of questions?" I began with deliberate hesita-tion, fiddling with my fingers to emphasize my supposed reluctance to bother her. I disliked manipulating the woman, but one thing I'd learned from my years on the force was to tailor my interview techniques to the suspect's personality. A timid character like Martha would respond well to my feigned apprehension.

"Sure. Grandmother told me she'd hired you to clear Dad's name." Her voice was less tentative than it had been before, confirming I'd been right to play the nervous card.

"That's right. I think your father's murder and Jimmy Wright's murder are connected." Again, I hesitated, allowing Martha time to gather her thoughts. "If the murders are linked, so is the attack on Sergeant Reynolds."

"Unfortunately, yes." Martha sighed. "I hope Liam is okay."

"He's still in the hospital." I didn't elaborate or mention the police guard outside his room. For all I knew, the dowdy woman sitting across from me had tried to kill Reynolds. "Did you happen to see anyone in the gardens before the attack? You guys went for a walk, right?"

Her eyes widened in surprise, and I caught a glimpse of fear before she blinked it away. "Of course. You were in the gardens just before Reynolds was attacked. I suppose you saw us."

I chose not to correct her assumption. Better to let her believe I'd seen her, and she'd be more likely to name whichever brother had been with her on that walk. "Yeah. I saw both of you on my back to the house. I was just wondering if either of you had seen anything suspicious?"

"No. Doug and I just wanted a chance to talk." Martha twisted her rings. "We knew the police would suspect the family."

"And you had an inkling they'd be right."

The woman nodded. "I don't think my father was killed by an intruder, and you and your family had no reason to kill him. So yes, it must have been one of us."

"Do you have any idea which one of you is the killer?"

Her lips twisted into an ironic smile. "I know it wasn't me."

*And you won't tell me if you suspect one of your brothers.* I chose another tack. "Did you notice anything odd on the day of your father's murder? Anything that stands out in your memory."

She raised an eyebrow. "Dad announcing he was changing his will was pretty memorable."

"Yeah. That must have upset you."

"The new terms wouldn't have made any difference to my situation."

"No, but it would have negatively impacted your brothers. You must have been upset on their behalf."

"Yes, but I didn't kill our father."

Martha's quiet certainty convinced me that she wasn't the killer. However, I couldn't rule out that she'd helped one or both of her brothers commit the crime.

"Where were you when Huff was killed?"

She raised an eyebrow. "In bed, of course."

"So you didn't see or hear anything strange?"

"I heard your friend fall over in the suit of armor. I'd imagine the whole house heard that."

*Touché.*

"In other words, you didn't see anyone walking around the house that night?"

"As I said, I was in bed. After the stress of the day, Candace had given me one of her sleeping pills, but I only took half, and it didn't really work."

"The gardeners said they put all the power tools back in the shed before they finished work on Saturday. Whoever killed your father broke the padlock off the shed's door and stole a hedge trimmer."

She shuddered. "That indicates premeditation."

"Exactly."

Martha took a sip from her iced coffee glass, frown lines creasing her usually smooth forehead. "I know you want me to speculate about the killer, Maggie, but I won't do it. Doug and Amb are my brothers. If one of them killed Dad, he didn't do anything all three of us haven't fantasized about at some point."

"There's a big difference between imagining killing a person and actually committing a murder. I can't tell you the number of times I've dreamed about inflicting fatal injuries on my ex, but I can guarantee you I wouldn't do it. If one of you killed your father, the police will find out, sooner or later."

The woman opposite me toyed with her spoon, avoiding eye contact. "I'm not so sure about that. The new guy on the case seems to think one of the gardeners did it."

I resisted the urge to roll my eyes. Typical O'Shea. What motive did he think the Hennessy brothers had to kill Huff? "Was your father in the habit of taking a late night swim?"

"Yes. He suffered from insomnia. If he couldn't sleep, he often got up and went for a swim in the pool at home. I guess the same must have happened the night he died."

"Who knew your father liked to swim at night?"

Her laugh was tinged with a note of bitterness. "We all knew. Family and servants."

I went over the scenario in my mind. Perhaps one of Huff's children couldn't sleep and went for a walk. They'd noticed Huff in the pool, and decided to take the opportunity to kill him. We'd all seen the Hennessy brothers using power tools earlier that day, and the Huffingtons knew where the shed was located. I swallowed a sigh. My conversation with Martha had brought me no closer to finding the identity of Huff's killer and Reynolds's attacker—assuming that person was one and the same. I glanced at my watch. Lenny would be talking to Carol by now. "Thanks for the chat, Martha. I'm sorry to ask you awkward questions."

She shrugged. "It's your job."

As I stood to leave, a snippet of my conversation

with Rob Hennessy floated to the forefront of my mind. "Do you know why the plant in front of your father and Brandi's room died?"

Martha blanched, her knuckles turning white around the handle of her iced coffee glass. "No."

*Liar, liar, pants on fire.* Finally, I was onto something. "Only Rob Hennessy says someone dumped weed killer into the pot." I paused for dramatic effect. "Weed killer that had been mixed with milk."

Martha's mouth opened and closed, but no words came out.

I slipped one of my newly printed business cards out of my pocket and slid it across the table. "If you think of any reason why poisoned milk would have been dumped outside your father's room, give me a call."

She didn't take the card, but she inclined her head, wordlessly.

I left Martha staring at my card, a stricken expression on her homely features. My gut said she'd call me. Whether or not she'd divulge the name of the murderer when she did so was another matter.

I retraced my steps back to the lobby. Lenny was lounging in one of the leather armchairs near the hotel exit. From his downcast look, I surmised that the interview with Carol had not been fruitful.

He leaped to his feet when he saw me. "Hey, Maggie. How're tricks? Did Martha have anything interesting to say?"

"No, but her reactions to my questions were interesting." We walked out the revolving doors and down the steps toward the parking lot. "How did the interview with Carol go?"

Lenny pulled a face. "She had nothing to add that Carl hadn't told us already. She overheard Huff screaming at his staff and firing a couple of them. The valet was one of the people fired, but he was still at the hotel the following day, so Carol assumes he sorted it out with Huff. The women left by the afternoon ferry."

"Jill and Alexis were the names Reynolds mentioned," I said. "Did Carol mention them?"

"Yeah. She said one was Huff's personal massage therapist, and the other was supposed to act as Hailey's nanny for the trip."

"Supposed to? What happened?"

"Apparently, Huff hired the nanny without consulting Amb and Candace. They objected, and opted to look after Hailey themselves."

We'd reached my MINI, and I unlocked the car. "Thanks for coming with me today and taking over the Carol interview. I'm sorry it turned out to be a bust."

"Not entirely." Lenny grinned. "I didn't learn much from Carol, but I did bump into Amb and Doug."

My hand froze on the ignition. "And? Don't leave me in suspense."

"*And* I persuaded them to come to the Unplugged Gamers meeting tomorrow night."

I blinked. "But tomorrow's Tuesday. The next club meeting isn't until Thursday."

"Yeah, but Doug and Amb don't know that. I called the others to make sure we had members present. Mack can't make it, but Julie and Günter will be there."

I cast him a sideways glance. "You sly dog. Where are we holding this impromptu meeting?"

"I told them to be at your place at eight." Lenny grinned. "I thought it'd give us a chance to chat with them in a relaxed environment. And my grandfather's poteen has a habit of loosening tongues."

I gunned the engine and eased the car out of the parking lot. "Okay Mr. Future Assistant, I guess I'd better stock up on snacks."

## 22

ON TUESDAY, my shift at the café ended at two o'clock, and I devoted my afternoon to chasing down Paddy Driscoll's missing sheep. My motivation was nonexistent, but I'd made a deal with Paddy, and I'd uphold my end of the bargain—even if I used the opportunity to sneak in a few questions relating to Jimmy Wright's murder.

I knocked on doors, drank endless cups of tea, and asked the same questions over and over again. And every time, I drew a blank. No one knew what fate had befallen Nancy the sheep, and no one knew any reason why Huff Huffington—or anyone else, for that matter—would want Jimmy Wright dead. The only silver lining to my day was scoring an appointment with Jimmy's neighbor, Noel Ahearn, who'd returned from his vacation. I was due to visit him tomorrow evening.

By eight o'clock, I was exhausted. The last thing I

wanted to do was play board games, but I'd stocked up on supplies and made the cottage semi-presentable for my guests.

Lenny was the first to arrive, rolling up to my door with a bottle of his grandfather's poteen and a plate of brownies.

I stared at the gooey chocolate confections and groaned. "Oh, no. I've seen the effects of your brownies in action. No way am I serving those."

He grinned. "They're just brownies, Maggie. No secret ingredient this time. I swear."

I sniffed at the plate. They smelled okay. Better than okay, actually. My treacherous stomach rumbled, making us both laugh. "All right. If you promise there's nothing illegal in these brownies, we'll keep them."

He followed me into the kitchen, where he allowed himself to be accosted by Bran, a dedicated crotch sniffer. "Hey, boy. How are you doing?"

Bran whined in excitement and danced around my friend's legs.

I folded my arms across my chest. "Unbelievable. The only other person he displays this much affection for is Reynolds."

Lenny scratched behind Bran's ears, sending the dog into paroxysms of delight. "Have you heard from the sarge? Timms is annoyingly discreet."

My stomach clenched at the memory of this morning's frustrating conversation with an officious nurse. "I've tried calling the hospital several times, but they won't give out information to someone who isn't a family member. I've been relying on Timms for updates."

"What does he say?"

"That Reynolds has a concussion and will be in the hospital for another few days. I've sent him text messages, but no reply so far."

This irked me more than I cared to admit. I was being irrational, but the weekend on Gull Island had propelled our relationship into unchartered territory. I had no clue where I stood with the guy, and I had even less of an idea of where I wanted to stand. "I'm close to tracking down his family members for more info, but I don't want to be stalkerish."

"Under the circumstances, I'm sure they'd understand. Unfortunately, I doubt they can tell you anything more than Timms reported. If the guy has a concussion, he needs rest."

"I need to pick up summer clothes," I said. "I finish work early on Friday, and I'll get the ferry over to the mainland. If I drive to Galway to go shopping, I can stop by the hospital and see how Reynolds is doing."

"That's smart. Hopefully, he'll be awake and alert by then."

My doorbell rang, sending Bran into a barking frenzy. He raced to the door, ready to sniff-test my guests. Amb and Doug stood on my doorstep. The former looked ill-at-ease, and the latter wore his habitual slick smile. For once, Bran hung back. An icy sensation settled between my shoulder blades. The last time my dog had disdained someone, they'd turned out to be a killer.

I swallowed hard and forced a smile. "Come on in."

I ushered them inside the cottage and through to my living room, where I spied my cousin and Günter through the window. "Help yourselves to snacks. I'll be back in a sec."

I had opened the door before Julie had a chance to ring the bell. My cousin's boyfriend carried a stack of board games in his arms.

He winked at me. "I brought the least complicated ones in my collection. I figured they'd be easy to explain to newbies."

"Are we doing a spot of investigating?" Julie whispered in excitement.

I placed a finger over my lips. "Amb and Doug just got here," I said in a carrying tone. "Want to come through to the living room and set up one of the games?"

While Lenny helped Günter to unpack *Settlers of Catan*, Julie joined me in the kitchen. "Wow, Maggie. Are you planning to feed seventy people for a month?"

I regarded the piles of salty snacks and sweet treats I'd arranged on trays for my guests. "Did I go overboard?"

"I'm not complaining." My cousin stole one of

Noreen's mini chocolate muffins from a tray and took a bite. "Yum. This is good."

Sukey and Felix slept peacefully in their basket, but Mavis rubbed herself against my cousin's legs.

"She's Jimmy's cat," I said, correctly interpreting my cousin's look of surprise. "I took her in after Jimmy died."

"She's gorgeous." Julie stroked Mavis's luxuriant fur, and the cat purred in contentment. "Are you keeping her?"

I regarded the tortoiseshell cat and shrugged. "Now that she's stopped marking her territory and bullying the other animals, she's kind of cute."

"Careful, Maggie. You'll turn into Noreen."

"I have no intention of acquiring eight cats. Three's my upper limit."

My cousin continued stroking Mavis. "When Reynolds gets back, you're going to have to make a decision. Do you want to make your fake relationship real? Or do you need more time to get over your break-up?"

I exhaled sharply. "I don't know. Well, perhaps I do know. Maybe that's the problem."

"Did you like being his pretend girlfriend for the weekend?"

"I liked it way more than I'd expected to, and trust me, I'd imagined it a time or two."

My cousin smiled. "I'm sensing a *but* here."

"I made a huge mistake marrying Joe. I don't trust myself to choose a man who'll treat me right."

"From your description of Joe, Reynolds is nothing like him."

"No, he's not, but I'm still not sure that making our relationship official is a smart move."

Julie squeezed my arm. "Come on. Let's get the Huffington men drunk and see what we can find out."

Back in the living room, I lined up the ingredients for the Blue Margaritas I'd decided to make as our cocktail option on the drinks table. While I prepared salt-rimmed cocktail glasses, Julie arranged the snack trays on the portable table I'd brought in from my garden. The next hour passed in a blur of cocktails, poteen, and the first round of *Settlers of Catan*.

Despite Doug's affable manner, his good humor seemed forced, and his jaw tense. Amb went through the motions of being polite, but his mind was not on the game. After Amb had downed his second Blue Margarita and Doug his third shot of poteen, I asked the question I'd been itching to pose since they'd arrived.

"Any news on the investigation? I heard the police brought someone in for questioning."

I'd heard nothing to that effect, but it worked as an opening gambit.

"The gardener," Doug said. "Sergeant O'Shea took him in for questioning earlier today."

I swallowed my gasp of surprise. "Rob Hennessy?"

Amb nodded. "He had the means and the opportunity, apparently."

"But no motive," I pointed out. "What does Rob stand to gain by your father's death?"

"Dad ordered Hennessy and his brother off the property on the day he died," Doug said. "The noise from their machines was disturbing him."

"That's hardly a motive to kill," I pointed out. "Your family was only staying at Marley House for the weekend. Rob's employed by the local council."

Amb took another gulp of Blue Margarita. "The guy must be insane."

I chose another tack. "Did either of you see or hear anything suspicious on the night your father died?"

They both shook their heads.

"My room was the farthest away from the swimming pool," Doug said. "I didn't even hear Lenny fall over in the suit of armor. The first I knew of something being wrong was when Martha pounded on my door and woke me up to say Dad was dead."

"I was asleep." A muscle in Amb's cheek flexed. "After the…events…at dinner, Candace gave me a sleeping tablet. I was out for the count."

"Did Candace take one, too?" I asked.

Amb looked at me sharply. "I believe so, yes. Until my sister woke us up to say Dad had been murdered, neither of us left our bedroom."

If Amb was asleep, how could he know for sure that his wife hadn't left their bedroom? As if sensing the direction of my thoughts, Doug intervened.

"How's your investigation progressing, Maggie?"

he asked, smoothly steering the conversation away from the topic he and his brother obviously didn't want to discuss. "Grandmother told me she'd hired you to clear Dad's name."

"I haven't uncovered any new info regarding Jimmy Wright's murder." I took a deep breath, crossed my fingers, and took a chance. "I'm still trying to track down a witness. I hope they can provide me with vital information."

"A witness?" Amb's tone was harsh. "Are you saying the cops accused Dad of murder and didn't bother to track down a potential witness?"

I gave a noncommittal shrug and sent a silent apology to Liam Reynolds. "Had Sergeant Reynolds remained in charge of the case, I'm sure he'd have gotten around to it."

"What witness?" Doug demanded. "Was it a man or a woman?"

I thought of Mavis the cat and stifled a giggle. "I'm afraid I'm not at liberty to say."

Amb tugged at his collar. "This O'Shea guy never mentioned a witness. I get the impression he's happy to roll with the idea of Dad being the killer."

"And it's not as if our father is alive to defend himself," Doug added. "Can't you dig up information to exonerate Dad?"

I looked from one brother to the other, noting the sheen of sweat on Amb's brow, and Doug's clenched fists. "I promised your grandmother I'd take another look at the case against Huff, and I'll keep my word."

I gave them a tight smile. "Tracking down the witness is my first priority."

THE DAY after our impromptu Unplugged Gamers meeting was the first sunny day of the week. When my shift at the café ended, I longed to avail of the sunny weather and go for a run with Bran. Unfortunately, duty called. I'd arranged to swing by Noel Ahearn's farm on my way home from work and ask him a few questions about his argument with Jimmy Wright. After stretching shoulders stiff from carrying trays all day, I climbed into the MINI and gunned the engine.

I eased the vehicle into Smuggler's Cove's evening traffic, which was heavier in the summer than it had been in the colder months. My progress down the main street of the town was at snail's pace. I was in line to turn at the crossroads when someone knocked on my car window. Startled, I rolled down the window. "Hi, Tom. What's up?"

The elderly ferry office attendant flashed his false teeth at me. "Could I trouble you for a lift, Maggie? My car's in for repairs, and I need to get to Carraig Harbour."

I reached across the car and opened the passenger door. "Jump in. I'll pass Carraig Harbour on my way."

"Thanks." The old man climbed into the car and

closed the door. "I missed the bus. You're my only chance of getting to work on time."

I gestured at the line of traffic in front of us. "I'm not sure about that. What time do you need to be there?"

"Not for another half an hour. I was working at the Smuggler's Cove Harbour ticket office until five, and they need me to cover a shift out at Carraig."

"I guess you work longer hours in the summer months with more frequent ferries."

"Yeah." Tom turned on his toothy smile again, and the laugh lines on his craggy face deepened. "Noreen tells me your new private investigation agency is involved in several investigations. Good for you."

"Two investigations to be precise." Huff's murder interested me greatly, but it wasn't my case, even if I wanted it to be.

"Those Huffingtons certainly know how to bring drama in their wake." Tom chuckled. "Helen Wright was gone from Whisper Island before I was born, but her reputation lingered."

"Reputation?"

"Yeah. She was a stunner, according to my father. Broke several hearts before she left for America."

"She's still a good-looking woman for her age," I said vaguely, not particularly interested in Helen's past as a heartbreaker.

"I'd say that grandson of hers has left a trail of broken hearts in his time. He's a handsome lad."

He must be referring to Doug. Amb wasn't ugly, but he no one would describe him as handsome. "I guess you've seen the family around the town."

"And on the ferry. I sometimes go over and back on the ferry as a steward during tourist season." Tom chuckled. "It's a change of scene from the ticket office, and it gets me a spot of fresh air."

"Right." I let him rattle on, only half listening. Tom was a nice guy, but he was a notorious talker.

"…but he looked quite different on Thursday. I had to look twice to recognize him."

My subconscious stirred, turning words I hadn't absorbed over in my mind. "Hang on a sec. Who didn't you recognize?"

"The Huffington lad," Tom said cheerfully. "He looked different without the baggy jeans and the baseball cap."

I blinked, trying to connect the dots. The outfit Tom had described didn't sound like the sort of clothes Doug Huffington would wear. He seemed to live in semi-formal attire. "When did you see him wearing baggy jeans and a baseball cap?" I asked. "The day the family came over on the ferry?"

"Ah, no. He was all dolled up the day he came over from the mainland with the rest of them. I was surprised because he'd looked like any other tourist the day before."

Now my instincts were on red alert. "The day before? Are you saying that Doug Huffington came over to Whisper Island last Wednesday?"

"Yeah. He caught the two o'clock ferry from the mainland." Tom turned the matter over in his mind. "I didn't see him catch a return ferry, but he must have done. He was on the ferry with his brother and sister the following morning."

Doug Huffington had visited the island on the day Jimmy Wright had been murdered. Did Reynolds know? I didn't think so. We'd discussed the investigation into Jimmy Wright's murder, and Reynolds had spoken to the Huffingtons. The younger members of the family had been ruled out on the basis that they hadn't arrived on Whisper Island until the morning after Jimmy's murder.

Why had Doug come over on the day before he was due to arrive with his siblings? It could be innocent. Maybe he'd wanted to explore without the rest of his family. But if that were the case, why hadn't he informed Reynolds? I was still turning over the implications in my mind when I pulled into the ferry terminal's parking lot at Carraig Harbour.

"Thanks for the lift, Maggie." The old man doffed his cap at me and gave me a roguish wink. "If I were ten years younger, I'd ask you out."

Make that thirty years younger, I thought in amusement. "Hang on a sec, Tom. I'd like to go over to the mainland later this week. Do I need to book tickets this time of year, or can I just show up?"

"Booking is smarter, especially if you want to bring your car. We sometimes have free places, but there's no guarantee."

I killed the engine and opened my door. "In that case, I'll come with you and buy my ticket now."

As Tom and I walked across the parking lot to the ticket office, a prickle of awareness made me tense my neck. I looked over my shoulder, but I didn't recognize anyone I knew among the crowds of tourists lining up in front of the ticket office. I gave myself a mental shaking. The two murders and the attack on Reynolds had made me paranoid.

With a wink and a chuckle, Tom let me in through the staff entrance and got me my ticket for Friday, neatly bypassing the long line.

"Thanks, Tom," I said when he handed me the ticket.

"No problem. I appreciate you giving me a lift."

I pocketed the ferry ticket and made my way back through the parking lot to my car. I glanced at the clock on the dashboard. In fifteen minutes, I was due to meet Noel Ahearn. In spite of the traffic and the detour to Carraig Harbour, I should still make it on time.

I started the engine and exited the parking lot, turning in the direction of the Ahearn's farm. With Tom out of the car, I turned up the music on the radio. It was an old Nineties song that I remembered from my childhood. I hummed along tunelessly and navigated the sharp curves of the cliffside road.

When I'd first moved to Whisper Island, the precarious state of the roads had terrified me, but I'd grown used to them. I reached the crest of a particularly steep hill and swore under my breath at the sight of the tractor coming up toward me. The road was too narrow for us to pass one another. I'd need to pull at a curved spot farther down and wait for him to pass.

I resumed my song and rolled down the hill, picking up more speed than I wanted. I pressed the brakes to slow my pace.

Nothing happened.

My heart lurched in my chest and I increased the pressure on the brakes. Still no response. Sweat beaded on my forehead. This wasn't good. This wasn't good at all. I forced myself to take a deep breath and tried the handbrake. No response. The car rolled faster and faster down the hill, drawing closer to the approaching tractor.

The driver of the tractor sat on his brakes and honked his horn, but his vehicle was too wide to avoid me. I tasted bile. If I didn't think of a solution quickly, I'd crash.

With seconds to spare, I angled the MINI in the direction of the cliff edge, opened the car door, and hurled myself out onto the road.

## 23

THE ROUGH ASPHALT tore at my bare arms, scraping them with ruthless precision. Ignoring the pain, I gritted my teeth and rode my adrenaline rush to scramble toward the stone wall opposite the cliff. An almighty crash behind me indicated that my MINI had tumbled over the edge and smashed on the rocks below. Had I delayed another second, I'd have been killed. Breathing hard, I slumped against the wall.

Farther down the road, a man climbed down from the parked tractor and ran toward me.

"Maggie? Are you okay?" Paddy Driscoll's rough-hewn face was a picture of horror. "What the heck happened?"

I heard a sob and it took me a moment to realize the sound was coming from me. Paddy gathered me into his arms and hugged me tightly. "Thank goodness you're all right. Noreen would be devastated if anything happened to you."

"I'm sorry," I said between gulps of air, "my brakes failed. They were in perfect working order before…" I trailed off, not wanting to reach the inevitable conclusion.

"Before what?" Paddy demanded.

I swallowed past the hard lump in my throat. "They worked fine before I left the car in the Carraig Harbour parking lot."

An ominous silence descended between us. Finally, Paddy said, "I'm calling the police, and then I'm taking you back to my place for a cup of tea."

I dabbed at my tears and nodded, too shocked to argue. I was dimly aware of Paddy's conversation with Reserve Garda Timms. When he put his phone back in his pocket, the big farmer led me over to his tractor and helped me up. Then he drove us the short distance from the scene of the accident to his farmhouse.

"I don't think I'm supposed to leave the scene of an accident," I said, realizing the stupidity of my words the moment they were out of my mouth. "Paddy, we need to go back. We'll get into trouble."

"No, we won't. I told Timms you were in shock and that they'd find us at my place. As for your car, that's beyond saving."

I choked on a sob and allowed him to lead me into his house and through to his living room. For once, Paddy's Bullmastiffs didn't snarl at me, their hostility held in check by a quelling look from their master.

After I was seated in one of Paddy's enormous overstuffed armchairs, he cleaned and bandaged my scrapes and supplied me with a cup of tea that had been liberally laced with whiskey.

"Get that down you," he said, shoving the cup at me.

I obeyed but balked when he offered me a second serving. Despite the man's blatant concern for my welfare, I ran through the vehicles I'd seen parked in front of the ferry ticket office. To my relief, a large green tractor wasn't among them. Besides, there was no way Paddy could have beaten me to that narrow pass in a tractor as slow as his.

The farmer sat in an armchair opposite mine and eyed me intently. "I hope this isn't because of your investigation into my missing sheep?"

I shivered and held my cup close to my chest. "I doubt it. It's more likely to be because I'm looking into Jimmy Wright's murder on behalf of Helen Huffington."

Paddy's smile was wry. "Two birds, one stone, eh? You can ask the same people about Jimmy and my Nancy."

"Yeah, but I'm afraid I haven't made any progress with Nancy. I was on my way to meet Noel Ahearn when my brakes failed."

The wrinkles on Paddy's brow deepened. "Noel didn't have anything to do with Nancy's disappearance."

"No, but he and Jimmy had a disagreement."

"Over Noel's plans to open a pay-to-play car park?" Paddy snorted. "Sure, everyone around here objected to that, including me. Several of us wrote letters to the council and the local newspaper."

My ears pricked up. "So Jimmy wasn't the only one to write to the paper?"

"Heck, no. Sean Clough must have received a flood of letters, but he only published a few of them. Jimmy's was one, and mine was another. You're barking up the wrong tree if you think Noel was responsible for Jimmy's death."

I looked the farmer straight in the eye. "Who do you think killed Jimmy?"

"I think Reynolds had the right of it. I'd say Ambrose J. Huffington III was the killer." Paddy pronounced Huff's name with disdain.

I raised an eyebrow. "Did you know Huff?"

"Never met the guy and I didn't want to," the farmer muttered. "I'd heard enough about the man from Jimmy to know to give him a wide berth."

My pulse kicked up in pace. "From Jimmy? But I thought you and Jimmy hated each other."

"Hate's a strong word. Before Nancy went missing, we were the best of pals. I was delighted when he moved back to Ireland after his stint in Boston, even if he was less than thrilled about the circumstances."

"I heard the Huffingtons fired him."

"It was more complicated than that," Paddy said and fell silent.

"Could you elaborate?"

The man shifted uncomfortably in his seat. "I'd rather not. I know Jimmy's dead and all, but we were friends once."

"If it's about him being Amb's father, I already heard."

Paddy's eyes widened in surprise. "From who? Jimmy told no one but me."

"Helen Huffington mentioned it when she hired me to take another look at the case against Huff."

Paddy guffawed with laughter. "I'll bet she didn't tell you the second kid's probably Jimmy's, too."

It was my turn to be surprised. "Doug was also Jimmy's son?"

"Jimmy certainly thought so. He came back from Ireland when Amb was a baby, right enough. Helen Huffington intervened and put a stop to his affair with Huff's wife. But what Helen didn't know is that Jimmy and Diana met up in France the summer after he left Boston. Nine months later, the second boy was born. Draw your own conclusions."

I sat back in my chair and contemplated this fresh slant on Jimmy's murder. Up to this point, I'd assumed that the only Huffington child with a reason to want Jimmy dead was Amb. If Jimmy was Amb's biological father, Amb's inheritance might be at risk. Until now, I'd reasoned that it would have been in Doug's interests for Jimmy to stay alive. If it transpired that Amb wasn't Huff's biological son, Doug's share of the inheritance would increase substantially. However, if Doug was also Jimmy's son, he had a compelling motive to want the farmer silenced.

In fact, if this scenario were true, the only Huffington who had a reason to keep Jimmy alive and well was Martha.

To my relief, Timms showed up without Sergeant O'Shea. I didn't think I could cope with the older policeman's snide remarks after the fright I'd just had. Once Timms had taken my statement, Paddy drove me home.

"Are you sure you don't want me to call Noreen? I don't like leaving you alone in the cottage, especially with all those Huffingtons lurking."

I stifled a grin. "If one of them were responsible for what happened to my car, I'd say the safest place I can be is near them."

"Hide in plain sight, like?"

"More like keep your friends close, and your enemies closer," I replied in a bone-dry tone.

Unlike my crazy ride earlier, the drive home was blissfully uneventful. When we arrived at the entrance to Shamrock Cottages, Lenny's vibrant purple van was parked outside the gates. I breathed a sigh of relief. "Lenny's here, so you have no need to worry about me."

Paddy snorted. "I'm not so sure about that, but at least you won't be alone."

The farmer drove me to my door. "Thanks for the lift, Paddy," I said as I got out of the car. "And for treating my scrapes."

The man grunted. "No problem. Make sure you stay out of trouble from now on."

"I can't make any promises, but this is the sort of trouble I'd happily avoid."

I waved goodbye to the farmer and went to join Lenny, who was waiting for me on my doorstep, bouncing from foot to foot in that excited manner that told me he had news.

"Whoa, Maggie." He looked me up and down. "What's with the scrapes and bruises?"

"It's a long story. What's new in your world?"

"Good news. I have a lead on Jimmy's internet hookup."

I perked up instantly. "You do? Come in and tell me everything."

When we were armed with iced tea and leftover cookies from the café, we sat out on my deck to chat.

"Keep your voice down," I warned. "Just in case one of the Huffingtons walks by."

"I took another look at kink dating sites operating in Ireland and tried a few variations of the user name Jimmy had chosen for the two sites I checked out last week," Lenny whispered. "On Kinks-n-Winks, I struck gold."

My pulse kicked up its pace. "Go on."

"Jimmy used to meet a woman called Judy semi-regularly, and they made many arrangements via PM on the dating site. Apparently, Judy didn't like giving out her phone number."

I toyed with my straw and absorbed this information. "Is there a mention of her arranging to meet Jimmy on Whisper Island?"

Lenny shook his head. "No, but they could have made the date in person at the end of a hookup. Here's the best bit: there's a party being held in Galway this Friday for mankini and Lycra fans. Judy intends to be there."

"So what's the plan? We gatecrash a kink party?"

"Exactly." Lenny beamed at me. "And the best part? I've already ordered our outfits."

## 24

I HELD the hot pink material up to the light. "Please tell me this is a joke."

"Nope. I've got one, too." Lenny whipped a neon-orange monstrosity out of the box and dangled it in front of me.

"Is it…" I struggled to contain my laughter, "… the same model as Jimmy's?"

"Even for you, I'm not strutting around in a crotchless mankini. No, this is Borat-style."

I busted out laughing. "We can't go out in these things. We'll get arrested."

"Nah. It'll be fine. We'll have coats on until we get inside the house."

"I've spent the last forty-eight hours dreading wearing this outfit." I wasn't exaggerating. Ever since Lenny's announcement about the kink party, I'd had nightmares about the barely there leotard he'd ordered for me.

"Your scrapes and bruises will cause more talk at the party than your outfit," Lenny said cheerfully. "Don't worry about it."

I glanced down at the scrapes on my arms and grimaced. In the two days since my MINI had made its inglorious descent down the cliff, the Whisper Island police had failed to turn up any clues as to who had sabotaged my car. In fact, the only piece of information Sergeant O'Shea had deigned to share with me was to confirm that my brake lines had been cut, a circumstance that came as no surprise.

I looked around the apartment belonging to Lenny's brother Jake. "Are you sure Jake isn't going to walk in at any moment?"

"I told you, he's away for the night. We have the place to ourselves. Besides—" Lenny picked up the box of my aunt's baked goods that I'd brought Jake as a gift, "—he'll love these."

"Well, I didn't make them, so they're more likely to be edible." I fingered the leotard again and sighed. "I'd better get this on."

"Yeah. The party starts in twenty minutes. We want to get there early and maximize our chances of finding people who knew Jimmy."

"How will we recognize this Judy chick?" I asked. "Do people wear their dating site monikers on a label?"

"I guess we'll find out." Lenny laughed. "At least we're not likely to run into anyone from Whisper

Island at the party. Can you imagine trying to live down these outfits?"

"Ugh." I tugged at a piece of my Lycra costume. "Not that I wish Reynolds a concussion, but I'm kind of glad he's not around. If he knew what we were up to, he'd freak."

"When I imagined us going undercover for Movie Reel Investigations, I was wearing a James Bond-style suit and cool shades. A mankini never entered the picture."

"Tell me about it. I thought the stripper-style maid's outfit I was obliged to wear during my previous stint undercover was an indignity, but this…" I looked down at the hot pink strips that barely covered my body. "At least Helen Huffington pays well."

"Yeah. The money is a definite bonus." Lenny grinned at me. "Sure you don't want to send old Tom at the ferry office a photo of you in that outfit?"

I gave him the evil eye. "No way."

"It was only thanks to your charms that we got the time of your ferry ticket changed to this evening," Lenny pointed out. "Tom's normally a bear about making changes during the tourist season."

Old Tom was not the man I wanted to exercise my charms on, but that particular individual's only response to my voice mails and text messages had been a curt one-line message to say that he'd gone to his brother and sister-in-law's house to recuperate for a few days. Although I was relieved to hear he was no longer in the hospital, his impersonal text message stung way more than I'd expected. On this gloomy thought, I stomped into Jake's bedroom to put on my party gear.

Twenty minutes later, Lenny parked his van outside a large redbrick house in an upmarket part of Galway city.

"This place looks way too respectable to be the site of a fetish party. Are you sure we have the right address?"

Lenny checked his phone. "It's correct, all right."

"How on earth did you score us invitations?" I asked. "People in the kink scene are usually very careful about who they let into their parties."

"Let's just say a guy owed me a favor, and he vouched for both of us."

"I have to say I feel kind of uncomfortable about deceiving our hosts."

"Yeah, but it's our only chance to find Judy." Lenny turned to me. "Are you having reservations because you don't want to lie to people, or are you worried about your outfit?"

"Both, I guess."

Lenny slapped me across the back. "You'll be fine. If you're worried about me looking at your boobs, I promise I won't...as long as you don't check me out in my mankini."

"Deal," I said, and we shook hands.

He reached for the door handle. "Ready to go in?"

"Wait." I was breathing hard, and my stomach

was a bundle of nerves. "This isn't… People won't be having sex in front of us, will they?"

Lenny spread his palms wide. "Dude, how should I know? I'm into board games, UFOs, and old movies. I don't do the kink scene."

"It'll be fine." I exhaled slowly. "No one will care what I look like."

"Heck no. I look like an extra on a comedy skit show, and I'm still going in." He held up his hand and gave me five. "We've got this, dude."

I took a deep breath and opened the passenger door of Lenny's purple van. "Let's do this thing."

Outside the car, I shivered in spite of the warm evening. I wasn't used to parading around half-naked. Lenny opened a wrought-iron gate, and we walked up to the front door.

The front door of the house was opened by a horsey-looking woman wearing leopard-print strips of tape across her nipples and other vital areas. Above her right breast, she'd stuck a label onto her skin.

"Hi, Naomi48," I said in as calm a voice as I could muster under the circumstances. "I'm Grace-Kelly5, and this is UFOsRock."

"Welcome." The woman displayed horsey teeth in an overlarge mouth. "Come on in."

I took off my coat and accepted the proffered name label. I tried very hard not to look at Lenny while I stuck the label onto the fabric that barely covered my right boob, but my eyes had other ideas. A split second's glance at Lenny's orange mankini was all it took to make me lose control. I snorted back a giggle and faked a coughing fit.

Lenny pounded me on the back. "It's her first time," he said to our hostess sotto voce. "She's a bit nervous."

"Oh, there's no need to be nervous, love. Sure, all we do is sit around half naked and get drunk." This was accompanied by braying laughter that triggered another laugh-coughing fit and more back-pounding from Lenny. "But I do have to ask you to leave your mobile phones at the door. We have a strict no photos policy." She dropped her voice to a whisper. "And whatever you did to get those cuts and bruises? I'm afraid we don't cater to that sort of malarkey here."

I stifled a grin. "Car accident. These were definitely not acquired in the pursuit of pleasure."

Naomi's eyes widened as she took in the full glory of my injuries. "Oh, you poor dear. Are you sure you're up to partying?"

"I'll be fine, thanks."

"Well, if you're sure…" Naomi handed each of us a bag to put our phones in, labeled with our fake names.

Once our phones were safely stored in a locked closet, our host led us into a living room that was packed with neon Lycra and dangling man bits. Most, thankfully, appeared to have opted for mankinis that covered the worst of what they had to offer, but my gaze was inevitably drawn to the two who hadn't.

I took a rapid step back, but Lenny stopped me.

"We've come this far, Maggie," he whispered. "Let's at least stay for a while and see if Judy puts in an appearance."

I swallowed hard. "Okay. But if things get weird, I'm out of here."

"Deal."

Lenny propelled me into forward motion and located free seats on a sofa. I sat and tried hard to concentrate on my fellow party guests from the neck up. One of the guys wearing a Jimmy Wright-style mankini droned on about stocks and shares and financial stuff that I should pay more attention to, but never did.

The woman to my left regaled her other neighbor with details of her daughter's upcoming nuptials, and Lenny found a fellow computer geek to talk bytes, RAM, and whatever else techies enjoyed. A glass of champagne appeared in my hand as if by magic. The entire scenario was tinged by the surreal.

After a generous gulp of champagne and a lull in the wedding talk, I made my move. "Excuse me," I said to my neighbor, "but do you know if Judy is coming tonight?"

"Judy?" The woman shrugged. "I don't know her well, but she's usually at these parties."

"Judy's the reason most of the single men show up," her neighbor proclaimed with a laugh.

The future mother of the bride snorted. "And the attached ones, too. Judy doesn't discriminate."

Poor Judy. Her name was being dragged through

the mud, and she wasn't here to defend herself. "She said she'd meet me here," I lied breezily, "but she's late."

The future wearer of a feather boa hat eyed me with blatant skepticism. "If you're a friend of hers, you'll know Judy is never on time."

I rallied quickly. "I know. She's dreadful, isn't she? And I made her swear she wouldn't leave me in the lurch tonight."

"You should know better than to believe anything Judy says," the other woman said with an acid bite. "She promised me she wasn't interested in my boyfriend. That certainly wasn't true."

"Judy and I have an acquaintance in common." I placed particular emphasis on the word "acquaintance." "I thought he'd be here tonight as well." It was possible that they recognized Jimmy's photograph from the news reports on his murder, but I considered it unlikely. The police had managed to keep the information about Jimmy's last outfit out of the press, and the photo that the media had gotten hold of bore little resemblance to the man I'd found dead in the crotchless mankini. People looked different with their clothes on. Of course, people also looked different alive.

"What's he called?" my neighbor asked. "If he's a regular on the local mankini scene, we'll know him."

"He has a couple of monikers," I said, trying to contain my excitement. "Does Bulldog2020 sound familiar?"

"Bullie? Oh, yeah. He sometimes shows up. He's

more of an occasional visitor than a regular guest, though."

"He's a farmer if I recall correctly," the mother of the bride said. "He bored me senseless about cows at one party."

Her friend straightened and grabbed my arm. "Oh, look. Judy's just walked in."

## 25

MY ATTENTION WAS RIVETED by the new arrival. Judy was at least ten years my senior, but her figure put most of my contemporaries to shame. Instead of Lycra, she wore neon green tape, similar to what our hostess was wearing. The tape had been applied in a haphazard fashion, leaving part of one nipple exposed. From Judy's confident strut, I surmised that the look was deliberate.

I jumped to my feet. "I'll go say hello to her." I took off before my neighbors could respond. I couldn't risk Judy failing to recognize me in front of them. I made a beeline for my quarry, but the large man wearing the hideous purple mankini got there first.

*Darn.* Now what? I ran through my options and decided to drop the social niceties my mother spent many years drilling into me with a modicum of success. I marched up and interrupted them. "Judy, there you are. I thought you'd never show." Ignoring her startled look and the man's irritated squawk, I grabbed her arm and dragged her into a corner.

"What's going on?" she demanded. "Who are you?"

"No one you know, but please play along. I know Jimmy." At her frozen expression, I elaborated. "Bulldog2020. He also went by Bullseye2020."

The instant she blanched, I knew my hunch had been correct. "I know his name. I saw it in the papers."

"Can you tell me—"

She held up a hand. "Stop. I don't want to talk about him."

The woman began to move away, but I held her in place. "Please, Judy. Listen to me for a sec. This is important. He was murdered. I discovered his body."

Her pale face grew even whiter. "Please, stop. I don't want to think about it."

"I know you don't. I don't either, but the man's dead, and I believe you may have witnessed the crime or its aftermath."

She shook her head violently. "No, no. Please stop talking about it."

I took a deep breath and crossed my fingers behind my back. "I know you were at the farm that day, Judy," I said gently. "I only want to help you."

The woman stared at her feet. The seconds ticked

by. I bit my tongue and gave her space to think. Finally, she spoke. "Okay, I was there that day, but I didn't see who killed him."

"But you found his body before I did," I guessed. "At around four-thirty?"

Judy shot a worried look around the room. "Yes," she whispered, "but please don't tell anyone. I have a long-term partner. He'd go crazy if he knew I'd been seeing Bullie on the sly."

"Can you run me through the events of that day?"

She regarded me with suspicion. "Are you a Guard?"

"I'm not with the police. I'm a private investigator."

The woman sneered. "Not much better, in my opinion."

"Please, Judy. I'm not here to out you to your partner or anyone else. All I want to know is what you saw."

She exhaled a sigh. "Okay, but let's go into another room. I don't want anyone overhearing."

I followed her out of the living room and down the hallway to a home office. After another quick look to make sure no one had followed us, Judy closed the office door.

She leaned on the desk and looked me straight in the eye. "Bullie was one of my regular hookups. We'd meet in hotels, or go away for the weekend. That sort of thing. Meeting him at his home that day was a first." She smiled sadly. "He got a kick out of the idea of sneaking me onto the farm without his neighbors knowing what we were up to."

*Or what you were wearing while doing it…* I stifled a laugh.

Judy paled underneath her heavy makeup. "I'd gone into the house to change when I heard shouting. An American guy was roaring at Bullie and accusing him of all sorts of shenanigans. In turn, Bullie was yelling back and saying the guy had cheated him out of his life savings." Judy bit her lip. "I was just about to call the police when they fell silent. A moment later, a car roared off. I waited for a few minutes to see if Bullie would come looking for me. When he didn't, I decided to go in search of him. Maybe he needed time to cool down, you know?"

"And then you found the body?" I asked gently.

"Yes. It was horrible." Tears formed twin rivulets down her rouged cheeks. "He had a rake sticking out of his chest. The instant I saw him, I knew he was dead." The woman choked on a sob.

I hated having to pressure her, but I didn't have the time or patience to be waylaid by a crying jag. "What did you do next?" I prompted. "Did you go back into the house?"

She shook her head, and her Marilyn Monroe-style wig bounced. "I panicked. I just ran. I have no idea where I was going, but I took off." She heaved a shuddery breath. "And then I remembered my clothes and my handbag. Without money or my ticket for the ferry, I wasn't likely to get home."

"Did you go back to the farm?"

"Yeah. I went straight upstairs to the bathroom where I'd gotten undressed and grabbed my clothes and bag." Her sobs grew louder. "I wasn't thinking straight. I just grabbed them and ran without getting dressed."

"Understandable." I handed her a fresh tissue.

Judy blew her nose and continued her tale. "I'd barely had time to get out of the house when I heard the sound of a car driving down the track and toward the house." She swallowed hard and began to wail again. "I thought the killer had returned."

"How awful for you," I said in a soothing tone. "What did you do next?"

"I ran back into the house. I looked out the kitchen window to see if the coast was clear, and I saw a man go into the barn."

My chest swelled with excitement. "How long did he stay in the barn?"

"I don't know. I lost track of time."

"Probably the shock. Did the man come straight out of the barn, or did you have the impression he stayed there for a while?"

Judy considered my question for several seconds. "He didn't come out straight away, but he can't have been in the barn for more than a few minutes."

"How did he appear when he came out?"

"Stressed. He ran his hands through his hair. I remember that. And then he started looking around the yard, so I ducked back under the windowsill." Judy's voice broke on a sob. "I was terrified he'd come into the house."

"But he didn't?" I prompted, keen to avoid more weeping and gnashing.

"No. I waited in the house until I heard him leave in his car, and then I ran." She hiccupped and dabbed at her eyes. "I had no idea where I was going, but I ran until my lungs were burning."

"Did you stop to get dressed?"

"Eventually. I kept going until I felt I was a safe distance away from Bullie's farm. Then I pulled on my clothes." She hiccupped. "I'd lost one of my shoes. I guess I must have dropped it somewhere in one of the fields I ran through."

"How did you get back to the mainland?"

"Once I was dressed, I searched for a bus stop but couldn't find one. I was getting desperate, so I decided to hitchhike to the harbor and catch the next ferry." She smiled ruefully. "I guess I got lucky. A woman with two small kids in the back of her car stopped and offered me a lift."

"Was she surprised that you were shoeless?" I asked. "I can't imagine many people wander around Whisper Island barefoot."

"Given the weather forecast that day, yes, but I told her one of my heels broke off, and she seemed to buy it."

I had to admire Judy's pluck. "Why didn't you go to the police when you got home?"

She hiccupped. "Because I'm a coward. If I'd been required to give evidence in court, my partner would've found out."

"Not necessarily," I said. "You could have given evidence on the condition that your name didn't appear in the media." I wasn't entirely sure how the Irish legal system worked, so this last part might have been baloney, but I sensed Judy's urge to get away from me, and I wanted to pump her for as much information as I could before she took off.

"Even if I got them to agree to give me anonymity, it would have been a risk. My partner is a barrister. Gossip spreads like wildfire on the legal circuit."

"Look, I can't say too much, but Jimmy Wright— Bullie—wasn't the only murder victim."

Judy's lips trembled. "Is there a killer on the loose? Do you think I'm in danger?"

I was tempted to say yes just to get her to a police station, but my conscience won out. "Not now. The person suspected of murdering Jimmy was the second murder victim."

"Oh my goodness," she gasped. "You're talking about that rich American guy who got bumped off on Gull Island last weekend."

I nodded. "Ambrose J. Huffington III was the prime suspect in Jimmy Wright's murder."

Judy blinked. "If Huffington killed Jimmy, who killed him?"

"That's the multi-million-dollar question," I replied in a dry tone. I slipped a business card out of my cleavage and handed it to her. "Regardless of Huffington's potential involvement in Jimmy's murder, both men deserve justice, and their families and friends want answers. Please come forward and speak to the police. I'll come with you if you like."

She bit her lip. "I'll sleep on it. Will you keep silent until then?"

"Okay. I won't tell them about you if I don't have to."

Judy eyed me curiously. "You said you're a private investigator. Which of the murders are you investigating, and why?"

"Huffington's mother wants me to clear his name."

"Ouch." Judy pulled a face. "From what you've told me, you consider him to be the guilty party."

"Yeah. The police are confident he did it, and I haven't found any evidence so far that contradicts that theory. You're sure the man you heard arguing with Jimmy had an American accent?"

"Definitely. He was loud. There was no mistaking the accent. What I can't tell you is if the man I heard arguing with Bullie is the same man who came to the farm a few minutes later."

"About that guy…" I chose my next words with

care. "If I ask Naomi to give me my phone back, would you please look at a couple of photographs?"

Judy's brow creased. "I guess, but the man was far away and I was in a panic."

"I understand, but you might recognize the guy if you saw his picture."

Her eyes darted to the side. "I can try, but I don't want the police involved.."

"I promised I wouldn't tell the police about you unless I had no choice."

"Define 'no choice.' If I identify the man from the photos you want to show me, you'll insist I talk to the police."

Judy was no fool. I needed to tread carefully, or she'd clam up and run.

"We can discuss our options after I show you the photos. I have a friend who's involved in the investigation. I can guarantee he'll be discreet."

What I couldn't guarantee was Reynolds being put back on the case anytime soon, but I left that tidbit out.

"Okay," she said. "I'll look at your photos and then we'll see about the police."

"Thank you, Judy. I appreciate your help."

We left the office and made our way back down the hallway. A thought occurred to me before we reentered the living room. "When you heard a vehicle returning to the farm, did the engine sound the same as the one you'd heard leaving?"

She considered this for a moment. "Now that you

mention it, it sounded a bit different, but that might have been because the car left with screeching tires and roaring engine. The one returning sounded, well, normal. I'm sorry I can't be more specific. I'm not into cars."

"Thanks. You've been very helpful."

Back in the living room, Lenny and his newfound friend had moved onto conspiracy theories and the darknet.

Our host was holding court at the drinks table, entertaining two guys in their fifties with a risqué tale of her recent vacation in Spain.

Keeping a grip on Judy's arm, I made a beeline for Naomi. But before we reached her, a dark-haired woman seated by the window let out a wail. "A squad car just pulled up outside."

Naomi swore fluently. "My neighbors must have complained again."

Judy and I exchanged panicked looks. "Is an event like this illegal?" I asked. "I haven't seen drugs on the premises."

At that moment, the doorbell rang, quickly followed by shouts in the hallway. The living room door burst open, and uniformed police officers poured in. Half-naked party guests ran in every direction, making it difficult to navigate a path toward the door.

In the chaos that followed, the dude in the crotch-less purple mankini managed to elbow me in the ribs with enough force to send me flying across a glass coffee table. I landed with a grunt and moaned at the stabbing pain in my side.

Strong arms hauled me to my feet, and I picked up the scent of a very familiar aftershave. "Oh, no."

"Hello, Maggie," Reynolds said, his voice brimming with laughter. "I didn't expect to see this much of you before our first official date."

"LIAM? WHAT ARE YOU DOING HERE?" I stared up into his twinkling blue eyes, and my cheeks burned with embarrassment at my lack of clothing. "I thought you'd gone to stay with your brother and sister-in-law to recuperate."

"I did, but Gavin was on duty tonight, and I decided to tag along."

"You're supposed to be resting," I said lamely, aware of his subtle scrutiny of my half-naked body, and kicking myself for wondering if he liked what he saw.

"And you're not supposed to be at a depraved, drug-filled sex party." His shoulders heaved with laughter.

"I haven't seen any sign of drugs or sex," I said dryly. "Just a bunch of middle-aged people who get a kick out of wearing weird outfits."

"The neighbors complained about the noise and

alleged that illicit activities were taking place."

I snorted. "If they are, I missed all the fun. Apart from locating Jimmy Wright's last booty call, the party's been about as interesting as watching two flies climbing a wall."

"You found the woman in the lime-green leotard?" Reynolds looked impressed. "Where is she?"

I scanned the room. "Gone. I suspect Judy's got a strong sense of self-preservation. She'll have been the first one out of here."

Reynolds dragged me over to a sofa. "Come on, Maggie. You can't leave me hanging. What did she say? And how did you get all those scrapes and bruises? Timms texted me this evening with a wild story about you jumping out of a moving vehicle, but it was so disjointed that I wondered if it was the meds making me hallucinate."

I grimaced. "No hallucination, unfortunately."

Over the next few minutes, I provided him with a detailed run-down of my car crash and my conversation with Judy. "Apart from the shoe she dropped, there were no clothes to find. When Lenny saw her, she was hunkered down behind a wall to avoid being seen by people in passing cars. What Lenny didn't realize is that she was holding her clothes and purse."

"That solves the mystery of the missing clothes," Reynolds said. "Unfortunately for you, Judy's story only cements our conviction that Huff was the killer."

"Huff's sons are men with American accents," I pointed out. "And even if Huff killed Jimmy, we don't know that he was the man Judy saw go into the barn later."

"Yes, but Huff's sons didn't arrive on Whisper Island until the day after Jimmy's murder."

I treated him to a smug smile. "That's where you're wrong. According to old Tom at the ferry office, Doug Huffington came over to Whisper Island on Wednesday."

Reynolds looked impressed. "Well, well. You have been busy."

"When you guys burst in, I was on the verge of showing Judy photos of all three Huffington men in the hope she could identify the guy she saw."

"Okay, but Huff's prints were on the rake, and we know he and Jimmy had good reason to hate one another. Even if Doug visited Jimmy, it must have been after the murder took place."

"I'm pretty sure Huff was guilty," I said. "I only took the job because I wanted an excuse to do some digging into Huff's murder."

Reynolds frowned. "It's too much of a coincidence for the murders not to be connected, but I haven't figured out what the link might be. What's your take on the situation?"

"I'm not sure. Yeah, there's a link, but how strong a one, I don't know." I looked at the bandage on his head. "How are you feeling? That was a nasty bump you got."

"Some headaches, but I'm otherwise fine." He grinned. "I'm back to work on Monday."

"O'Shea won't like that."

Reynolds's smile faded. "He can lump it. From what Timms tells me, he's making a mess of all our current investigations, including the one into my attack. And if I'm back on the island, I'll make sure you're kept safe."

"Speaking of which, Timms said you kept mentioning the color pink."

"Yeah." Reynolds frowned. "I saw a figure lurking in bushes just after you left me. I got the impression they'd been eavesdropping on our conversation. I went back to the Japanese garden and checked behind the pagoda. I'd just come back when someone wearing a bright pink coat appeared and whacked me over the head. That's the last thing I remember."

"I'm pretty sure the pink coat was Julie's."

Reynolds's eyebrows shot up. "Why would Julie attack me?"

"She didn't. When I got back to the house after leaving you, I met her outside. She was on her way back through the gardens in search of her missing rain poncho. Do you remember she'd tied it around her waist on our way back from the lighthouse?"

"Vaguely."

"She thought it must have fallen off near the Japanese garden, so I said I'd go look for it, seeing as it had started to rain. Instead of her poncho, I found you." I shivered at the memory of seeing him face down and bleeding in the stream.

"And I'm grateful you did," he said quietly. "You saved my life."

My cheeks burned again. "You've helped me out a time or two. Just returning the favor."

"I'm going to check to see if anyone found that poncho, and where." A muscle in his jaw flexed. "And then I'm going to throw all my effort into tracking down who tampered with your car. If we find that person, we'll have our killer."

"I tracked down the Hennessys while you were out of it on painkillers at the hospital, but they hadn't seen any sign of Julie's coat."

"All the same, it's worth taking another look. There are plenty of hiding places in the Marley House gardens, and we can presume that my attacker didn't waltz back to the house wearing bright pink."

"I'm relieved you'll be back on the case," I said. "Or should I say, back on all the cases."

Reynolds's mouth twitched. "I hear you gave Sergeant O'Shea a piece of your mind the day you made your statement."

"Just told him a few home truths. The only reason he wants to cling to these cases is that he wants to show you up."

"As for me being back in charge, I'll have to talk to my superintendent. Last I heard, he thought I could help O'Shea rather than take back the reins."

My jaw descended. "That's outrageous. It's not your fault you got hit on the head."

"No, but the boss has a point. Passing cases back

and forth isn't a great idea. Unfortunately, if O'Shea stays in charge, he'll do his best to conceal information from me. I might need your help, but only if it doesn't involve you putting yourself in harm's way again."

"It's not like I took out an ad for the killer to cut my brake lines."

"I know, but I feel terrible that you were in danger." He shifted his weight and his gaze softened. "You mean a lot to me, Maggie. I don't want to see you hurt."

I blinked, searched for the appropriate response, and came up blank. Before I could jolt my dazed brain into cooperating, Lenny ambled back into the living room, carrying our coats, my purse, and two rainbow-colored party bags.

"We get party bags?" I asked in incredulity. "In the middle of a raid?"

"Looks like Naomi prepared in advance. I put your phone in your party bag, by the way." Lenny turned to Reynolds and grinned. "Hey, Sarge."

The policeman's eyes stood out on stalks at the sight of my friend in a mankini. "I got to hand it to you, Logan. You can wear that thing without a blush."

Lenny grinned. "Why not? Everyone else at the party was wearing similar—or worse. Besides, this was my first official undercover job for Movie Reel Investigations."

"Are you now on staff?" He cast me a warning

look. "Careful about regulations. He'll need a license if he works too many hours."

"Yes, Sergeant. I'll get on it as soon as I get some cash."

"We'll be like *Magnum, P.I.*," Lenny said, unself-consciously freeing one of his butt cheeks of a stray piece of Lycra. "We can train Bran to be a sniffer dog and bust criminals."

"That's a frightening thought," Reynolds said, trying not to laugh. "Maybe I need to rethink my decision to go back to Whisper Island if you two will be scouring the place for lawbreakers."

"You'll be delighted to have our help," I said with a grin. "Just think of all the information we'll be able to weasel out of people that you can't."

"We'll see about that," he said, but his tone was teasing. "Come on. Let's get out of here."

When we stepped outside the house, a younger, blonder version of Reynolds leaned against a squad car.

"Maggie and Lenny, this is my brother, Gavin. Gavin, these are friends of mine from Whisper Island."

If Gavin were surprised to be introduced to two attendees of the kink party he and his coworkers had just raided, he didn't show it. He pumped my hand. "Nice to meet you, Maggie."

"You're very relaxed," I remarked. "I take it you aren't arresting anyone tonight?"

Gavin Reynolds laughed. "Nah. We've given the

house owner a stern lecture about keeping the noise down, but other than that, it's her house. There were no signs of illegal activities on the premises, just a bunch of people in ridiculous outfits."

"I don't think the neighbors appreciate the parties," Reynolds added. "They probably feel they lower the tone of the neighborhood."

While Gavin chatted with Lenny, Reynolds sidled over to me. "It's still pretty early. Want to have a proper brainstorm about Huff's murder?"

My chest swelled at the prospect of being included in the investigation again. "Definitely. Lenny and I are staying the night at his brother's apartment. You could come back with us and we can pool our information."

"I suspect you'll be able to tell me more than I can tell you." He indicated his head. "I've been out of the loop."

I frowned. "Are you sure you shouldn't go back to your brother's place and get some sleep?"

"No way. All I've done these last few days is sleep." He dropped his voice to a whisper. "I love my sister-in-law, but she fussed. I'm going stir crazy. That's why I persuaded Gavin to let me come with him tonight."

"Bet you didn't expect to participate in a raid and find me there."

He chuckled. "That was a very pleasant surprise."

"When you two are finished flirting. Maggie and I'd better make tracks." Lenny tugged at the thin material of his jacket. "It's not like we're wearing much underneath our coats."

"Would it be okay if Reynolds came back to Jake's apartment with us? We want to compare notes."

"Fine by me," Lenny said, "but what about his head?"

"That's exactly what I was about to say," added Gavin. "Susie will kill me if you go off boozing."

"No alcohol for me," Reynolds said, winking at me. "This is strictly work."

Gavin shrugged. "Okay, but don't say I didn't warn you. Susie's not happy that I took you with me tonight."

"I won't be late. I'll get a taxi back to yours and be in bed by eleven."

"Okay." Gavin grinned. "Don't do anything I wouldn't do."

"That doesn't eliminate many options," Reynolds whispered into my ear, making me laugh.

Lenny unlocked the van and slid behind the wheel. I threw my purse into the back and was about to climb in when the clickety-click sound of a person running in high heels drew my attention. Reynolds and I turned to see a frantic Judy running toward us.

She staggered to a halt when she reached us, breathing heavily. "I saw him. I saw the man you're looking for."

Reynolds shot me a bewildered look, but I focused on Judy. "Where?"

The woman pointed back the way she'd come.

"He was lurking in the bushes at the end of the street. Scared the daylights out of me."

I was in motion before I'd fully registered the significance of her words, my coat flapping around me, the party bag still in my hand. "Come on," I yelled over my shoulder to Reynolds. "Judy's talking about the guy she saw go into Jimmy Wright's barn."

"Maggie, wait—" he shouted.

But I kept running. I tore down the pavement in the direction of the bushes Judy had mentioned and scanned the terrain. No guy was lurking.

Ignoring the shouts and pounding feet behind me, I hung a left and sped down a narrow side street. My coat was half off, but I had no time to secure the belt. Sure enough, a man in a baseball cap was ahead of me, running at full tilt. I accelerated into a sprint.

My quarry was quick, but I'd spent months running after Bran, and I was in good shape. I was gaining on him fast. And then disaster struck. My foot caught on the end of my trailing coat, catapulting me forward. I landed with a thud. My injuries from the incident on Wednesday burned anew.

Swearing under my breath, I disentangled myself from the coat and threw it onto the ground. The guy I was chasing had reached the end of the lane. He swerved to the right, out of my line of vision. No way was I losing him. I forced oxygen into my lungs and took off.

When I got to the end of the lane, the man in the baseball cap was crossing the street, his progress slowed by an oncoming car. I leaped into action. He jerked his neck, reeled back at the sight of me in my barely there leotard, and reacted too late when I charged. I accelerated my speed, leaped through the air, and hit him in the chest with both feet.

We crashed to the ground in a tangle of limbs. The contents of my party bag spilled onto the asphalt, revealing my phone, an array of flavored condoms, and a pair of fluffy pink handcuffs.

Winded, I stared down into the face of Doug Huffington. He squirmed beneath me and tried to push me off him, accidentally brushing against my chest in the process.

"Hey," I yelled. "Keep your paws to yourself."

"How else am I supposed to get free? You're naked." Doug's face was a maelstrom of rage and confusion.

I seized the opportunity of his distraction to show off my excellent right hook, connecting with his jaw with expert precision. On instinct Doug's hands flew to his face, leaving his torso exposed. I punched him hard in the stomach. He roared and rolled into the fetal position. I yanked his arms behind his back, felt around for the handcuffs, and secured them his wrists.

"Holy wow, Maggie," a voice said behind me, "your boob's hanging loose."

"A gentleman wouldn't mention my state of undress, Lenny." I staggered to my feet and regarded the fluffy handcuffs. "I need to thank Naomi for that party bag."

Strong arms slipped a coat around my shoulders. "Much as I appreciate the view, I suspect you're cold." Reynolds's voice shook with laughter. "Once again, Maggie Doyle takes down a suspect in a spectacular fashion—pun intended. I predict Movie Reel Investigations will be flooded with clients come Monday morning."

I huddled into the jacket, comforted by its traces of his spicy aftershave. "As long as they don't need me to track down missing sheep, bring it on."

## 27

THE MORNING after Doug Huffington's arrest, Lenny and I caught the first ferry back to Whisper Island. I'd arranged to meet Reynolds at the station for a late breakfast, so we swung by the Movie Theater Café on our way to stock up on freshly baked scones and takeout coffees.

"Promise me you'll fill me in on all the details," Lenny said when he dropped me off at the Whisper Island Garda Station parking lot. "I hate not being involved."

"I'll tell you whatever I can, I swear, but you know Reynolds. Unless a detail is public knowledge, he'll make me promise not to share the info."

"I know," he grumbled. "You need to hurry up and make money so you can hire me to be your official assistant."

I leaned across the transmission and gave him a kiss on the cheek. "I'm working on it. Thanks again for your help in tracking down Judy. Without her input, we'd never have caught Doug."

My friend grinned. "No problem. I've gotta impress my future boss."

I laughed. "Consider her impressed."

I waved goodbye to my friend and bounded up the steps to the station's entrance. Despite last night's dramatic events, I'd woken early, and I couldn't wait to pump Reynolds for the details of his conversation with Doug Huffington. I shoved open the station's door, and my excitement dimmed at the sight of Sergeant O'Shea's florid complexion behind the front desk.

The man's eyes bulged when he saw me. He jabbed a meaty finger in my direction. "You—"

"Morning, Maggie." Reynolds appeared at the door of his office, cutting short whatever blistering diatribe his coworker had intended to deliver.

My gaze fell to the extra coffee I'd purchased for the person on desk duty. I'd hoped it would be Timms. In the war between my dislike of O'Shea and my compulsion to do the right thing, good manners won out. I shoved a latte across the counter. "Here."

His jaw dropped, and he stuttered something unintelligible.

"I think the words you're looking for are 'Thank you.'" Reynolds's mouth twitched with amusement at O'Shea's belligerent expression. "Come on, Maggie. Those scones smell heavenly."

He ushered me into his neat office where he'd

already cleared his desk and set it with plates and cutlery. When our scones were cut, buttered, and piled high with strawberry jam and clotted cream, I pounced.

"Don't leave me in suspense. What did Doug have to say?"

"A lot, as it happens. We took him to Gavin's station in Galway for his initial questioning, and he'd blabbed most of the pertinent information on the way in the squad car. He clammed up after his lawyer arrived, but we already had enough to charge him with obstructing justice and for being an accessory to murder after the fact."

I leaned forward, eyes wide. "Ooh…more details, please."

"Doug admits to visiting Whisper Island on the day Jimmy was murdered. He says his mother revealed that Jimmy was Amb's biological father, and more than likely Doug's father as well."

"Interesting. So Doug wanted to confront Jimmy?"

"Not confront," Reynolds corrected. "Doug wanted to visit the man without the rest of his family knowing. He'd discussed the matter with his brother, but Amb wanted nothing to do with Jimmy. He was of the opinion that contacting their real father could jeopardize their inheritance if Huff were to find out, but Doug was curious to meet the man who was probably his real father."

I took a bite of my scone. I was sure it was delicious, as Noreen's baked goods always were, but I barely tasted it with this morning's excitement. "You mentioned charging Doug with being an accessory to murder after the fact. Did Doug help Huff cover up his involvement in Jimmy's death?"

"Not exactly. After he'd killed Jimmy in a fit of rage over Jimmy threatening to tell the world he was Amb and Doug's biological father, Huff drove away from the farm at speed, and almost crashed into Doug's rental car. When he recognized who was behind the wheel, Huff slowed down, and Doug persuaded him to tell him what had happened."

"Whoa. So Huff confided in Doug?" I asked, intrigued by this unexpected turn of events. "He must have been panicking."

"Yeah. Huff admitted to killing Jimmy on the spur of the moment. Doug pumped him for details, and then agreed to return to the scene of the crime to get rid of the rake—Huff knew his fingerprints would be on it. Meanwhile, Huff disposed of his bloodstained shirt—we're still looking for that, by the way."

I scrunched up my forehead. "I don't understand. The rake was still in Jimmy's body when I found him a couple of hours later. What went wrong with the plan?"

Reynolds grinned. "Nothing went wrong. Doug went to the farm as he'd promised Huff. As Judy described, he went into the barn, stayed a few minutes, and left."

"Without disturbing the rake?"

"Doug had no intention of touching the rake. He said he was never sure he'd help Huff and was certain he wouldn't the instant he saw Jimmy's body."

"It was the sight of the mankini," I said. "That would bring anyone to their senses."

Reynolds chuckled. "Doug wasn't too keen on discussing his biological father's choice of attire. What he did make clear was that Huff's actions had destroyed any chance for him to get to know Jimmy."

"So Doug left the rake untouched in the hope that Huff's fingerprints would incriminate him?"

"Pretty much."

I turned the matter over in my mind. "Okay," I said finally. "That wraps up the Jimmy Wright murder case, but if Huff killed Jimmy, who killed Huff? You didn't mention charging Doug with that crime."

Reynolds grimaced. "Not yet, but I'm working on it. He admits to bashing me over the head, but he denies deliberately leaving me to drown."

I let loose a string of unladylike expletives. "He left you facedown in a stream," I said in searing tones. "What did he expect would happen?"

"I know. I have no intention of letting him wriggle off the hook." He took a sip from his coffee cup. "We found Julie's pink poncho, by the way. Or rather, Rob Hennessy found it."

I raised my eyebrows. "Where was it?"

"Doug had stuffed it into the compost heap." A wry smile twisted his lips. "I'm sure you heard that

Sergeant O'Shea dragged Rob in for questioning several times, but couldn't amass sufficient evidence to charge him?"

"I heard. The man is a total fool."

"Unsurprisingly, being a suspect for a murder he didn't commit infuriated Rob. He and his brother tore up the Marley House gardens looking for that poncho in the hope it would exonerate him."

"And they struck gold in the compost heap," I finished for him. "Did the poncho contain any evidence to link Doug to your attack?"

"Oh, yeah. We found two sets of fingerprints, as well as a trace of my blood. One set belonged to Doug Huffington, and we presume the other is your cousin's, although we'll have to check to be sure."

"If Doug denies trying to kill you, what was his motive for attacking you?"

"He claims he did it because he was afraid I'd identify the real killer. He'd heard O'Shea was incompetent and wanted him in charge of the case."

I winced. "Nice guy. Do you believe his denial about killing Huff?"

Reynolds spread his palms wide. "I'm not sure. If Doug wanted to protect someone, it points to the killer being his brother or sister. He'd gladly throw Brandi to the dogs."

"Or Candace," I added. "He might try to protect Candace for Amb and Hailey's sakes."

"True, but my money is on Amb or Martha."

A memory nagged at me. "Hang on a sec. Rob Hennessy said he saw Martha walking in the gardens with one of her brothers just before you were hit over the head. Martha confirmed that the brother she was with was Doug. So if Martha and Doug were together, wouldn't she have known he attacked you?"

"Possibly," Reynolds said. "I haven't spoken to her yet, but I intend to."

"And then there's the business of the dead plant," I murmured, sifting through the oddities in the case.

Reynolds raised an eyebrow. "Dead plant?"

"Rob Hennessy told me he found the plant outside Huff and Brandi's room dead."

"How is a dead plant relevant to Huff's murder?" Reynolds asked, perplexed.

"I'm not sure that it is, but it's odd. Rob said the soil smelled of sour milk and weed killer."

Reynolds's sharp mind seized on this information without my needing to spell out the implications. "Someone poisoned milk with weed killer. Why dump it in the plant? Did they intend to kill Huff or Brandi and change their mind?"

"That's what I suspect. Either they got a crisis of conscience, or they were disturbed and needed to get rid of the poisoned milk fast."

"I'll ask Amb and Martha about that when I see them later."

"Are they still staying at Shamrock Cottages?"

Reynolds shook his head. "After they learned of

Doug's arrest, Helen was very distressed. Doug, Martha, and the others chose to move to the hotel to be near her."

"In other words, Shamrock Cottages is a Huffington-free zone?"

"Exactly." He eyed me carefully. "However, I want you to be careful. Doug was prepared to follow you all the way to Galway to see what you and Lenny knew about the murders. It's likely that Doug killed Huff, but we can't rule out the others just yet. Don't be alone with any of them. Actually, I'd prefer if you weren't alone at all. Could you move back in with Noreen until I wrap up this case?"

"I'll ask her, but I'd rather stay in my own home."

"Just for a couple of days, Maggie." His eyes pleaded with me. "I'd feel more comfortable if I knew you weren't out there all alone without a car. I'm going to be working long shifts to wrap up the Huff murder case, and I won't be around if something goes wrong."

In other words, if someone tried to hurt me. In spite of the stuffy air in his office, I shivered. "Okay. I'll pack a bag when I get home and find somewhere to stay. Julie's place might be more convenient for working at the café. I'll call her after our breakfast."

His relief was palpable. "Thanks, Maggie. I'll sleep better knowing you're safe."

After Reynolds and I had finished our coffee and scones, I left to go in search of my cousin. Julie taught

Irish classes at the school on Saturday mornings, and she'd mentioned finishing at eleven o'clock. I glanced at my watch. If I walked quickly, I'd make it on time.

I speed walked through the town, navigating my way through crowds of tourists, and hurrying past islanders who wanted to pump me for details on last night's dramatic arrest. When I reached the elementary school, my cousin was climbing into her new SUV. I flagged her down before she exited the parking lot.

Julie rolled down her window. "Hi, Maggie. What's up?"

"Could you give me a ride out to Shamrock Cottages?"

"Sure. Hop in." She reached across and opened the passenger door for me.

I climbed up and fastened my seat belt. "I have another favor to ask. Could I crash at your place for a couple of nights? Reynolds doesn't want me staying on own my until he wraps up both murder cases, and I have to admit I don't feel comfortable being out there with no car."

"No problem, but I don't have room for all your animals."

"Noreen looked after them while I was in Galway last night. I'm sure she won't mind keeping them for a day or two."

Julie's phone rang as we pulled up in front of my cottage. She glanced at the display and pulled a face.

"It's my boss. Go on in and get packed. I'll take the call out here."

"Okay. I'll make it quick."

I jumped down from the SUV and jogged over to my front door. I slid the key into the lock, but to my astonishment, the door opened before I'd finished the last twist. That was odd. A cold dread froze my limbs, but I shook it off. Noreen had a spare key. Maybe I'd forgotten to give her something for the animals, and she'd come back to get it.

I glanced over my shoulder, but my cousin was still on the phone. Shaking off my nerves, I pushed open the door and stepped inside. A quick check assured me that the cottage was empty. Relief washed over me and the heart rate I hadn't noticed increase returned to normal. I went into my bedroom and threw a few essentials into a bag. I'd already packed toiletries for my overnight trip, so I only needed a few extra items as well as more clothes.

When I was sure I had everything I'd need for the next few days, I zipped the case closed and went back into the hallway.

Under my home office door, a sliver of light spilled onto the floor. I frowned. Knowing the weather forecast for the weekend predicted hot temperatures, I'd closed all my shades before I'd left with Lenny yesterday. I was certain I hadn't left a light on in the office. I looked through the open front door. Julie was still on the phone. I glanced back at the office door.

Cursing myself for my paranoia, I sidled down the hallway and eased the office door open.

Sure enough, the light was on, and my laptop was open. My heart lurched in my chest. No way had I left it open. Time to get the heck out of here. I spun on my heels and collided with the hard chest of Amb Huffington.

## 28

THE IMPACT WINDED ME. I staggered back, giving my opponent the advantage. Amb shoved me against the desk and kicked the door shut. I groped for a weapon and my fingers closed around a paper knife.

"Drop it," Amb snarled, his eyes manic.

"Why should I?"

His sneer turned my blood to ice. "Because I have this."

The instant he pulled the gun, I let the paper knife fall to the ground with a clatter. My heart pounding, I backed behind the desk.

"I'm not planning to shoot you, Maggie. Not unless you make me." Amb turned the key in the office door, locking me in the room with him.

"You killed your father," I said dully. "Why threaten to shoot me? The police already suspect you and Martha."

Amb's laugh rang hollow. "Did Doug tell them we

killed Dad? Typical. He'd sell us all down the river to save his own neck."

"Why are you here, Amb? What were you hoping to find on my laptop?" I said a silent thanks to Lenny for insisting I used strong passwords.

"Whatever dirt you've dug up on my family an me. Grandmother should never have hired you. As soon as she told me she'd asked you to look into Jimmy Wright's murder, I knew you wouldn't stop there."

"And you knew I was a more competent investigator than Sergeant O'Shea," I added. "The person you were sure would take over both murder cases once you'd ensured Sergeant Reynolds was out of the way. Doug took the blame for that, you know."

Amb shrugged. "He was stupid enough not to wear gloves when he took the poncho off me. If the police found his prints on it, he only has himself to blame."

"Doug didn't know you'd left Reynolds face down in the stream, though. He thought you'd just hit him over the head."

"The policeman fell into the water. I didn't put him there."

"I don't believe you. I think you'd killed your father less than twenty-four hours before and you figured one more death wouldn't make a difference." I swallowed past my rage and kept my voice steady. "Just like you thought nothing of cutting my brake lines when you felt I was getting too close to the truth.

Sweat beaded on Amb's upper lip. "You have no proof. It'll be your word against mine."

"I have you in my cottage, pointing a gun at me," I snapped. "That's not the action of an innocent man."

"You were supposed to be away. Candace said you'd gone to Galway for the weekend."

"For one night, not the whole weekend." I took a deep breath and tried to steady my nerves. Julie was outside the cottage, safe in her car. What would Amb do when she came into the cottage looking for me? "Does Candace know what you've done?"

A look of revulsion passed over his face. "Of course not. I'd never involve her in anything this sordid."

"When you're hauled off in handcuffs, she'll be involved," I said tartly. "Candace *and* Hailey. How will your daughter feel growing up knowing her father is a murderer?"

Amb's Adam's apple bobbed. "I regret any pain my actions will cause my daughter and my wife, but I can't change what I've done. I had no choice."

*I had no choice.* The words echoed in my mind, creating a kaleidoscope of memories. "The weed killer in the milk," I whispered. "That's why you had no choice. Candace was going to kill your father before he had a chance to change his will."

Amb's jaw dropped. "You knew about that?"

"The gardener found sour milk and weed killer in the soil of the potted plant outside your father's

bedroom. I put two and two together." Well, I had…
just this instant. It made perfect sense. Candace would
have considered her husband too weak to get the job
done. Amb, in an act of twisted loyalty, chose to kill
his father so that his wife wouldn't be convicted of
murder.

"I couldn't let her do it," he said, his voice shaky.
"The guilt would have destroyed her."

"How did you find out what she intended to do?"

"After the drama at dinner, I was agitated and
couldn't sleep. Candace wanted me to take one of her
sleeping pills and said she'd take one as well."

"But you didn't take yours."

"No." His mouth twisted into a wry smile. "I hate
sleeping pills. I only told her I'd take one to give her
peace of mind. I guess she didn't take hers, either."

"You saw her sneak out of the room and you
followed her," I prompted.

"Yes. I thought she was just going down to the
kitchen to make hot chocolate. She sometimes does
that when she can't sleep. I decided I'd join her."

"But when you got there, you saw her use the back
door to go out to the shed where she broke the
padlock and stole a container of weed killer."

He nodded wordlessly.

"And then you saw her add a dose of the weed
killer to a glass of milk."

He shuddered and took a step back. "My father
was in the habit of going for a late night swim if he
had insomnia. When he dried off, he always drank a

glass of warm milk before he went back to bed. George, his valet, prepared it for him and left it in front of his bedroom door."

"And Candace intended to swap George's milk for her poisoned version?"

"I guess so." He stared at his shoes, the gun no longer pointing straight at me, but still very much present.

"So you got rid of the poisoned milk and decided to kill your father yourself."

Amb's sneer returned. "And I don't regret it. My father was a horrible man. He made my mother's life a misery, and he delighted in torturing his children and his employees. The world is a better place without Ambrose J. Huffington III."

"Maybe, but murder is murder," I said quietly. "It doesn't matter how loathsome he was. You took his life. We have a justice system for a reason."

"I don't intend to be around to try out your justice system," Amb said, his voice eerily high. He pulled back his shoulders and straightened the gun.

A cold sheen of sweat trickled down my back. Any second, he'd pull the trigger, and I'd be dead. And then he'd go after Julie. I had to stop him. But how?

In one fluid motion, I bent down to retrieve the paper knife from the floor and hurled it at Amb. Startled, he leaped back and fired, splintering the window frame.

Taking advantage of his distraction, I sprinted to the door, turned the key, and raced down the hallway toward the still open door. Outside, Julie had climbed out of her car and was running toward me. "I heard a shot."

"Hit the deck," I roared. "He's got a gun."

Wide-eyed with fear, my cousin threw herself onto the ground and covered her head with her hands.

I'd almost reached the door when I spotted a pair of large green orbs on top of my hallway closet. In a leap worthy of an acrobat, Mavis jumped down from her perch with a hiss and landed in front of Amb. He tripped over her and sent his revolver flying.

In a move my former gym teacher would have approved of, I caught the revolver with one hand, twirled it, and pointed it at Amb. "Hands where I can see them."

He didn't move a muscle.

"I'm serious. Hands up. And no funny business, or I might shoot you anyway."

The man held up both arms. His fingers were curled into fists. "Please. I didn't mean to hurt you and your friend."

"Open your fingers," I demanded. "Right now."

In the distance, sirens drifted in the warm breeze.

Amb stared at me, dumbfounded. "You called the police."

No, but my cousin must have done so. Thank goodness for Julie's quick thinking. "Open your fingers."

In a split second, Amb opened his hand and hurled a knife at my right arm. I got off a round before I registered the pain, but I must have only grazed him.

"Julie, stay down," I yelled.

Amb charged out of the cottage and ran to Julie's SUV. He leaped behind the wheel, and I let off another round, shattering the front windshield. With my injured arm, my aim was lousy. Quick as a flash, I switched to my left.

He gunned the engine and sent gravel flying as he roared down the drive. I fired twice, hitting one of the back wheels as well as the back windshield.

Only two rounds left. I had to make them count. Keeping my arm steady, I fired my last rounds, hitting one of the tires twice.

The SUV swerved all over the drive, but Amb kept his foot on the gas pedal.

"Can he keep going with the tires in that condition?"

I flashed her a grin. "Not for long."

The sound of the approaching sirens grew louder. Julie and I ran to the end of the drive. The flashing lights of one of Whisper Island's two squad cars zoomed toward us, closely followed by Lenny's purple van.

My heart was in my throat as I watched Amb aim the SUV at them.

"He's going to stop, right?" Julie whispered beside me. "Reynolds will swerve at the last second?"

I opened my mouth to reply, but no words came out. My throat was bone dry.

The SUV was almost to the squad car, at the narrowest point in the road. I heard a scream and realized belatedly that it came from me. In the next instant, Amb swerved the SUV toward the cliff, slowed briefly, and then accelerated.

Julie's car flew over the side of the cliff, appeared to hang in the air for a second, and then began its perilous free fall to the rocks below.

## 29

In SUBDUED SILENCE, Julie, Reynolds and I stood at the cliff edge and stared down at the wreckage of the SUV.

Only Lenny seemed thrilled by the action-packed turn of events. "Dude, two wrecked cars in one week? That's epic, even by your standards, Maggie."

"I only crashed one," I pointed out. "Amb is wholly responsible for wrecking Julie's car. And before he took off in it, he confessed to attacking you, and killing his father."

"And himself," Reynolds said quietly. "No one could survive that fall."

We fell silent for a moment. Then Reynolds turned to me, tears in his eyes and pulled me close. "I thought you were in that car."

Enveloped in the comfort of his arms, I leaned in and rested my head against his chest. "I'm fine, and so is Julie."

"Fine apart from a cut on your arm," a gruff voice said.

I whirled around to see Paddy Driscoll leaning against the passenger side of Lenny's van.

"Paddy?" I asked in confusion. "What are you doing here?"

"I hitched a ride over to your place with Lenny. I was going to talk to you about Nancy."

Guilt gnawed at my stomach. "I'm sorry I couldn't help you find the answers you wanted."

"On the contrary." Paddy pulled a thick envelope out of his shirt pocket. "You asked questions and jogged someone's conscience. That person came forward to confess they'd hit Nancy with their bicycle and buried her in the woods."

I slow-blinked. "Nancy was hit by a *bike*?"

"By *a kid* on a bike." Lenny nodded to Paddy in a silent acknowledgment of an agreement they must have struck on their way to meet me.

I cast my mind back to my odd conversation with Carl Logan at Marley House, and the pieces fell into place. "Carl?" I mouthed to Lenny.

He gave me the briefest of nods, and solved the mystery of what had befallen Nancy the sheep.

Paddy stepped forward and shoved an envelope of cash into my hand. "This is more than we agreed on, but your work was worth it to me."

"I can't take your money," I protested. "I didn't solve the case. I had nothing to do with the person responsible coming forward."

"But you did," Paddy said firmly. "The fact I hired a P.I. made him realize how much the incident still bothered me, and he decided to confess. There are no hard feelings. He was only a kid."

Reynolds laid a hand on my good arm. "Come on, Maggie. There's nothing you can do here now. Go with Lenny and get your arm checked out. I'll wait for the rescue team to arrive."

I bit my lip and wondered if I should tell him about Candace's intention to kill Huff. In the end, my sense of justice overcame my reservations. "Amb claims he only killed Huff because Candace intended to kill him with weed killer."

Reynolds raised an eyebrow. "Is that the weed killer Rob Hennessy found in the potted plant?"

I nodded. "What are you going to do with the information?"

"I'll question Candace, obviously, but at the moment, I don't see how I could charge her with the intention to kill her father-in-law."

The breath I hadn't realized I'd been holding came out in a whoosh. Even if Candace had contemplated murder, I didn't want to see Hailey left with no parents. "Will you let me know what happens?"

His slow-burn smile turned my knees to jelly. "I'll fill you in on all the details, Maggie. If I didn't, you'd never let me hear the end of it. Now go with Lenny and get your arm checked by a doctor. I'll see you tomorrow."

THE FOLLOWING MORNING, Reynolds knocked on my door holding a bag of Noreen's muffins. "It's my turn to come bearing breakfast and gossip."

I inhaled the scent of my aunt's banana chocolate muffins. "My favorite flavor. I'm starving, too."

I dragged him through to the kitchen and fixed us coffees to take outside. When we were settled on the deck, and I was armed with a muffin, I demanded, "Spill. I want to know everything."

"There's not much to tell. Candace was devastated, but Martha and Helen seemed resigned. Martha seems to think she'll be able to persuade Candace and Hailey to join her on her trip to Italy next month."

"I hope they take her up on the offer. A change of scene before they go home sounds like a good idea."

"And Helen Huffington asked me to give this to you." Reynolds drew an envelope out of his breast pocket.

I took the thick cream envelope gingerly.

"You're looking at it as if it contains anthrax," Reynolds said dryly.

"I'd rather not hear from any of the Huffingtons ever again," I admitted. "I'm perfectly happy to go back to my mundane, murder-free existence."

He grinned. "Aren't you going to open it?"

"Oh, all right." I tore open the envelope and removed the single sheet of paper it contained. A check fell into my lap. I glanced at the amount and gasped. "Fifty thousand euros? Is she out of her mind?"

"What does the note say?"

With a pang of regret, I read the final words I'd ever hear from my late grandmother's oldest friend.

*Dear Maggie,*

*I hired you to do a job, and you performed it to the best of your ability. I might not like the outcome, but we had a deal, and I always honor my debts. Consider this recompense for services rendered.*

*Regards,*

*Helen Wright Huffington*

I looked at the check and felt Reynolds's eyes watching me. Fifty thousand euros would enable me to hire Lenny. I swallowed past a hard lump and made my decision. In swift movements, I shredded the check. "I'll make my business a success, but I won't do it with money from a woman whose grandson tried to kill us."

Reynolds leaned across the table and cupped my chin. "Well done, Maggie. I knew you'd say that."

And then he kissed me, and I forgot all about my banana chocolate muffin for a long time.

## THE END

## A NOTE FROM ZARA

•Thanks for reading **How to Murder a Millionaire.** I hope you enjoyed Maggie's third adventure on Whisper Island! Maggie and her friends will be back in September 2017 for more murder and mayhem in **The Thirty-Nine Cupcakes.**

•In the meantime, I'm publishing a mailing list exclusive serial called **To Hatch a Thief**, featuring an adventure that occurs between **Dial P For Poison** and **The Postman Always Dies Twice**. Sign up for my mailing list to access the episodes.

**Happy Reading!**
**Zara xx**

**Join my mailing list and get news, giveaways, and an exclusive FREE Movie Club Mystery serial! Join Maggie and her friends as they solve the mystery in *To Hatch a Thief*. http://zarakeane.com/newsletter2**

•I also have **an active reader group**, **The Ballybeg Belles**, where I chat, share snippets of upcoming stories, and host members only giveaways. I hope to join you for a virtual pint very soon!

Would you like to try Maggie's recipe for the Blue Margaritas that she served at the impromptu Unplugged Gamers meeting? Here's the recipe!

## BLUE MARGARITAS

- 1 teaspoon coarse salt
- 2 oz (60ml) Tequilla
- 1 oz (30ml) Triple Sec
- 1 oz (30ml) freshly-squeezed lime juice
- 1 oz (30ml) blue Curacaco liqueur
- 1 teaspoon sugar
- 1 lime, cut into wedges

1. Half-fill a cocktail shaker with ice cubes.
2. Put in the Tequilla, Triple Sec, lime juice, blue Curacaco, and sugar in the shaker and shake vigorously.
3. Strain into a cocktail glass and and garnish with a lime wedge.

*Maggie's tip: To create a perfect salt-rimmed cocktail glass, use a lime wedge to rub the rim of the glass. Then dip the rim of the glass into coarse salt and twist.*

**ALSO BY ZARA KEANE**

## MOVIE CLUB MYSTERIES—Cozy Mystery

Dial P For Poison

The Postman Always Dies Twice

How to Murder a Millionaire

The Thirty-Nine Cupcakes (September 2017)

## BALLYBEG SERIES—Contemporary Romance

Love and Shenanigans

Love and Blarney

Love and Leprechauns

Love and Mistletoe

Love and Shamrocks

## BALLYBEG BAD BOYS—Romantic Suspense

Her Treasure Hunter Ex

The Rock Star's Secret Baby

The Navy SEAL's Holiday Fling

Bodyguard by Day, Ex-Husband by Night

The Navy SEAL's Accidental Wife

## DUBLIN MAFIA—Romantic Suspense

Final Target

Kiss Shot

Bullet Point (2017)

## ABOUT ZARA KEANE

*USA Today* bestselling author Zara Keane grew up in Dublin, Ireland, but spent her summers in a small town very similar to the fictitious Whisper Island and Ballybeg.

She currently lives in Switzerland with her family. When she's not writing or wrestling small people, she drinks far too much coffee, and tries—with occasional success—to resist the siren call of Swiss chocolate.

Zara has an active reader group, **The Ballybeg Belles**, where she chats, shares snippets of upcoming stories, and hosts members-only giveaways. She hopes to join you for a virtual pint very soon!

To join the Ballybeg Belles, go here:
**https://zarakeane.com/belles**

zarakeane.com

**HOW TO MURDER A MILLIONAIRE**